MIRAGE OF DUST

Three men risked their lives in a search for gold in the Mexican desert. They struck lucky, and worked like the devil to amass a fortune. Attacked by bandits, they fought a running war until they reached the border. But at the border their troubles really began. Bandits, the sun and the desert were not such deadly enemies to three desperate men as each one of them to the others . . .

B. Traven

The Treasure of the Sierra Madre

PANTHER
GRANADA PUBLISHING
London Toronto Sydney New York

Published by Granada Publishing Limited
in Panther Books 1974
Reprinted 1980

ISBN 0 586 04078 1

First published in Great Britain by
Jonathan Cape Ltd 1934
Copyright © B. Traven 1934

Granada Publishing Limited
Frogmore, St Albans, Herts AL2 2NF
and
3 Upper James Street, London W1R 4BP
866 United Nations Plaza, New York, NY 10017, USA
117 York Street, Sydney, NSW 2000, Australia
100 Skyway Avenue, Rexdale, Ontario, M9W 3A6, Canada
PO Box 84165, Greenside, 2034 Johannesburg, South Africa
CML Centre, Queen & Wyndham, Auckland 1, New Zealand

Set, printed and bound in Great Britain by
Cox & Wyman Ltd, Reading
Set in Intertype Times

Granada ®
Granada Publishing ®

The seat on which Dobbs was sitting was a thoroughly bad one. One rail was missing and another had caved in. It was a punishment to sit on it. It did not occur to Dobbs to consider whether he deserved this punishment or whether, like the majority of punishments, it was unjustly inflicted. Probably he would not have realized he was uncomfortable unless someone had asked him how he liked his seat. His preoccupation was the one usual with so many of us – how to get hold of some money. If you have a little money already it is easier, because you have some to lay out. But when you have nothing whatever, there are difficulties in arriving at a satisfactory solution of the problem.

Dobbs had nothing. It may safely be said that he had less than nothing, for he was not even adequately or completely clothed, and clothing, to those in need, is a modest start towards capital.

But there is always work for those who want it. Only it is as well not to go to the man who says so; for he never has any work to offer and never can point to the man who has. He makes his assertion merely to prove what a lot he knows of the world.

Dobbs would have wheeled stones if he could have got the job. But he could not even get navvy work. There were too many after it, and the natives always stand a better chance of getting it than a foreigner.

At the corner of the Plaza a shoe-black had his high iron chair. The other shoe-blacks, who could not afford a chair, ran about round the Plaza like weasels with their little boxes and folding stools and left no one in peace whose shoes did not shine like the sun. Whether you sat on one of the numerous seats or walked about, you were pestered all the time. It wasn't easy, then, even for the shoe-blacks to make a living, and compared with Dobbs they were capitalists; for they possessed an outfit which might cost three pesos at least.

Even if Dobbs had had the three pesos, he could not have been a shoe-black. Not here among the natives. No white man has ever attempted to clean shoes on the streets, here at least. The white man who sits on a seat in rags and starves, the white man who begs of other white men, the white man who commits burglary is not despised by other white men. But if he cleans shoes in the streets, or begs from Indians, or lugs round ice water for sale in buckets, he sinks far below the dirtiest native and starves all the same. For no white man will patronize him and the natives will treat him as an unfair competitor.

A gentleman in a white coat took his seat on the high iron chair at the corner, and the shoe-black set to work on his brown shoes. Dobbs got up and strolled across and muttered a few words in a low voice. The gentleman scarcely looked up, but feeling in his pocket he took out a peso and gave it to Dobbs.

Dobbs stood still for a moment, quite taken aback. Then he returned to his seat. He hadn't reckoned on anything at all, or only on ten centavos at most. He kept his fingers on the coin in his pocket. What should he do with it? A dinner and a supper, or two dinners, or ten packets of Artistas cigarettes, or five glasses of coffee and milk with a pan Frances, which is an ordinary roll?

After a short time he left his seat and followed the two or three streets that led to the Hotel Oso Negro.

The hotel was really only a Casa Huéspedes, a lodging-house. The front of it was occupied on one side by a shop selling shoes, shirts, soap and musical instruments, and on the other side by a shop selling wire mattresses, easy-chairs and photographic apparatus. Between these two shops was the wide entrance leading to the courtyard. In the courtyard were the mouldering wooden huts which formed the hotel. These huts were all divided into small, dark, windowless compartments, and in each of these cabins there were from four to eight bunks. Each bunk was provided with a dirty pillow and an old worn blanket. Light and air came in through the doors, which were always open. In spite of this the air in the rooms was always stale, for they were all on the ground level and the sun could penetrate only a short way into them. There was no current of air either, because the air in the courtyard was stagnant; and it was not improved by the latrines, which had no water system. Besides this, a wood fire burned night and day in the middle of the yard, and on it clothes were boiled in large jam tins. For the hotel also accommodated a laundry run by a Chinaman.

On the left of the entrance passage which led into the courtyard was a small room occupied by the porter. Leading out of it was another room with a grill which went up to the ceiling. The trunks, chests, packages and cardboard boxes which were left in charge of the hotel were stored here on shelves.

There were trunks belonging to people who had perhaps only slept there for a night, and many of the trunks and chests were thickly coated with dust. The money perhaps had only run to one night. The next night the man had slept out somewhere and the following nights too. Then one day he would come and take out a shirt or a pair of trousers or whatever it might be, lock the trunk and leave it in charge again. Later he might set off on a journey. As he had no money to pay for a ticket either by rail or ship, he had to go on foot; and so his trunk was no use to him. By this time he was in Brazil, perhaps, or had perished long since of thirst in a desert somewhere, or starved, or been killed on a forest track.

After a year, when the storage space became so congested that there was no room for the effects of new arrivals, the proprietor made a clearance. Sometimes there was a label on a chest or package, but often the owner of it forgot what name he had given and, having changed his name in the meantime, he could not recover his chest, because he was unable to recall the name he had used at the time. He might point out the article. The porter then asked the name, and when the name did not tally with the label which was stuck on to the chest with a pin, he refused to give it up to him.

Often too the label had fallen off. Sometimes the name

was written in chalk and had got rubbed out. In other cases, the porter had been in a hurry and had forgotten to ask the name, and there was a cardboard box with nothing but the number of a bed written on it in blue chalk. Its owner, however, had never known the number of his bed, and if he had, he wasn't likely to have remembered it. A note of the date was never included.

It could never be ascertained, therefore, how long a chest or a trunk had lain in store. The length of time was judged by the thickness of the layer of dust which had collected on it. And according to its destiny the proprietor could say pretty accurately how long a trunk or a sugar-bag had been in his keeping. No charge was made. But when there was no more room, the articles which had the thickest coating of dust to show were thrown out. The proprietor looked through the contents and sorted them. They were mostly rags. It very seldom happened that anything of value was found; for no one who possessed anything of value put up at the Oso Negro, or he only stayed there a night. The proprietor gave these rags away to the more ragged of his patrons, who eagerly begged for them, or to any other tramps who passed by. No trousers are so ragged and no shirt so worn and no boots so trodden down that no one can be found who thinks them still good enough; for no one on earth is so poor that there is not another who can say he is poorer still.

Dobbs had no trunk to give in charge, nor even a cardboard box or paper bag. Even if he had owned anything of the kind, he would not have known what to put into it; for all he possessed was in his trouser pockets. It was months since he had had a coat.

He entered the porter's office. True, it had a counter in the wall which divided it from the passage, but no one, not even the porter himself, ever made use of it. On this counter, just in front of the sliding-window, stood a water-bottle and a small earthenware jar. This water-bottle was for the use of the whole hotel. If anyone was thirsty he had to come to this window shelf to drink. There was no water and no water-bottles in the sleeping compartments. Some of the more experienced lodgers, particularly those who were often thirsty during the night, took old Tequila bottles full of water to bed with them.

The porter was a young man, not yet twenty-five perhaps. He was small and thin and had a long sharp nose. His hours of duty were from five in the morning to six at night. At six the night porter took on; for the hotel was never shut, night or day. This was not on account of arrivals by train, as no trains came in after nightfall, unless they were late. It was because there were men sleeping in the hotel who were employed in restaurants or other trades where the working hours ended late at night, or sometimes in the early morning.

At all hours of night and day there was somebody stirring in the hotel. At any hour there was somebody who had to get up and go to work. Among those who slept there were private night watchmen, bakers, paviours, newspaper sellers, bakers' roundsmen and many more for whose occupations there is no precise description. Many of them could have afforded to rent a room where they would have slept more comfortably and in cleaner surroundings and without the company of strangers, foreigners and tramps. But for the sake of being called and getting off punctually to work they preferred to sleep in the hotel, where they could rely on being called to the minute. Both porters were very efficient. Every day there were arrivals and departures. Every day there were changes. All nationalities were represented. White, yellow, black, brown and reddish-brown faces passed by the porter's window. But the porter on duty always knew whether they had paid or not. If he had any doubt he looked at once in his book and followed the man from the window which looked on to the courtyard, to see into which room he went.

There were a few smaller rooms available in which there was only one fairly wide bed with a mattress. The mattress was very hard, but the guests were not particular. These rooms were for two persons and each paid a peso. They were taken by those who were accompanied by a woman. For women and girls who came alone there were huts with a number of bunks at fifty centavos apiece. There were two doors to them, but they did not lock and hung so askew from the hinges that they would not even shut. The bunks, however, were furnished with mosquito-nets under which the girls could conceal themselves and undress. Indian girls and others of humble origin are astonishingly adroit at dressing and undressing under these nets and can pass the night under them as invisibly as though they were within the four walls of a house. The ones who stayed there were mostly kitchenmaids and scullerymaids from the restaurants.

A girl slept in this hotel, where not a door was ever locked or shut, much more safely than in many places which have the name of good family hotels, for the men were far too much occupied with their own concerns to take any notice of them; and the tramps and vagrants of the Oso Negro would have killed the man who dared to interfere with them.

There were clients of the hotel who had been there for two, three and even five years. As they always occupied the same bunks in the same corners, they were able to live here as cleanly as in a private house. Only, of course, their companions changed most nights. But sometimes there were enough of these permanent lodgers to fill a whole room. Their life there was much freer than in a private house. They could come in when they liked without putting a landlady into a temper, and they could go out when they liked without anybody bothering about them; and if they came home very drunk no one took the slightest notice of them.

The rooms had no cupboards. You hung your clothes on nails in the walls. Many of those who had been there some while and were in regular work kept their Sunday clothes in wooden boxes which they could padlock. Others made a curtain of sacking to protect their clothes from the dust. Others again laced them across and across with thick string so tightly that it would have been a difficult matter to abstract a pair of trousers. It was very seldom that anything

10

was stolen; if a man went past with anything under his arm he was scrutinized suspiciously by the porter, and if he was carrying another man's trousers, the porter would know it and not let him go far. And the porters were very well acquainted with the coats and trousers of the regular inmates.

The porter had very little room in his office, for it was crowded out with all manner of things – small packets and boxes and handbags for which it was hardly worth while opening the iron cage, as they were only handed in for a short time. It might be for half an hour or so, and generally they were called for within the time stated, but sometimes they were left for weeks and then forgotten. The owner left the town unexpectedly, perhaps as a seaman on a ship bound for the other side of the world. For if a ship just about to sail found itself shorthanded, the man had to go aboard in what he stood up in, or else lose the job.

This confined space also accommodated some high pigeon-holed shelves for towels, soap and loofahs, which were supplied to those who wanted baths. There were only shower-baths. The water was not heated and there was little of it.

Then there were pigeon-holes for letters and papers of all sorts, on which the dust accumulated.

Lastly, there was a safe. To this were consigned the articles of value handed in by the visitors to the hotel – money, watches, rings and valuable instruments. Among the latter were compasses, surveyor's instruments and others used by prospectors for gold, silver and minerals generally. For even owners of such instruments were often down and out and turned up here for a bed. Rifles, revolvers and fishing-tackle, too, were hung round the walls.

The thick hotel register occupied the only part of the table which was not littered up with papers, packets and boxes. Every visitor was entered in it, but only the surname, the number of his bunk and the sum paid. What his other names might be, or his nationality or calling, or why or whence he came, did not interest the proprietor at all. These particulars interested the police even less. They never so much as looked at the book. It was of interest at most to the revenue authorities when the proprietor desired to prove that his receipts were assessed at too high a figure. It is only when state-paid officials tumble over each other for something to do that the police find nothing too paltry for their notice and want to know, even to the colour of the one hair on a mole, who the arrival at an hotel is, where he has come from, what he is there for and where he intends going when he leaves. These officials would not know otherwise what to do with themselves, and the taxpayers would soon find out that they were superfluous.

Dobbs went in to the porter and, putting down his peso on the table said: 'Lobbs, for two nights.'

The porter turned the pages of the book until he found a vacant bunk, wrote down 'Jobbs' because he had not quite caught the name and was too polite to have it repeated, and then said: 'Room seven, bed two.'

'Good,' said Dobbs and went out. There was nothing now to prevent him lying down right away and sleeping for the rest of the afternoon and all night and all next day and the night after and on till the following midday, if he wanted to. But he was hungry and so had to go hunting or fishing.

But the fish were not biting. No one gave him anything. Then walking in front of him he saw a gentleman in a white coat. He overtook him and muttered a word or two, and the man gave him fifty centavos.

With these fifty centavos he went to a Chinaman's for dinner. It was long after midday, certainly. But there is always dinner going at a Chinaman's, and if it is too late to call it Comida Corrida, then the same meal is simply called Cena, and that turns it into supper, even though the Cathedral clock has not yet struck four.

Then Dobbs took his ease on a seat for a bit and finally thought of coffee. His stalking was fruitless until he saw a gentleman in a white coat. And this gentleman gave him fifty centavos. A silver piece.

'I'm in luck with gentlemen in white coats today,' thought

Dobbs, and went to the round coffee kiosk on the side of the Plaza de la Libertad nearest to the customs and passenger quay.

He sat down on the high bar-stool and ordered a glass of coffee and two croissants. The glass was three parts filled with hot milk and then hot black coffee was added until it was full to the brim. Then the sugar-bowl was set before him and the two lovely brown croissants and a glass of ice water.

'Why have you robbers put another five centavos on the coffee?' asked Dobbs, while he stirred the mountain of sugar which he had shovelled into his glass.

'Costs have gone up,' said the waiter, busying himself with a toothpick. After which he leant indolently against the bar.

Dobbs asked the question merely for the sake of something to say. It mattered a lot, certainly, to a man like him, whether coffee cost fifteen or twenty centavos. But he wasn't going to excite himself over the raising of the price. If he could run to fifteen, he could run to twenty; and if he hadn't got twenty, he certainly wouldn't have fifteen. So really it all came to the same thing.

'I'm not buying any tickets, damn you. Leave me alone, can't you?' he shouted at the Indian youth who for the last five minutes had been fluttering the long, thin lottery tickets in front of his nose.

But the boy was not so easy to shake off.

'It's the Michoacan State lottery. Sixty thousand pesos first prize.'

'Get out, you thief. I'm buying no ticket.'

Dobbs dipped his roll in the coffee and pushed it into his mouth.

'The whole ticket's only ten pesos.'

'Curse you, do you think I've ten pesos?' Dobbs wanted to drink a mouthful of coffee, but the glass was too hot to hold.

'Then take a quarter. That's only two fifty.'

Dobbs had managed to get the glass to his mouth. But just as he was going to drink, he burnt his tongue and had to put it down again quickly, because it was getting too hot for his fingers too, after holding it so long.

'If you don't get out with your stolen tickets, you'll have this water in your face.'

Dobbs was in a temper by this time, not so much with the boy's importunate salesmanship as because he had burnt the tip of his tongue. He could not take vengeance on his tongue, nor on the coffee, which he took the greatest care not to spill. So he vented his rage on the boy.

This did not worry the boy at all. He was used to such outbursts. Also he was a good salesman and knew his man. A man who could drink coffee at that time of day and eat two fancy rolls with it was well able to buy a lottery ticket for the benefit of Michoacan State.

'Take a tenth then, señor. Only one peso.'

Dobbs took the glass of ice water and gave the boy a threatening look. The boy saw it, but did not budge from the spot.

Dobbs drank a mouthful of the water. The boy waved the tickets about in front of his nose. With one flick Dobbs threw the water in his face and the tickets were soaked.

The boy was not in the least put out. He only laughed as he shook the water from his tickets and his torn shirt. He took the shower-bath more as a friendly way of opening up a deal than as an expression of hostility, and he had it firmly fixed in his small head that the man who could have a glass of coffee and milk and two rolls was bound to buy a lottery ticket as well, in order to win a prize and so find the means to repeat such extravagance.

The largest glass of coffee comes to an end in time. Dobbs drained his to the last drop, and when he had also picked up the last crumb of the rolls, he pulled out his fifty centavo piece. He got twenty back in a small silver coin. The boy had only been waiting for this moment, apparently.

'Now señor, just buy a twentieth in the Monterrey lottery. Only twenty centavos. First prize twenty thousand pesos. Here you are. This is a lucky number.'

Dobbs weighed the silver piece in his hand. What should

he do with it? Cigarettes? For the moment on the top of the coffee he had no desire for a cigarette. Money was thrown away on lottery tickets. All the same, once gone never missed, and for a day or two you could hope. It wasn't a matter of months. The draw was in a few days.

'Give me your ticket then, you son of a bitch – if it's only to see the last of you and your tickets.'

The little salesman tore the twentieth part of a ticket off the long slip without the loss of a moment. The paper was as thin as a gossamer – so thin that the print showed as clearly on the back as on the front.

'That's a very lucky number, señor.'

'Why don't you try it yourself, then?'

'I haven't the money for that, señor. Here it is. Many, many thanks, señor. Remember me next time.'

Dobbs put it in his pocket without looking at the number. Then he went off to have a bathe. It was a long way out of the town, beyond the cemetery, and then down the hill to the river. You had to jump ditches and pools and wade through morasses before you got there.

There were Indians by the dozen splashing in the water as well as white men of the same social level as Dobbs, men who lived on what others let fall. No one was in bathing drawers, but there was no one either who worried about that. Women and girls went past these bathing-places, and thought nothing of men bathing entirely naked. They saw nothing in it to offend or disgust them. Only the smart American and European women would have thought it beneath their dignity to walk past. They watched the bathers with good prismatic glasses from the balconies and windows of their houses high above. Ladies who lived on the other side of the Avenida Hidalgo, in the Colonia Guadalupe and in the other colonies, got themselves invited to tea by the ladies who lived here. Each one brought her prismatic glasses, so as to have a better view of the landscape from this commanding height. That is why the colony here had the name of Colonia Buena Vista.

The bathe was refreshing and Dobbs saved the five and

twenty centavos he would have had to pay for a shower-bath in the hotel. But bathing here had its disadvantages too. There were the gigantic crabs which lay in wait in the mud. These crabs sometimes thought the toes of bathers were tasty morsels which they could not afford to despise, and it hurt like the devil when a fine full-grown crab got a proper hold on your toe and tried to make off with it.

The river was divided into many channels, and the crab-fishers were dotted about on the different banks. It was a wearisome business, and only those whose patience was quite inexhaustible could do any good at it.

The crab-fishers were mostly Indians or the very poorest of half-breeds. The bait was decaying, stinking flesh. The more it stank, the better it was. A big bit of meat was put on the hook with a very long line, then the bait was thrown far out into the channel.

It was left lying there a good while. Then the fisherman began to draw it in slowly, very slowly, so slowly that the movement was scarcely perceptible. It took an eternity before the baited hook reached the bank again. Then the line was still drawn slowly up the flat slope of the muddy shore. A dozen times it might be all to no purpose. The hook had to be thrown out again, often with fresh bait, because the old one had been eaten off; and then once more with infinite patience it was drawn slowly in.

The crabs seized the lump of flesh in their claws and held on to it with such a fierce tenacity that they let themselves be drawn out of the water with it rather than release their grip. But if the pace were too fast the crab could not keep up, or else became suspicious and let go. Often it took such a firm hold of the bit of flesh that it severed it from the hook, and then the crab had won.

With patience a fisher could do a good day's business, for many of the crabs weighed half or three-quarters of a kilo, and the restaurants paid good prices, as crab is esteemed a great delicacy by the gourmet.

Dobbs watched the fishermen, but decided it was not a job for him. He had not got the patience for it. One little jerk and the booty was lost. It was a kind of fishing which required calmer nerves than Dobbs, who had been brought up in the racket of a large city in America, could command, even though he were offered five pesos for every crab he landed.

He strolled back to the town. The bathe and the walking to and fro had given him an appetite and now there was his supper to think of. Again for a long time he had no luck, and all he got in reply were insulting remarks which he had to put up with in silence. But a man gets callous when he's hungry and when his supper depends on a thick skin.

At last he saw a gentleman in a white coat. He thought to himself: 'I'm in luck today with gentlemen in white coats, I'll try it on again.' He guessed right – fifty centavos, and there was his supper at last.

Afterwards, while he took his well-earned repose on a seat, it came into his mind that it would be just as well to have something in his pocket, because you never know when you may need it. This thought did not come quite unprompted. It was the sight of a gentleman in a white coat going by on the other side of the Plaza. Dobbs went straight up to him.

Sure enough he put his hand into his pocket and brought out a fifty centavo piece. Dobbs held out his hand, but the man kept a tight hold on his coin.

'Now, listen to me, young man,' he said with annoyance. 'I have never in the whole course of my life come across impudence to equal this, and if anyone had told me such a thing could happen, I wouldn't have believed him.'

Dobbs stood there dazed. He too had never in the whole course of his life had such a lengthy speech made to him. He scarcely knew whether to stand his ground or to make off. But as the coin was still in the man's hand, he felt that sooner or later it was destined to come into his own and that the old boy was only enjoying the excuse for a sermon. I can very well, he thought to himself, listen to a sermon for the sake of fifty centavos, and that's all I have to do. And so he stayed where he was.

'This afternoon,' the man went on, 'you told me you'd had no dinner. Whereupon I gave you a peso. Then I came across you again and you say you had no money for a bed. Whereupon I gave you fifty centavos. Then you came along again and said you had had no supper, and again I gave you fifty centavos. Now just tell me what it is you want money for now?'

'For breakfast tomorrow,' Dobbs replied with presence of mind.

The man laughed and gave him the fifty. Then he said: 'This is the last time I'll give you anything. You can go to somebody else now for a change. It's beginning to get monotonous.'

'You must pardon me, sir,' said Dobbs, 'but I never knew you were the same person. I never looked at your face till this moment. I won't come to you again.'

'I'll give you another fifty to make sure you keep your word and don't plague me any more. That will give you a dinner tomorrow. After that you must support yourself without my assistance.'

'Then that well's pumped dry,' said Dobbs to himself; and he came to the conclusion that he had better leave the town and see what he could make of it farther afield.

Chapter Two

That night a man in Dobbs's room said to another that he thought of going to Tuxpam, but he had no mate to go with. The words were scarcely out of his mouth before Dobbs said: 'I'll go with you to Tuxpam.'

'Are you a driller?'

'No, pumpman.'

'Right,' said the other, 'we can go along together if you like.'

Next morning they set off intending to scour the numerous oil-fields in the Tuxpam district in search of work. Before starting they had their glass of coffee and two rolls at a coffee stall.

It isn't so easy, though, to get to Tuxpam. There is no railway. You can only go by air. And that costs fifty pesos. But there are plenty of lorries going that way, and perhaps they might get a lift on one of them. As for doing it on foot – it is more than a hundred miles under a blazing tropical sun and very little shade all the way.

'First of all, we have to get across the river.' said Barber, 'and that's the least of our troubles.'

The ferry cost twenty-five centavos and they had no wish to spend this sum.

'There's only one thing to do,' said Barber, 'we must wait for the Huasteca freight ferry. They'll take us over for nothing. But one may not come until eleven o'clock. They go when they have a load, not by time-table.'

'Then we'll sit on the wall here and wait,' Dobbs replied.

He had bought himself a packet of fourteen cigarettes for ten centavos with the change he got when he paid for his breakfast, and they brought him luck. In the packet was a coupon for fifty centavos, which he cashed at once at the tobacconist's. So now he had, all told, one peso ten centavos.

Barber had about one fifty. They could have paid the fare,

but as they had plenty of time and no occasion to hurry, they thought they might just as well wait for the freight boat and save the money.

It was a lively scene at the ferry. Motor-boats by the dozen, big and small, stood by for passengers. Special ones, for which a higher fare was charged, brought over the directors and managers of oil companies who were in too much of a hurry to wait while the ordinary boats collected the five or six passengers without whom they would not start. And as there were always people waiting, particularly workpeople, who lived on this side and worked in their hundreds, and even thousands, on the other, the banks near the ferry, at certain hours of the morning and evening, were like a perpetual fair. There were stalls where you could get a meal, or coffee, or roasted bananas, or fruit, or cuchilladas, or hot tamales, or cigarettes, or sweets. All this trafficking owed its life to the ferry. Motor cars and trams were always discharging passengers for the ferry in a ceaseless stream. It went on all day and all night without stopping. There on the other side were the hands, here on this side the brain – the head offices and banks. On the other side it was labour, and here refreshment, rest and enjoyment. On the other side lay the wealth, the gold of the country – oil; but over there it was worthless. It was here on this side, in the town, in the tall blocks of offices, in the banks, at the board meetings, in the All American Cable Service that oil, which on the other side was quite valueless, acquired its value. For oil, like gold, is worthless in itself. Its value is only the result of a commercial process.

Dollars by the milliard were ferried across. Not in notes, not in coined gold, not even in cheques. These milliards went across as figures jotted down in little note-books, or sometimes merely on scraps of paper, by men who generally – but not always – took a special boat plying for hire at a fare above the prescribed tariff.

At half past ten the freight boat came over, loaded up with barrels, cases and sacks. A number of Indians, men and women, crossed in her, heavily laden with baskets, in which

20

they had country produce for the town, mats, bast bags, poultry, fish, eggs, cheeses, flowers and kids.

Barber and Dobbs climbed in, but they had an hour to wait before the return journey was made. It was a long crossing, as the quay was a long way down stream. Up stream, one behind another, lay the tankers ready to take in the oil and carry it across the ocean.

On the far side the scene was just as lively, and the appearance of a fair in full swing quite as striking. Down stream too there were tankers, reaching almost to the river's mouth. Back from the river bank were the huge tanks filled to the brim with the precious oil. It was taken from the tanks to the river's edge by numerous pipes. From here it was pumped into the tanks of the ships through wire tubing. While the oil was being taken in, or when a ship was loaded with it, the red flag was flown as a danger signal. For the raw oil gives off a gas, and if there is any carelessness with a match or a naked flame the ship may burn out to the water-line.

Sellers of fruit, parrots, tiger cats, tiger and lion skins, monkeys, buffalo horns, and models of palaces and cathedrals formed of shells were here in crowds, offering their wares to the sailors. If they could not get money they would take clothing, waterproofs, leather trunks or anything else they valued in exchange.

The refineries discharged clouds of smoke and gas. The gas got into lungs and windpipes and stung like sharp needles. Then everybody coughed, and when the wind carried these fumes over the city the whole population felt it lived in a lethal chamber. Newcomers who were not used to it felt apprehensive and nervous. They clutched their throats all the time and tried to sneeze or snort it out, and wondered what was up. Many of them felt as though they would die of this smarting poison in the throat and lungs.

But those who knew it of old were glad to put up with it. So long as this acrid poison gas pervaded the town, gold ran through its streets and life was rosy, look at it how you liked.

The saloons were on this side too, one touching another. They all lived on the ships' crews. The American seamen were their best customers, for in their own country they could get neither beer, wine nor brandy. They found here all they lacked at home, and they took in enough to keep them going for long enough in their own dry and stupid land. They were used to paying through the nose for bootleggers' brandy, and so here where prices were normal they felt that whisky and beer cost nothing at all and were simply being given away. One dollar went the way of the last in the canteens and bars. And not far off were the beautiful ladies who relieved them of what was left. But the sailors never thought they were being taken advantage of. They were happy, and if anyone had forbidden them their drink and their beautiful ladies they would have cursed him all sides up. They had the utmost contempt for the Mission to Seamen, which thought only of offering the sailor a clean bed and a comfortable room where he could read the newspapers. Anyone who wants to go to church can always find a church to go to, and there is no need to bring it to the sailor at his dinner time or to his bedside and sicken him here too of what little religion his schooldays have left him. Seamen and prisoners are always regarded as fair game by those who want to stuff in religion to the retching point. But overfeeding never comes to any good. And because it does no good and produces a result the opposite to what is hoped of it, the convict and the seaman only get more and more religion pumped into them. The convict in prison and the sailor on land, once all his money is spent, fall an easy prey to religious exploitation. They would both prefer a rousing film, but they cannot have that for nothing.

'It's just midday,' said Barber, 'we might board a tanker. Perhaps we might find dinner going.'

'Not a bad notion,' Dobbs agreed. 'We can only be fired out at worst.'

They saw two men with shirt sleeves rolled up standing at a fruit stall. Barber went straight up to them and asked: 'Which is your ship?'

'The *Norman Bridge.* Why?'

'Have you had dinner?' Barber asked.

'No, we're just going to have it now.'

'What about dinner for us two?' asked Barber.

'Come along. They're all across in the town. Tons of it.'

When Dobbs and Barber left the ship an hour later they were so full they could hardly walk. They leant against the side of a hut to give time for digestion. But they soon became restive, because they wanted to get on and make sure of shelter for the night.

'There are two roads we might go,' said Barber. 'We might take the big road here, keeping close to the lagoon. But I don't advise it. It's the road everybody travels on. There'll be nothing for us in the camps as they're all overrun with tramps; and we'll find no work either, because they get men in plenty.'

'Then what did we come across at all for if there's no point in it?' Dobbs asked in annoyance.

'No point? I didn't say that,' Barber said indignantly. 'I only say that on this road where all the traffic goes there isn't much doing because there are too many others already. In my opinion we'll do better on the inland road. We'll come on more oil-fields, which no one knows of and which lie off the beaten track. We'll hit on camps too which are just being started. There, there's always a job to be got. We'll follow the river up for a bit, then turn left, and half an hour'll bring us to Villa Cuauhtemoc.'

'Off we get then if you think that way's the best,' said Dobbs.

The whole way it was oil and nothing but oil. To the left on the high gradient the tanks were marshalled like soldiers formed up in line. The river was on the right. Soon there were no more ships and the river banks were vacant. But the water had a thick film of oil, the banks were covered with it and any object which the river or the incoming tide had thrown on to the banks was coated too with black glutinous oil. The road they walked on was turned to mud in many places where an abandoned pipe still exuded thick oil or where oil oozed from the ground. Oil and nothing but oil wherever you looked. The sky itself was shrouded in oil. Thick black clouds of smoke heavy with oil gases belched out from the refineries.

Then they came to higher ground which had a more pleasing aspect. Here were the wooden dwelling-houses of the engineers and clerks. They had good air and pleasant surroundings and made up for the lack of town life by gramophones and the radio. For it was difficult to get back from the town at night and not always very safe. The neighbourhood was infested by ruffians who were on the look-out for easy chances and thought little of doing a man in.

Villa Cuauhtemoc is the old town, a prehistoric Indian town, which was there before the Spaniards came. It has a healthier situation than the new town and it occupies the shores of a large lake which abounds in fish, duck and geese. The drinking-water is better there than in the new town. But the new town quickly left the old town far behind. For the new town is close to the sea at the mouth of a river which takes the largest ocean-going ships right up to the railway terminus, and they can anchor there as safely in the wildest hurricane as though they lay in an enclosed dock. In the new town the old town is scarcely ever mentioned. Thousands even tens of thousands, of the inhabitants of the new town have no idea that the real and original town lies across the river and only half an hour's journey inland. These two, mother and daughter, drift farther and farther apart. The new town, just a hundred years old, with its hundred thousand inhabitants and its chronic shortage of houses, is in Tamaulipas State, while the old one is in Vera Cruz. The old town becomes more and more provincial, the new one takes a more and more important place among the great cities of the world and its name is known to the ends of the earth.

The two were now in a hurry to get on and had reached the end of the town facing the lagoon where the road climbs up into the hills; and there they saw an Indian crouching by the roadside. He was wearing good trousers, a clean blue shirt, a tall conical straw hat and sandals. A large bast bag containing almost all he possessed was in front of him on the ground.

They paid no attention to him and went on without slackening their pace. After a time Dobbs looked round. 'What does he want, that Indian? He's following on behind us.'

Barber turned round. 'Looks like it. He's stopped now and he's pretending to look for something in the bush.'

On both sides of the road was thick impenetrable bush.

They went on, but when they turned round they saw the Indian following them. He seemed to be walking faster and catching up.

'Had he a revolver?' Barber asked.

'Not that I saw,' Dobbs said.

'I didn't see one either, but I wondered if you had seen anything of the sort perhaps. Doesn't seem to be a bandit, then.'

'We can't be too sure,' Dobbs said after looking round again, and seeing the Indian still on their tracks. 'He may be a spy of bandits who've told him to keep us in sight. When we camp for the night he'll fall on us or else the rest of the gang will come up.'

'Don't like the look of it,' Barber went on. 'We'd do well to go back. You never know what these fellows may be up to.'

'But what can they get from us?' Dobbs asked to reassure himself.

'Get?' Barber answered. 'But we don't carry a placard to say that we have only a peso apiece. And if we did they wouldn't believe it. They'd fall on us first, hoping to find we had bags full of it. Anyway, two pesos are a fortune to these fellows, not to mention boots, trousers, shirts and hats. All worth something.'

But they went on. Whenever they looked round the Indian was behind them, now only about fifteen paces away. When they stopped the Indian stopped. They began to feel nervous. The sweat broke out on them.

Dobbs breathed hard. 'If I had a revolver or a rifle,' he said at last, 'I'd shoot the fellow. Then we should be quit of him. I can't stand much more of this. How'd it be, Barber, if we caught him, tied him up to a tree and gave him one on the head. He wouldn't come after us any more then.'

'No,' Barber said. 'But perhaps he means no harm. I'd be glad to be rid of him, though.'

'I'll stand still and let him come up,' Dobbs said suddenly. 'I can't go on like this. It drives me crazy.'

They halted as if they wanted to knock something down from a tree – a fruit or a bird.

The Indian stood still too.

Dobbs now had an idea. He got more and more excited about this tree, as though there were something up there of uncommon interest. As might be expected, the Indian was taken in by the ruse. He came slowly nearer, step by step, with his eyes fixed on the tree. As soon as he was close up to them, Dobbs shouted out in great excitement: 'There it goes!' He caught hold of Barber and pointed to some creature which had apparently made off.

Then he turned abruptly to the Indian and asked him what he wanted. 'Why do you keep on following us?'

'I want to go there,' said the Indian, pointing in the direction in which Barber and Dobbs were going.

'Where?' Dobbs asked.

'There. Where you're going.'

'You don't know where we're going,' said Dobbs.

'Yes, I know all right,' the Indian replied quietly. 'You're going to the oil-fields. I want to go there too. I might find work.'

Barber and Dobbs were relieved. That was the truth, no doubt. The man was only after a job. He had not the look of a bandit either.

But to set their minds completely at rest, Dobbs asked: 'Why don't you go by yourself? Why do you run after us?'

'I've been sitting for three days from morning till night at the end of the town there, waiting for white men on their ways to the camps.'

'You know the way yourself though, surely?'

'That's true,' said the man, 'but I'm scared of tigers and lions. There are so many round here. That's why I can't go alone. They might eat me.'

'I don't see that we're any safer from tigers ourselves,' Dobbs said.

'Oh, yes,' replied the Indian. 'They don't like white men. They'd rather have Indians. But if I'm with you they won't come for me and won't eat me.'

Barber and Dobbs laughed over their fears now they knew that the Indian whom they had been afraid of was more afraid than they were themselves.

The Indian now kept pace with them. He spoke little and trotted along beside or behind them as the path allowed.

Just before sundown they came to an Indian village and counted on shelter for the night in one of the huts. The Indians are very hospitable, but in this case they were passed on from one man to the next always with the same excuse, that there was no room. There were only a few huts in the village, and when they came to the last one they met with the same refusal.

The man seemed troubled and upset and said: 'It will be better for you to go to the next village. It's a big one of more than thirty huts. There you'll find all you want.'

'How far is it?' Dobbs asked anxiously.

'How far? It is not far,' said the Indian, 'only two kilometres. You will be there long before tonight. The sun hasn't gone down yet.'

There was nothing for it but to go on to the next village. They walked the two kilometres, but they saw nothing of any village. They went on two more kilometres, and still there was no village in sight.

'That fellow was making fools of us,' Barber said angrily. 'I'd like to know why they wouldn't let us stop there instead of sending us out into the wilds.'

Dobbs, no less annoyed, said: 'I know something of Indians. And I should have known better. They never refuse anybody shelter. But they were afraid of us. That was the whole trouble. There are three of us and we might have made short work of the whole family in a hut during the night.'

'What bunk!' Barber replied. 'Why should we kill the poor devils? They have nothing, less even than we have, I dare say.'

'All the same, they were afraid. There's no other way of looking at it. They don't estimate wealth the way we do. It's a matter of a horse or a cow or two or a few goats. That's their wealth. We might have been bandits. How were they to know? And they fear bandits more than they fear the devil.'

Barber nodded and said: 'Maybe so. But what'll we do now? Here we are in the bush, and in ten minutes it'll be pitch dark.'

'All we can do now is to make a halt where we are.'

Dobbs saw no other way out of it. 'Surely there's a village not far off. The track is well trodden, and ox and horse dung about. But it may be an hour away, and we can't go on in the dark. We might get off the track and land in a marsh or a thicket and lose ourselves. And if we did come on the village they'd set the dogs on us. It would only be looking for trouble for three men to arrive at a village at this time of night and ask for shelter.'

By the light of matches they examined the ground to find a suitable spot where they could lie down and sleep. But there was nothing but great cactuses and other varieties of prickly scrub. The ground itself was creeping with insects which would make rest or sleep unlikely. The Indian, too, had spoken of tigers and lions being common in the district. The Indian belonged to the district and must know what he was talking about.

They stood about for a time, and then when standing tired them they lay down after all. Dobbs lay next to Barber, but they had scarcely settled down before the Indian squeezed in between them like a dog, cautiously and slowly, but persistently. He did not feel safe until he lay between the white men; for the tiger would not go straight for the one in the middle. He would take one from the outside. And one would be enough for that night.

Dobbs and Barber, however, were not at all willing to make room for him. Their shouldering and elbowing must have bruised him all over. But he let himself be buffeted to and fro without protest. If they ejected him with their fists and feet, he only waited until he thought they had fallen asleep, and as soon as one or the other of them turned on his side, leaving the least space, he forced his way in again and kept on till he lay extended full length between them once more. At last they gave it up as useless.

Barber was awakened by some animal crawling over his face. He sat up and brushed it away, but while he sat listening to the singing and chirping in the darkness of the bush, he suddenly caught himself together in a spasm of fright.

He heard quite distinctly the cautious approach of a prowling beast. It was without doubt some large animal. When he heard it again and knew he was not deceived, he gave Dobbs a shake.

'What's up?' Dobbs asked sleepily.

'There's a tiger or lion on the prowl. Just behind us.'

'You must be dreaming,' Dobbs said, waking by degrees. 'It isn't likely that a tiger would venture to attack us.'

He listened. When he too heard the sound he sat up. 'I believe you're right. It's some large beast. A man wouldn't be creeping about here at night. He'd be more afraid than we are. It's an animal, and a big one judging from its tread.'

If the Indian had been awake all this time, he must have thought it safest to say nothing and lie quiet. But now he sat up with a jump and then sprang to his feet. Nothing could be seen of his face in the blackness of the night, but no doubt it was distorted by fear. From the sound of his voice the other two could imagine what his face must look like.

'It's a tiger close to us,' he said in a shaking voice. 'We're finished. He'll spring any moment. He's there in the undergrowth, waiting.'

Dobbs and Barber held their breath. The Indian knew the tread and smell of a tiger. He belonged to the country.

'What can we do?' Dobbs asked.

'We'd best shout and make all the noise we can,' Barber suggested.

'No good. Noise won't worry a tiger. It'll only aggravate him all the more.' They stood there breathless and listened. For a minute nothing was to be heard, and then two or three steps. . . .

'I know,' Dobbs said softly. 'We'll climb up a tree. We'll be as safe there as anywhere.'

'Tigers can climb a tree too,' Barber said, also in a whisper. 'They're cats. They climb and jump like nothing on earth.'

'All the same, it'll be the safest place.' Dobbs stuck to his plan.

He felt his way and after a step or two came to a mahogany tree. Without thinking twice about it he started to climb.

When the Indian realized what was going on, he was up the tree after Dobbs in a flash, if only not to be the last and lowest. But he took his bag with him.

Barber did not wish to be left all by himself down below, and so finally he climbed up after the other two.

When they had settled themselves as comfortable as they could in the darkness, they breathed again and took a calmer view of the situation. They felt safer up there than on the ground. Barber was quite right when he said: 'Down on the ground the tiger could drag you away. Here you can hold on.'

'Hold on, yes,' said Dobbs. 'But he can take an arm or a leg away with him.'

'Better than if he took all the lot,' said Barber.

Gradually weariness got the better of fright. The Indian was again in the middle, with Barber below and Dobbs above. He felt doubly secure. They had all strapped themselves to branches with their leather belts in case they fell off in their sleep.

The night was long in spite of oppressive dreams and halfwaking visions. At last the day dawned.

In the light of the sun everything looked perfectly normal

and nothing remained of the night's horror and dread imaginings. Even the surface of the ground looked much more inviting than it had seemed at night. Only thirty yards away there was a clearing and the grass there looked very reassuring through the trees.

They climbed down and each had a cigarette by way of breakfast. The Indian brought out a few dried tortillas and gave one to each of the other two.

While they sat there smoking and munching in silence, again they heard the tiger's tread. All three jumped. They knew its tread as well as if it had been the step of their nearest and dearest. If ten years had elapsed they would have known it every bit as well; for it had eaten into the very fibre of their beings, and could never be dislodged.

A tiger in full daylight? Why not? But so close to three human beings? That seemed very improbable.

Dobbs turned in the direction from which the sounds came the night before and came now too. He peered through the trees at the clearing, and there was the tiger.

They could all see it distinctly now. It was grazing, tethered by a long rope to the stump of a tree in case it ran away. It was an amiable tiger, who was glad to be left to graze in peace. It was a donkey.

The Indian said nothing. He knew a tiger, and he knew that it was a tiger he had heard in the night.

Dobbs and Barker looked at each other. They said not a word, but they went red in the face. Then they laughed till they cried.

At last Dobbs said: 'Don't you ever tell this to a soul, or we'll never dare to show our faces anywhere again.'

Chapter Three

The village, of which the Indians had told them the evening before, was not twenty minutes away. The discovery of a tethered donkey was already an indication that a village was not far off. But it is not always a certain indication, for it may easily be a donkey belonging to a woodcutter or a charcoal-burner.

In the village they were given something to eat, beans, tortillas and tea made out of citron leaves. Late in the afternoon they came to the first camp. Dobbs went straight to the foreman, but there were no jobs going.

'Do you want anything to eat?' asked the foreman.

'Yes,' said Dobbs. 'And we should be glad to spend the night here too, if we can.'

'We'll find room for you,' said the foreman, and went back into his hut after showing them the kitchen with a jerk of the head.

The Indian stuck closely to them. He might have been spliced to them. So when they went across to the kitchen, the Chinaman who ran it gave them a look and then decided that they would have to have their meal in the kitchen. It was on the Indian's account. Had Barber and Dobbs been alone they would have had their food in the white men's canteen. But, with the Indian, that was impossible, because the Indians had their own kitchen quarters.

'We must give him the shove,' said Dobbs, while he chewed. 'We can't take him round all the camps with us. It's got to stop.'

'We'll send him home first thing tomorrow morning,' replied Barber, who did not want to spoil his appetite by a more immediate solution of the problem.

Later Barber and Dobbs had a talk with the workmen, to hear what was going on here or in camps near by.

'Nothing doing,' said a tall Swede. 'All dud wells. Four have salt water, two sand and eight nothing but clay.

They're all closing down. You needn't go any farther. New borings farther south. But you can't get there from here. You'll have to go by Panuco, or else by Ebano, if you want to reach that district.'

They dossed down in a store shed on old sacks, where they were safe from donkeys, and made up for the sleep of which the tiger had deprived them the night before.

In the morning they were given a light breakfast and then they set off again.

'Now then,' said Dobbs, when they were barely an hour from the camp, 'before we get to these other two camps, where there may be a job for us or at least our grub, we've got to settle this Indian.'

'Listen to me,' Dobbs went on, addressing the Indian, 'we're going on alone now. We've no use for you.'

The Indian looked up in alarm and said: 'But the tigers, Señor!'

'You must settle with tigers on your own,' Barber interposed. 'We want to be quit of you.'

'That's the fact,' said Dobbs, 'and if you don't go peaceably, then you'll get it in the neck.'

The Indian stood there, irresolute. It did not enter his head to plead or expostulate. They had told him to leave them and with that he had to be content. There was nothing to show whether he understood that he was a nuisance to them, and that they had a perfect right to choose their company for themselves. He quietly stood there and said nothing.

Dobbs and Barber went on. But the Indian still followed behind like a dog which, though it has been driven away, refuses to be parted from its master. It was not from devotion or loyalty or any such feelings. He knew that the two were bound for the oil-fields; he knew that they would always contrive to get something to eat; and he knew that as long as he hung on to them he could never starve. If he went alone he would not get even a crust in any of the camps, not even from his fellow Indians, many of whom he was sure to find working there. The fear of tigers, too, was genuine. At any cost he had to get to the camps in order to look for work; but he was afraid to go alone or in the company of other Indians. He knew the terrors of the bush and jungle better than the white men did.

After they had proceeded for half an hour, Barber turned round. 'There's that brown devil slinking along behind us still,' he said.

Dobbs picked up some stones and began to bombard the Indian with them. But he dodged them, and after that kept farther behind so as to be out of range whenever Dobbs or Barber picked up a stone and hoped to fire it off at him unawares.

'We shall never be quit of him,' said Barber. 'I don't know what else we can do.'

'Kill him like vermin,' Dobbs said in a rage, picking up another stone.

Sure enough, when they came to the next camp the Indian trotted into the cook-house with them and got his grub too. The foreman made a face when he saw the two coming along with the Indian at their heels.

Dobbs and Barber told him that the Indian followed them wherever they went, but he only shrugged his shoulders. He did not know what to make of two white men who went from camp to camp with an Indian.

Now was their chance to get hold of him and give him a good thrashing. But it wouldn't have answered, for the foreman would have thrown all three out on the spot if they came to blows; and Dobbs and Barber had no desire at all to spend the night in the open.

It was the same thing next day. The Indian jogged along happily behind them, always keeping out of range; and it was useless to say anything, because he gave no sign of understanding what they said. He merely stuck to them.

So at last they made up their minds to take the shortest way back to the town. There did not seem to be much prospect of finding work in any of the camps round about, and there was no other way of getting rid of the Indian.

Towards evening they reached Villa Cuauhtemoc where

they had come on the Indian on the road that led to the oil-fields. He showed no surprise that the trip was so soon at an end. He squatted down again where they had found him three days before, and waited there for new victims on their way to the camps.

That night Dobbs and Barber reached the river bank. It was too late to cross. They slept by the riverside under the shelter of a large tree, where they came on three more who had picked up a living there for the past four weeks, sleeping under the tree in the open and cadging their meals from the tankers. They had had lean day and days of plenty. There were days when not a ship would give them a bite of bread, and there were days when there were three or four they could go to for dinner and supper. It was a toss-up.

Next morning, the two of them crossed to the town by the ferry. Nothing had changed there during their brief absence. At the bank, in front of the Imperial and the restaurants which the oil magnates patronized, there were just the same people coming and going and firing off the same wisecracks as they had two and three and six weeks before.

Barber went his own way again and Dobbs had gained nothing in the interval except the knowledge that work was as hard to find in the oil-fields as in the city. That was something. He did not need to reproach himself with having left a stone unturned in his search for it. He could not do more than he had done. But in the oil-fields there were no more jobs going than there were here.

But one morning a job turned up. Loading machine parts. It was hard work and he earned only three pesos a day, which left him nothing over. And after five days the job came to an end. Then one day he was standing near the ferry which crosses to the railway station for the Panuco line, when up came five men who were apparently in a great hurry.

One of them, a thick-set, weather-beaten fellow saw Dobbs standing there. He stopped and after a word to the others called out to Dobbs: 'Say – do you want a job?'

'Yes,' Dobbs shouted back and came a step nearer.

'Come here – sharp! I can give you a job if you're not afraid of work.'

Dobbs had now come up to him.

'I've got a contract to rig up a camp. I'm a man short. Got fever or malaria or something, and I can't wait for him. So you can have his job.'

'Right,' said Dobbs, 'I'll come. What's the pay?'

'Eight dollars a day, keep deducted; that'll come to one-eighty or two dollars. Can't say for sure yet. Six dollars clear anyway. Well, what do you say?'

'I'll come.'

Dobbs, who ten minutes before would have given his eyes for a job worth two dollars a day, now spoke as though he did the contractor a favour.

'But you've got to come right now,' the contractor said sharply. 'Just as you stand. There's no time to go after your kit. The Panuco train starts in a quarter of an hour and we're not across the river yet. So pick 'em up, my lad, and come along.'

He gripped Dobbs by the arm and pulled him towards the ferry.

Chapter Four

Pat McCormick, the contractor, was an Irish-American, and no longer a young man. He had spent most of his life among the oil-fields of Texas and Mexico. He had worked as driller, tool-dresser, truck-driver, teamster, timekeeper, bodega-man, pumpman and in every other capacity the oil-fields had to offer. Of late years he had worked on his own, rigging up camps as a contractor. He made a tender after a careful inspection of the site where the camp was to be erected; and it needed a man of his long experience to make a proper inspection of the ground. You had to reckon the distance from the nearest railway station, the distance from a road on which lorries could be driven and also whether the site was bush or jungle or prairie. Then there was the question of water and a supply of cheap native labour. Everything had to be taken into account before the price was fixed. If it was too high, the contract probably went to another man; if it was too low, the contractor lost money by cutting things too fine. But the American companies are not niggardly; if it could be shown that circumstances had been overlooked, or had arisen since, which justified an addition to the estimate, they were willing to pay it.

From Panuco they went on south by lorries loaded up with material, until the road, which was already bad enough, came to an end. From here a track had been cut through the bush for another three miles. This track was just wide enough for the pack-mules of the Indians employed on the job. The track ended in a clearing with a diameter of about a hundred metres, which had been cut in the bush. This was the site on which the camp was to be erected, for the company's mineralogists had come to the conclusion that oil was in all probability to be found there.

Twenty Indians from villages a few miles away had already cleared the site and were now employed in widening the track to the road, so that lorries could come along it.

For the first few days the six men slept in a tent. Two Chinamen cooked their meals.

Timbering and planks, tools, nails and screw-bolts had already been brought along on mules and donkeys, and every two hours a fresh caravan arrived. The caravan drivers also worked by contract. They got paid so much a load, not by time. If they had been paid by time, they would have lain down for a sleep on the way. The clearing of the bush was also done by contract. The men earned good money, much better than if they had been paid by the day. And now the first job was to erect a hut for the accommodation of the white workmen. Then came the kitchen and canteen. That was all completed in two days.

One of the workmen was now put in charge of the whole gang of Indians and set to work erecting the rest of the huts, while the remaining five constructed the derrick under Pat's orders.

That was a hell of a job. Dobbs had never before taken a hand in erecting a derrick. He had to carry timbers weighing a hundredweight on his shoulders while the sun beat down without mercy. After three days his shoulders were raw. The skin, grazed by the timber and burnt by the sun, hung in strips about his neck.

When the timbering had been carried, there were the holes for the screw-bolts to be drilled. And all at top speed. There was scarcely time to eat, as not a moment of daylight could be wasted. From the first gleam of the sun to the last glow of red in the sky they hauled and toiled like slaves. Even after sundown the work went on by lanterns if there was anything that could be done by artificial light. There was no electric light till much later when all the machinery was installed.

The more experienced men put the timbering in position, riveted it with bolts and fixed the struts, and as the framework rose higher and higher the work went on at a dizzier and more dangerous height. The derrick builders gripped a strut with their knees, while with hands and arms they hoisted another of the massive balks, supporting it with their thighs, until hanging by their knees at this dizzy height, they directed the swaying bulk to the required position and there had to hold it fast while the bolt was pushed in and screwed tight. They had to be as nimble as monkeys, or they would have fallen headlong and broken their necks, or their arms and legs.

At last the derrick, the boring tower, was built and could be equipped. The heavy iron rollers, over which ran the stout wire cable that raised and lowered the chisel and scoop, were hoisted by a windlass and fixed in position.

The most arduous labours were now completed. Next came the machine-house, then the tool and store sheds.

Meanwhile, the road had been cleared and the first lorry came through on a straight run from the railway.

There was a small stream three miles away in the bush. Pipes were laid to it and a shed erected on the bank to accommodate a motor pump. Up to then, water for the camp had been carried in tins by donkeys. Now it was pumped and stored in tanks.

Next, the steam engine arrived, loaded on a powerful tractor. The following day, the tractor, with a commotion which could be heard for miles across the bush, fetched the boiler.

The next day, again, the great wooden driving-wheels were hauled along. They were like the wheels of a water-mill, and the cables and chains for the chisel, scoop and pipe were coiled on them. And the dynamo came, the wires were connected, and one evening there was an island of brilliant illumination which turned night into day, where only a few weeks before the bush had lain undisturbed in its tropical isolation since the creation of the world. The quiet of night was destroyed and all life in the bush within the radius of the perpetual illumination began to sicken. In the morning million upon millions of insects were piled up in heaps beneath the electric globes.

The rattle of machinery, which now never ceased day or night, drove the occupants of the bush from their homes, and they had to invade new territory in search of food and rest.

After this the real work of oil-getting began. The work of the camp riggers was done. They went back to the city and waited for a new contract, which might turn up in three days, or in six weeks; or again, they might still be waiting for it when six months had gone by. Oil is a gamble. Ten, twenty, or fifty thousand may be sunk in an oil-field, and then, when the boring has been taken to the utmost practicable depths, there is no oil – nothing but salt water, or sand or clay. The bush is restored to its rightful owners, who resume possession so swiftly and thoroughly that within a year every trace of human occupation has been swept away.

Oil is a gamble. You can lose a fortune or make five million dollars with five thousand. Hence all who have to do with oil are rich today and poor tomorrow. For weeks and months they labour in the heart of the bush or the jungle. And then they squander in three days in the town all that their hard work has earned them. The prudent and saving who do not squander it lose it just as surely. They wait and wait for work until their last peso has gone; then they beg from the people who go in and out of the Imperial, the Southern, and the banks. In the oil countries it is just as much a matter of luck to find work as to strike oil.

So it was with Dobbs. There he stood with no thought of a job. And then a job dropped from the sky.

'What about my money?' Dobbs asked the contractor.

'What's up with you?' said Pat. 'Don't be in such a hurry. You'll get your money. I shan't run away with it.'

'Well, give me some of it, anyway,' Dobbs asked.

'Right you are,' Pat replied, 'you can have thirty per cent.'

'And the rest?' asked Dobbs.

'Can't say. I haven't been paid myself yet.'

Dobbs got thirty per cent of his earnings. The others had not been paid up either. Those who pressed hard enough got forty or fifty per cent. Two others who wanted to stand well with Pat, so as to be taken on for the next contract, got only five per cent, and that only when they told him very humbly that they had not had a meal that night and could not pay for a bed.

'I'd just like to know whether the stiff has had his money or not,' Dobbs said to Curtin, who had worked on the contract too.

'Yes, if we knew that,' Curtin replied. 'The companies are often slow in paying because they're short of the ready and when the boring starts it eats money.'

For a week neither Curtin nor Dobbs could run McCormick to earth. He was not in his hotel. But one day they saw him on the other side of the street.

'On to him,' Curtin called out to Dobbs, and shot across the street. Dobbs was after him like a streak.

Curtin caught Pat by the sleeve of his shirt. He had no coat on.

'Where's our money, you swine? If you don't pay up we'll smash your face in. See?' Curtin took care to speak loud and flourished his fists.

'On the nail and no more of your put-offs,' Dobbs shouted. 'It's three weeks we've waited for our money.'

'Don't make such a damned noise about it,' said Pat in a low voice, and taking them into a bar, he ordered three large glasses of Habanero without delay. 'We can settle up quietly. Listen to me, I've another contract next week, and another after that's done; one in Amatlan, the other in Corcovado. I'll take you both on. You're good workers and I'd be glad to have you. Here's to it!'

He raised his glass and they all drank. Then Curtin said: 'It's all very well taking us on for your new contracts. But we don't work for nothing. Where is our money?'

'I haven't had it myself yet. I'm still waiting for the cheque.' He turned to the barman as he spoke and ordered three more large Habaneros.

'Look here,' Curtin said impatiently, 'you're not going to get away with it like this and put us off with a drink or two.'

'Put you off?' Pat said in astonishment. 'I put you off with drinks? That's not very ...'

'What it is doesn't matter,' said Dobbs. 'We want our money. We've worked hard enough for it. What's the good of being taken on again for your next contracts if you don't pay?'

'Damn you, where's our money?' Curtin suddenly bawled out as if he had lost his senses. Perhaps the spirits had had an effect just the opposite to what Pat had expected.

'I haven't had my money myself yet, I tell you.'

Curtin took him by the throat and shook him. 'Pay up, you thief, or I'll smash your skull on the bar counter.'

'Quietly, gentlemen, quietly,' the barman put in, but took no further notice of the proceedings. He wiped away the rings left by the glasses and then lit a cigarette.

Pat was a hefty fellow, and he defended himself. But Curtin had the advantage of rage. Dobbs came nearer and made as though to join in.

But now Pat got loose from the grip on his throat and, stepping back, said mulishly: 'You're nothing but a couple of bandits, and I ought to have known it before. But I'll see myself cut in pieces before I take on such a pair of scoundrels in future. Take your money and don't let me see you again.'

'We don't want your permission for that,' said Curtin.

Pat pulled out a handful of crumpled dollar bills from his trouser pocket.

'Here's your money,' he said to Dobbs. In a moment he had counted out the correct sum. He knew in his head to a cent what he owed each of them. He pushed the money over to Dobbs, and then, dealing out the bills with one hand, he counted Curtin's and shoved the heap towards him.

'There,' he said in the tone one uses in getting rid of importunate beggars for charity. 'Now be so good as to leave me alone. You have your money and I shall be very careful in future not to take on any more odd-job fellows who know nothing.'

He threw down three pesos for the drinks. Then he shoved his hat on to the back of his head and went out, ignoring them as though they had deeply insulted him.

Chapter Five

'What do you stop at the Cleveland for?' Dobbs asked Curtin when they were in the street again and mooching past the Southern Hotel. 'You pay three pesos the night there, at least.'

'Four,' Curtin replied.

'Come along with me to the Oso Negro. Fifty centavos,' Dobbs advised him.

'It's too dirty there for me, and nothing but beachcombers and such guys,' said Curtin.

'As you please. When your money's gone you'll land up at the Oso Negro like the rest of us. I don't need to go there myself either, but I want to make what I've got go as far as I can. Who knows when we'll touch any more. I'm going to eat at a Chink's, too, as per usual.'

They had got to the corner of the Plaza, where there was the big jewellery store, La Perla. They stopped and looked at the display in the window. It was a blaze of gold and diamonds. There was a diadem that cost eighteen thousand pesos. They said nothing, but, as they looked at the treasure collected there and thought of its value, they thought too of the money some people in the town must have to be able to buy such things.

Perhaps it was the sight of all this that finally turned their thoughts from oil. For to live here was to think of oil and nothing but oil. There was not a way of gaining a living which was not oil, directly or indirectly. Labour or speculation, all was oil. They leant against the big plate-glass windows and looked indolently across the Plaza, beyond which the masts of the shipping could be seen. That took their thoughts to voyages and reminded them that there were other lands than this and other resources than those which this city offered.

'What's your notion now, Curtin?' asked Dobbs after a while. 'It's a poor look-out to stand about and wait for something to turn up. You can wait and go on waiting, while your money runs out. Then it's the old story again – begging from fellows who have come in from the camps for a day or a night. I've a damned good mind to try something different. Now's the time while we have the dough. Once it's gone, you're planted.'

'It's not the first time I've thought the same thing,' Curtin answered. 'I know all about that. But I'm damned if I know what to do – unless it's gold-digging.'

'That's the very ticket,' Dobbs agreed. 'I was just thinking of it. Come to look at it, it's no more of a speculation than waiting for a job in the oil-fields. There's no country on earth with so much gold and so much silver waiting to be scratched up as this country here.'

'Let's go over and sit on that seat,' Curtin said.

'I don't mind telling you,' Curtin began when they had sat down, 'that I didn't come down here for oil, but for gold. I only meant to work in the oil district till I had the money to go after gold. It costs a bit. There's the journey, and the shovels and picks and washing-pans and the rest of the outfit. Then you've got to live for six or eight months before you make anything. Then when all's said and done, it may be that you've lost everything, your money and your labour, because you find nothing.'

Dobbs waited for Curtin to go on, but Curtin said no more. Apparently he had no more to say. So Dobbs spoke up.

'It isn't the risk. There's just as much risk in hanging round for work. With luck you may earn three hundred dollars a month, perhaps more, for six or eight or eighteen months together. If you don't have luck you don't get work, and then you've lost everything just the same. We all know that gold's not lying about in heaps to shovel into a sack. I know that. But if it isn't gold, it may be silver; and if it isn't silver, it may be copper or lead or precious stones. If you can't work it yourself, there's always a company that'll buy you out, or take you into partnership on good terms. Anyway, it's worth thinking over.'

They went on to talk of something else. It is not a very serious matter, here, to talk of going to look for gold. Everybody speaks of it, everybody plans it, and of ten thousand there's only one who goes and does it, for it isn't quite such a simple matter as going out to shoot rabbits. There's not a man here who hasn't once at least made up his mind to go and look for gold; and of all the hundred of mines worked for other metals there is not one which was not found and started by men who were on the search for gold and took what came. Many a mine which produces neither gold nor silver yields its owner greater riches than an ordinary gold-mine could. With the extension of electricity the value of copper increases. The time may come when gold will be quite superfluous; one can scarcely venture to say the same of copper, lead and several other metals.

No man has ever originated an idea. Any new idea is the crystallization of the ideas of thousands of other men. Then one man suddenly hits on the right word and the right expression for the new idea. And as soon as the word is there, hundreds of people realize that they had this idea long before.

When an enterprise takes definite shape in a man's mind, one can safely say that numbers of men all round him cherish the same or a similar plan. That is why movements catch on and spread like wildfire.

Something of the sort was occurring here.

Curtin determined to stay one more night at the Cleveland and moved into the Oso Negro the day after. When Dobbs turned in, there were three Americans in his room besides himself. The other bunks were not occupied, apparently. One of the newcomers was an elderly man whose hair was turning grey.

When Dobbs came in the three men stopped talking. But after a while they went on. The old man was in bed, one of the others was lying down in his clothes and the third was sitting on the edge of his bunk. Dobbs began to undress.

At first he did not gather what they were talking about. But soon he found that the old man was telling the younger ones about his experiences as a gold-digger. These two had come to search for gold; for in the States they had been told marvellous tales of the abundance of gold in this country.

'Gold is the devil,' said Howard, the old man. 'It alters your character. However much you find, even if it's more than you can shift, still you think of getting more. And for the sake of getting more you forget the difference between right and wrong. When you set out you make up your mind to be content with thirty thousand dollars. When you find nothing, you put it down to twenty thousand, then to ten thousand, and lastly you declare that five thousand would be quite enough if only you could find them, no matter how you have to labour. But the moment you come on gold, you are not to be contented even with the thirty thousand you originally hoped for, your expectations mount higher and higher and you want fifty, a hundred, two hundred thousand dollars. That's how you get entangled, and driven this way and that, and lose your peace of mind for good.'

'That's not my game,' said one of the other two. 'I can take my oath for that. Ten thousand and then I'm finished. Finished even though another million lay there to be picked up. That's the exact sum I need.'

'Nobody believes it till he's been out himself,' Howard replied in his leisurely way. 'It's easy to get away from a gambling table, but no man has ever got away from a heap of gold which was his for the taking. I've dug for gold in Alaska and found it, I've dug in British Columbia, in Australia, in Montana, in Colorado. And made my pile, too. Well, here I am in the Oso Negro and through with it. I've lost my last fifty thousand in oil. Now I have to beg from old friends in the street. Perhaps I'll go out and have another try, old as I am. But I haven't the money. Then there's always this to consider: if you go alone it's the best, but you must be able to stand the solitude. If you go two or three together, there's always murder at your elbow. If it's a dozen of you, then each man's share is diminished, and you have quarrelling and murdering without any disguise. As long as you find nothing, you're all brothers. But as soon as the little heaps of dust get bigger and bigger, the brothers turn cut-throats.'

In this way the old man got going on those tales about gold which are listened to more eagerly by those who drift in and out of such places as the Oso Negro than the most bawdy love stories. When an old gold-digger like this began on his stories he might keep it up all night. Not a man would sleep a wink and not a man call out: 'Give us a chance to get to sleep.' In any case, whether the tales were of gold or robbery or love, such a request would be in vain. A man might express his desire to sleep. But if he expressed it too often or too emphatically there was trouble, because the story-tellers maintained they had as good a right to be there as those who were there to sleep. A man has the right to spend the night telling stories if he chooses. If you don't like it you have the right to go and find a quieter place. No one should travel at all or put up in hotels who can't sleep in peace amid the thunder of guns, the rattle of wheels, the chumping of motor engines, and the coming and going and laughing and singing and chaffing and quarrelling of his fellow men.

'Have you ever heard the story of the Green Water Mine in New Mexico?' asked Howard. 'You can't have. But I knew Harry Tilton who was there, and I had it from him. A band of fifteen men went off to find gold. They didn't go quite in the dark. There was an old tradition that in a certain valley there was a prolific gold-mine which the Mexicans had found and worked and which later on the Spaniards took from them after the Indians had been forced by merciless tortures – tongues pulled out, skulls gimleted and other such Christian attentions – to betray its where-abouts.

'Close to the mine in a hollow among the mountains there was a small lake, and the waters of it were as green as an emerald. That's why the mine was called the Green Water Mine. La Mina del Agua Verde. It was an uncommonly rich mine. The gold was in thick veins, you had nothing to do but extract it.

47

'The Indians, however, had laid a curse on the mine, so the Spaniards said, because every Spaniard who had anything to do with it came to grief. Some by snake-bite, others by fever, others again through terrible skin diseases and other diseases of which the cause could never be discovered. And one day the mine was lost. Not a man could be found who had ever been there.

'When the consignments of gold ceased and no report either came through, the Spaniards sent an expedition. The position of the mine was accurately marked on maps and the way to it was easy to follow, and yet the mine was not to be found. And there was no difficulty in locating it. There were three sharp rocky peaks, and when you had them in a line with each other you were on the right track, and when a fourth peak, of a shape you couldn't mistake, came into view and stood at a particular angle to the line of march, then you were so close to the mine that you could not miss it. But though the search went on for months, neither the mine nor the mountain tarn was ever found. That was in 1762.

'This prolific mine has never been forgotten by anyone interested in gold-mining.

'When New Mexico was annexed by the Americans, there was a new rush to find it. Many never returned. And those who did were half crazed by the vain search and the delusions that came on them while they hunted around among the rocks in that valley.

'It was in the 'eighties, 1886, I believe, when some more went to look – these same fifteen men I am speaking about. They had transcripts from the old reports and copies of the old Spanish maps. There was no trouble with the four hilltops. But however they took their bearings by them, there was nothing to be seen of the mine. They dug and blasted here and there and not a trace could they find. They worked in gangs, three men to each, so as to quarter the whole territory. Their victuals began to run short, but they would not give up.

'One evening one of the parties of three was preparing a

meal. The fire burnt up, but the coffee didn't boil, because the wind was strong and cooled the can. So one of them started to scoop a deeper hollow for the fire. And as he dug and got down a foot or a foot and a half he came on a bone. He threw it aside without looking at it and then pushed the fire down into the hole after he had made flues to give it air.

'While they sat eating their food, one of them took up the bone without thinking and drew a figure with it in the earth. The man nearest him said: "Let me have a look at that bone." After a look he said: 'It's the bone of a man's arm. How did it get here?"

'The one who had dug the hole now said that he had come on it while digging and thrown it out.

' "Then there must be a whole skeleton here. Why should there be just an arm bone?" the other said.

'It was now dark and they wrapped themselves in their blankets and lay down to sleep.

'Next morning, the man who had found the arm bone, whom I'll call Bill, because I don't know his name, Bill, then, said:

' "Where that arm bone came from there must be a skeleton. Now I had an idea in the night. I asked myself, how came this skeleton to be here?"

' "That's easy," said one of the other two. "Someone killed or died of hunger."

' "That's possible, of course," Bill said. "There have been plenty of guys about here. But I don't believe they were killed or died of hunger just here. It's occurred to me that the mine was buried by a sandstorm or an earthquake or a landslip or something of the kind, and that explains why not a Spaniard ever came back. They were all buried close to the mine. It's true this bone may just as well belong to someone who was searching before us and lost his life here, but it's just as likely it belongs to one of the buried Spaniards. And if his arm is here so is his skeleton. And if we dig down to the skeleton we'll perhaps come on the mine. What I say is, let's dig a bit here where the fire was."

They dug and, sure enough, they found the skeleton, bone by bone. They dug in a circle round about and found another, and further on a third. And so they got the direction which the landslide or the earthquake had taken. They followed it and came on tools and at last on nuggets of gold which had clearly been scattered abroad.

' "We've got the mine all right. And what now?" asked Bill.

' "Let's call the others," said one.

' "I never credited you with a lot of sense," said the third, "but I didn't know you were quite such a dam' fool. We'll hold our tongues and go back with the rest in a few days. Then in a few weeks we'll come back, us three by ourselves, and open the mine up."

'They all three agreed to this. They collected the few nuggets and pocketed them. With the proceeds they would be able to fit themselves out well for the job. Then they shovelled all the earth carefully back. But before they had done, one of the other gangs came up. They looked suspiciously at the signs of digging and then one of them said: "Hey, you guys, what's the game here? You want to keep us out of it, do you?"

'The first three stoutly denied having found anything and having meant to play a dirty trick. There was a quarrel, and as though the very air had betrayed them, two of the other gangs came up in the midst of the argument. They were just in time, for the first two gangs were on the point of coming to terms and agreeing to shut out the other three.

'Now, of course, the second gang drew back and accused the first of its treachery. A man was sent to summon the remaining one and when it arrived a council was held. It was resolved to hang the three members of the first gang for having intended to conceal their find.

'The three were hanged. There was none to dissent from the verdict, for now there were their three shares to divide among the remaining twelve.

'Then they set to work and the mine was opened up, and sure enough it was almost inexhaustible. But very soon provisions ran so short that five men were sent off to replenish them.

'Harry Tilton, who told me the story himself, decided that as he was satisfied with his share up to date, he would not go with these five men. So he took his share and went. A bank paid him twenty-eight thousand dollars for his gold, and he bought himself a farm and settled down.

'The five men bought pack-horses, good tools and a plentiful supply of provisions and had the claim registered. Then they returned to the mine.

'But when they got there they found the camp burnt to the ground and all the men who had stayed behind murdered, or, rather, killed by the Indians. There were signs of a terrible fight having taken place while they had been absent. They buried the bodies of their dead comrades and started working the mine again.

'They had not been at it more than three or four days when the Indians came back. They were more than sixty strong. They attacked at once and killed them all. One of them, however, was not killed outright but severely wounded and left for dead. When he recovered consciousness he set off to crawl away – for days or weeks – he didn't know. At last he was found by a farmer who took him to his house. He told his experiences, but he died of his wounds before he had been able to give an exact account of the place where it had all happened. The farmer set off to find the mine. He searched for weeks, but he never found it. Harry Tilton, who was in one of the northern states, heard nothing of all this. He was content to live on his farm and bothered no more about it; he imagined that all his comrades on the expedition were wealthy or prosperous men, who after they had got all the gold they wanted had gone east. He himself was a silent man. He had spoken of having made his money gold-mining. But there was nothing uncommon in that. And as he made little of his gold-digging days, the existence of this rich mine was again forgotten.

'But as time went on, the rumour grew that Tilton had made his money in a very few days. He did not deny it. And so it was plain that the place where he had dug must have been very rich in gold. He was pestered more and more by gold-diggers to work out a map that would make it possible to find the mine again. This at last he did. But more than thirty years had passed. His memory was no longer fresh. I set out with one of the parties which went by his map.

'We found all the places which Tilton had described. But the mine itself we never found. Perhaps it had been buried again by a landslip or earthquake, or else the Indians had obliterated all trace of it, and done it so well that nothing was to be seen. They did not want anyone in their territory; for a mine like that would have drawn men in hundreds to the spot, and thrown the whole neighbourhood into such a tumult that nothing would have been left of the life they were accustomed to.

'Yes, if one could find a mine like that,' Howard ended, 'one would be a made man. But you might search for it for a lifetime and find nothing. It is the same in any other line of business. If a man hits on the right business and has luck, there's his gold-mine. Anyway, old as I am, if anyone's after gold, I'm his man. But you need capital first, just as for all else.'

The story Howard told had nothing in it to act either as an inducement or a deterrent. It was the usual gold-digger's story; true, no doubt, and yet sounding like a fairy story. But all stories which tell of great winnings sound like fairy stories. If you want to win a fortune, you must take a risk. If you want gold, you must go and look for it. And Dobbs determined that night to go and look for gold, even though he were armed only with a pocket-knife.

There was only one perplexity. Was he to go alone, with Curtin, with old Howard, or with them both?

Chapter Six

Next morning Dobbs told Curtin the story he had heard from Howard. Curtin listened attentively and then said: 'I dare say it's true.'

'Of course it's true. Why should he have been telling lies?'

Dobbs was surprised that any should doubt the truth of the story. But the doubt which Curtin implied made an effect upon him. Its truth had seemed to him to follow as obviously as night after day. There was nothing in the story which need have been invented. Yet the doubt which lay behind Curtin's words turned it into an adventure story. And though so far Dobbs had looked upon the search for gold as no more than the search for a pair of boots in the various stores of a town, or as the search for work, he now suddenly realized that looking for gold must necessarily have something mysterious about it. He had never before had this queer feeling of something uncanny, mysterious and strange when the talk fell on gold-diggers. When Howard told the story in his matter-of-fact way, he had not felt that there was any difference between gold and coal. They were both in the ground, and coal could make a man just as rich as gold.

'Lies,' said Curtin. 'I didn't say that. The story itself is no lie. There are hundreds such stories. I've read them by the yard in the newspapers that print such yarns. But, whatever else in this story may seem improbable, I'm certain that bit of it's true where those three fellows try to get away with it and put the rest of them off the scent.'

'You're right.' Dobbs nodded. 'That's the curse that hangs over gold.'

As he said it he realized that he would not have made such a remark an hour before, because the thought of a curse resting on gold would never have occurred to him.

Curtin had not undergone this change, perhaps only

because he had not been confronted by such an unexpected doubt as the one with which he had just confronted Dobbs.

This inner experience of Dobbs parted the two without their knowing it. It was a parting within their emotional life. From now on their lives sought different goals. The destiny of each began to define itself.

'A curse on gold?' said Curtin. 'I don't see that. Where's the curse? There's just as much of a blessing on it. It depends who has it. It's the character of the man turns it to a curse or a blessing. Give a knave pebbles or dried sponges and he'll be up to some knavery with them.'

'Greed – that's the thing gold brings out.' Dobbs wondered how he came to say this. But he persuaded himself that it was only for the sake of contradicting Curtin.

'It's silly to talk like that,' Curtin replied. He spoke his intimate thought unintentionally, and Dobbs did the same without appearing to notice the change.

'It just depends,' Curtin went on, 'whether a man loves gold for itself or whether he regards it as a means to an end. There are officers in the army who are so keen on seeing a belt well polished that they forget what a belt's really for. Gold is not necessary in itself. If I can make a man believe I have plenty of gold, it's as good as if I really had it. It isn't gold that alters a man's character. It's the power gold gives him; and that's why people get excited when they see gold or even hear it talked about.'

Dobbs leant back on the seat. He looked up and on a roof opposite he saw two men laying telephone wires. Their footing was so precarious that you might have expected to see them fall headlong any moment. All for four pesos or four-fifty the day, Dobbs thought, and with the prospect of a broken neck or broken bones. It's just the same building a derrick, except that the risk is rather better paid.

He went on to think what a dog's life a labourer lived, and pursuing the thought, he asked: 'And would you do the dirty on your pals and get all the gold for yourself, like those three wanted to?'

'I can't tell you before hand,' Curtin replied. 'I don't believe there's a man who can say for certain what he might do if he had the chance of getting a heap of gold for himself by jockeying his pals out of their share. I'm pretty sure no man ever behaved as he expected when he came in for a lot of money, or saw the chance of raking in a heap of gold by a movement of his hand.'

Dobbs was still looking up at the men laying the wires. Although he wished them no harm, he had half a hope that one of them might fall, if only to break the monotony of life.

When none of them fell, it occurred to him that he was uncomfortable and that the seat hurt his shoulders. He straightened himself and lit a cigarette. He watched the smoke and then said:

'I'd do like Tilton. That's the best way, and then you don't need to slave and hang around and starve. I'd be content with a little and then go my way. The others might fight it out as they liked.'

Curtin had nothing to say in reply. They had said their say, and now they talked about something else, just for the sake of saying something instead of sitting there like dummies.

In the afternoon, however, after they had come back from bathing in the river, grousing all the way because they had to walk the whole length of the dusty Avenida just to save the fifteen-centavo tram-ride, the topic of gold came up again. The thought of gold was intertwined with the longing for a square meal, the thirst for a glass of ice water, the discomfort of bad nights on the hard bunks. It was really the thought of their present situation and how to alter it. Only money could alter it, and money was closely connected with gold. Thus the thought of gold gained on them until they thought of little else. Finally they saw that money was no use. Only gold, a great mountain of it, could release them from a life in which, even if they didn't starve, they could never eat their fill. The country they were in held an untold wealth of gold. They saw it gleaming in front of their eyes even when they shut them in the blinding glare of the white and dusty Plaza. Perhaps it was not gold. Perhaps it was the white streets, the white dust, the white houses that made them so impatient. But whatever they thought of they always came back to gold. Gold was ice water, gold was a full belly, gold was a suite of cool rooms in the tall and smart Riviera hotel. Gold and only gold could put a stop to the loitering about for ever in front of the American Bank in the hope of cadging a stray peso or a job from the manager of an oil-field. It was a degrading, shabby life. You couldn't go on like that for ever. It had to end. After three days had passed, and when there was still no prospect of a job, and when as far as they could see months might go by without any prospect of one, Dobbs said to Curtin: 'I'm going after gold, even if I have to go on my own. What does it matter whether I'm done in here or by Indians in the Sierra? I'm off.'

'I was going to make the same suggestion to you,' said Curtin. 'I'm ready for anything.'

'You don't care whether it's robbery or Santa Maria?'

'Santa Maria? I'm not a Catholic.'

'They won't ask whether you're a Catholic or not. But if you come to grief picking pockets you'll soon know who Santa Maria is. That's the penal settlement on an island off the west coast. They don't ask what your religion is – only how many years you've got. When you make the acquaintance of this particular Santa Maria you'll know why the Holy Virgin there has the blade of a knife in her heart. A man who got away live from the island drove it in.'

'We must get off tomorrow.'

Dobbs thought over this and then he said: 'I was thinking we might take old Howard with us. We'll ask him tonight what he thinks of it.'

'Howard? Why? He's too old. We might carry him on our backs, perhaps.'

'He's old,' Dobbs agreed, 'but he's as tough as the sole of a boot. When it comes to a pinch he'll stand more than both of us put together. I don't mind saying I know damn all about gold-digging, and shouldn't be any the wiser if there was gold in the ground under my eyes. Howard knows what he's about, he's been gold-digging and has made his fortune at it. He's lost it all in oil. It's half the battle to have an old hand with us. The only thing is, would he come?'

'We can ask,' said Curtin.

They went to the Oso Negro. Howard was in bed reading stories of bandits in the 'Western Story Magazine'.

'Will I come?' he said at once. 'There's no need to ask. Of course I'll come. You've only got to say gold and I'm your man. I've still three hundred dollars in the bank. I'll put up two hundred. It's all I've got. When that's gone, I'm finished But one must risk something.'

After they had pooled all their money, Dobbs remembered his lottery ticket.

'Don't be so superstitious,' Curtin said laughing. 'I've never seen anyone yet who won anything in a lottery.'

'Never mind,' said Dobbs. 'I'll go and look at the list all the same. That can't do any harm.'

'I'll come along with you. I'd like to see the long face you'll pull.'

The list was everywhere. It was in every street where lottery tickets were for sale. It was printed on linen. As no one ever bought a list the lottery could make no profit from the sale of them, and each list was handled by hundreds of people. They had to be very strong to withstand the eager grasp of all those who were sure that they must have won at last.

They found one of these lists at the corner of the Madrid Bar. It was the size of a handkerchief.

Dobbs glanced at it and said to Curtin: 'It's you to be laughed at for superstition, not me. Do you see that number there in heavy type? That's my number. For my twentieth part I get a hundred pesos.

'Where from?' Curtin asked in astonishment.

'We go and cash it at once at the Agency.'

Dobbs put his ticket on the table. The agent examined it

and without making any deduction handed Dobbs two fat gold fifty peso pieces.

When they were in the Plaza again Curtin said: 'Now I'll put up a hundred dollars. Then we'll have enough. I have a friend in San Antonio over in Texas. He'll send me the money.'

He telegraphed and the money came by return. They took the night train to San Luis and from there the next train on to Durango.

Here they studied maps of the district.

'There's no use going anywhere near a railway,' Howard said. 'It's not worth while. Where there's a railway or even a good road, every corner which might yield anything is already known. We must go into the wilds if we want to get anything. We must snoop round where there's no tracks, where no mineralogist has ever been, where nobody has ever heard of a motor car. That's the sort of place to hit on.'

He fingered his way about the map and then said: 'Round about here. Just where, doesn't matter. Once we're there we must keep our eyes open. That's all. I knew a man once who could smell out gold as a thirsty donkey smells out water.'

'Right,' said Dobbs. 'And that reminds me, we must buy donkeys in one of the villages hereabouts to carry our traps.'

Curtin and Dobbs soon saw that they would have been helpless without old Howard. You don't find gold so thick on
the ground as to trip over it. You must know how to see it.
You can easily walk right over it and never know it's there.
But Howard saw the least trace of it, if any trace was to be
seen. He saw from the look of the ground whether there was
the likelihood of gold or not, and whether it was worth while
untying the shovels from the pack and panning a few shov-
elfuls of sand. Whenever Howard gave a blow with a pick
and turned up the ground, or even washed a little earth in
the pan, at once they were in the promised land, which ought
by rights to be rich in gold. Four times they found gold. But
the quantity was so small that it would hardly pay them a
day's wage. Once they came on a very promising spot, but
the water which they would need for the washing was six
hours away, and so they had to give it up.

On and on they went, deeper and deeper into the mountains.

One morning they foud themselves wedged in a narrow
track. They crawled and clambered and panted, and could
hardly get the donkeys forward. Their tempers were getting
short.

And Howard made things no better by saying: 'I've taken
two fine passengers on, damned if I haven't.'

'Hold your jaw!' Dobbs shouted angrily.

'Fine passengers,' Howard repeated scornfully.

Curtin had a powerful retort on the tip of his tongue, but
before he could let loose Howard continued: 'You're so
damned silly that you can tramp on millions with both feet
and see nothing.'

The other two, who were in front, stood still and did not
know whether Howard was making fools of them or
whether the exertions of the last few days had affected his
mind.

But Howard grinned and said quietly without any sign of excitement: 'There you go, walking on naked gold and can't see it. Till the end of my life I'll never know how I came to go looking for gold with such a pair of skunks as you two. I'd just like to know what I've done to have to put up with you.'

Dobbs and Curtin stood there. They looked down at the ground at their feet, then they looked at each other, and then at Howard with an expression which left it doubtful whether they were barmy themselves or only thought Howard was.

The old man bent down and scooped up a handful of loose sand. 'Do you know what I have in my hand?' he asked, and added without waiting for an answer: 'Gold dust. And there's more of it than we three could carry away on our backs.'

'Let's see,' they both yelled at once and started forward.

'You needn't come any nearer. You only need to bend down and pick it up. Then you'll see it and have it in your hands.'

Incredulously they picked up handfuls of sand.

'Perhaps you can't see it,' Howard said, grinning. 'But you can tell by the weight what's there.'

'That's true,' Dobbs shouted out. 'I see it now, too. We could fill our sacks and go straight back.'

'So we could,' said Howard with a nod. 'But that would be bad business. Better to wash it out clean. Why drag a lot of useless sand about with us? We shan't get anything for that.'

Howard sat down. 'The first thing is to fetch a few bucketfuls of water. I'll test the percentage of gold.'

And now the real work began. They had to find water. They found it, but it was about a hundred and twenty metres lower down and had to be carried up by the bucketful. To carry the sand down and wash it straight away would have been more laborious and certainly more wasteful of time; for the water could be used again and again. And though it was diminished by each washing, there was only this loss to make good; whereas all the sand would have to be carried down every time, and it might be that in two heavy sacks of sand there would be scarcely a grain of gold.

They made their camp, made the cradle and the puddling trough, dug channels for the fall of water, excavated a tank, which they lined so well with chalk and clay that the leakage was not worth talking about.

After two weeks they were able to proceed to productive work.

Work it was, without any doubt. They toiled like convicts. It was very hot by day and bitterly cold by night. They were high up in the mountains of the Sierra Madre. No road led there, only a mule track as far as the water. The nearest railway station was ten or twelve days distant by donkey. And to get there you had to go over steep passes, by mountain paths, through water-courses and ravines, along the edges of precipitous cliffs. The whole way there were only a few small Indian villages.

'I've never had to work like this in my life,' Curtin said one morning when Howard knocked him up before sunrise. However, he got up, saddled the donkeys and fetched the day's supply of water, although it was seven o'clock before he got a bite of food.

By that time they were all three sitting at breakfast.

'I wonder sometimes,' Howard said, 'what you two actually imagined gold-digging was. I've come to the conclusion you thought the gold would be lying around like pebble-stones, and nothing to do but bend down and pick it up and go off with it by the sackful. But if it was as simple as all that, gold wouldn't be worth more than pebblestones.'

Dobbs growled to himself. 'All the same,' he said after a while, 'there must be places where there's more of it and you don't need to break your heart to rake an ounce together.'

'So there may be, but they're like first prizes in a lottery,' the old man replied. 'I've seen places myself where you come on gutters with nuggets as big as my fist turned up with the pick or puddled out. I've known three, four and eight pounds got in the day. And I've known it when, in the same place, four men have racked their guts for three months and ended up with less than five pounds among the four of them. Take my word for it – the safest is washing out productive dirt. It's hard work, but when you've done your eight or ten months you pocket a good sum. And if you can stick it for five years, you're made for the rest of your life. But I'd like to see the man who'll do his five years of it. Generally speaking, the yield gives out altogether after a few months, and then you have to go on trek again to find a fresh place.'

The two greenhorns had never thought gold-digging was such hard work; and this was rubbed into them four times every hour. Digging and digging from sunrise to sunset in the sweltering heat; then up with the dirt into the trough; then rock and puddle and sift. And all to do over again three and four and five times – back and back with it into the cradle, because it did not come out clean.

So it went on day after day without a break. Their backs were so stiff they could neither stand nor lie nor sit. Their hands were like horny claws. They could not bend their fingers properly. They did not shave, nor cut their hair. They were too tired and they couldn't be bothered. If they tore shirt or trousers, they sewed a patch on, but not unless the things would otherwise fall to pieces.

There was no Sunday; for the only day of rest they had was a necessity in order to tinker up their primitive machinery, to wash themselves, to shoot a few birds or a buck, to find new grazing for the donkeys and to go to an Indian village for eggs, ground maize, coffee, tobacco, rice and beans. They were lucky if they could get such things at all. Flour, bacon and white sugar were not to be thought of except when one of them made a day's journey to the larger village where these rarities could sometimes, by no means always, be procured. When one of these expeditions produced a bottle of Tequila as well, it was a red-letter day.

Next, the question arose what they were to do about a licence. Prospecting was permitted without a licence, but not digging and washing out. But there were difficulties connected with a licence. You had to go to a government office and say exactly where the diggings were situated and pay a good sum. You also had to surrender a percentage of the yield. And it might take weeks before it was all settled.

All that might not have been so bad. The worst was that by taking out a licence, however careful you might be, you were pretty sure to bring bandits about your ears – those bandits who reap without sowing, who lie in wait for weeks and months while their victims do the hard work, and then fall upon them as soon as they load up to go, and take their gold from them. And not only their gold, but their donkeys and even the shirts from their backs. It is not easy to find the way back to civilization without donkeys or trousers or shirts or boots. Often the bandits, realizing this, are kind enough to take their lives too rather than leave them in such a perplexity. Who is to say where the poor wretches have got to? The bush is so vast and so impenetrable and its dangers so many. Sometimes there is a search for a missing man. And before the search is even on foot, the bush has disposed of the body almost to the last bone. From this last bone it has to be made out who the man was to whom the bone belonged. And the culprits, of course, will be brought to justice. But for that, they must first be caught. And because of this, the bandit's trade is an easy one, much easier than getting gold by the sweat of his brow.

Whenever a licence is taken out, the news gets round. It has happened before now that the robbers are not bandits, but the representatives of a large and respectable mining company, who put the fortunate prospector out of the way. Then when the gold-field is not worked, the licence lapses after a few months, and the company take it up. The licence will be given them on the ground that the first licensee has lost his rights owing to absence.

It is far better therefore not to bother with a licence. When you decide to give up and be content with what you have got, you can convey your treasure unobtrusively away. No one will think of searching such ragged vagrants, and if you meet with bandits, or any who might turn bandits for the occasion, you can disarm them by begging for tobacco.

So much for a licence. If you have one, bandits will take your gold. If you haven't one, and the government gets to know it, they take half your little pile or the whole of it as a penalty. There you are in the vast silence of the bush. But there is so much else as well. The moment you possess anything, the world takes on another aspect. In any case, from that moment, you belong to the minority, and all who have nothing, or who have less than you, become your deadly enemies. From that moment you must be continually on your guard. There is always something to keep you on the alert. As long as you have nothing, you are the slave of an empty belly and of any who can fill it. But when you have anything, you are the slave of your possessions.

Chapter Eight

These three men whom chance had brought together had never been friends. They had scarcely ever given a thought to the possibility of being friends. At best, they were partners in an enterprise. They had come together simply from motives of gain. And as soon as this motive ceased, their partnership would be dissolved. They got across each other and quarrelled as it was, and as always happens after a time when people are thrown together. Their quarrels might have ended by making them friends. It would not have been very surprising. When people who are not friends begin to quarrel and dispute, it is often the beginning of an enduring friendship.

The common labours and worries and hopes and disappointments ought, according to all the laws of human intercourse, to have made friends of these three men during the months they spent together. They were war comrades, closer comrades, indeed, than any war could have made them. There was not one of them who had not saved the life of each of the other two on more than one occasion. Each was always prompt to help another and to risk his life or broken bones to rescue him from danger. Anything might happen. Once a tree they were felling fell too soon, and Dobbs caught it on his shoulder and send it to one side; otherwise Curtin would have been crushed. As it was, Dobbs's shoulder was badly bruised.

'Bully for you, Dobbs,' was all that Curtin said. What else was there to say?

Two weeks after this, the slabbing gave when Dobbs was in the trench and Curtin rushed forward and hauled him out, although a great slice of gravelly earth swayed above him. Had it fallen a moment sooner, Curtin would have been so completely buried that Howard, who was trying to pin the slabbing at the other end, would have been too late even to guess where the two of them had got to.

When Dobbs had been pulled out and had got his senses and his breath back, he said: 'If you two had stopped to spit on your hands, I would never have spat on this heap of dirt any more.' As he spoke he spat out a mouthful of soil.

No words were wasted over incidents of this kind. It was all in a day's work and brought them no nearer together. If they had saved each other's lives for ten years together, they would never have become friends.

They could not see themselves with unprejudiced eyes, but if anyone else had seen them sitting round the fire before turning in, he would have had the impression that they were ready to spring at each other's throats at the first opportunity. Yet it was not murder that gleamed from their eyes. Perhaps it was jealousy. And yet if any one of them had been asked what he felt, he would not have said it was jealousy or greed. It certainly was not that. Each had the same as the others, each knew that the other two, like himself, had sunk their all in the common enterprise, and, like himself, had toiled and suffered privations and put up with every expected rebuff in order to achieve their common purpose. How could they feel jealousy or covetousness? A normal man doesn't have such unnatural feelings.

Every evening before the light began to fail, the day's yield was carefully weighed up and divided into three shares, and each took his share. They had done this from the start. 'We'd best share out every evening and each take his share,' Curtin suggested on the second evening after their labour began to show its first results.

'Then at least I won't need to be treasurer,' said Howard.

The other two looked up at once.

'Who the devil asked you to take charge of the funds? We'd think twice before trusting the lot to you.'

'Is that how the wind blows?' Howard said laughing. He was not at all put out. He had been through too much to be worried by such outbreaks. 'I was only thinking,' he said good-naturedly, 'that I was the most trustworthy man here.'

'You?' Dobbs shouted. 'And what about us – escaped convicts, I suppose?'

And Curtin joined in. 'How do we know where your palmy days were spent?'

Howard was not to be put out.

'You don't know that, of course. And it doesn't count for much between the three of us out here. I haven't asked either of you where you came from or where you spent the days of your innocence. It wouldn't have been at all polite of me. You should never tempt a man to tell lies. Out here, where not a cock crows, what's the use of deceptions? Whether we tell each other lies or the bleeding truth doesn't make a cent of difference. But of the three of us, I'm the only one to be trusted out here.'

The other two grinned, but before they had time for a juicy reply, Howard went on: 'You needn't excite yourselves. What I'm saying's right. We've only facts to think of here. Suppose we'd put the lot in your charge,' he said with a jerk of his head at Dobbs. 'But then when I was in the bush cutting props and Curtin had ridden down to get provisions, you'd pack up and clear out.'

'It's an insult to say that,' Dobbs broke out.

'Maybe. But it's just as insulting to think it. And if you wouldn't think it, you're the first man I ever came across who wouldn't. Out here it goes without saying that a man will make off with the lot, if he has the chance. He's a fool who doesn't. You're only a couple of hypocrites not to confess it. But let me see what you think about it when we have twenty kilos of pure gold in our hands. You're no better and no worse than the common run. And if you tie me to a tree one of these days and pack up and clear out, leaving me to my fate, so as to have my share, you'll only be doing what any man would do, unless the thought came to him that perhaps it mightn't pay him in the end. I can't get away with your two lots. I'm not quick enough on my legs. You'd be on me within twelve hours and hanging me from the nearest tree without scruple. I can't clear out. I'm at your mercy. That's why I say I am the only trustworthy man among us.'

'Looked at that way,' Curtin said, 'no doubt you're right.

But in any case it'll be best to divide out every evening, and each man can look after his own share and go when he likes.'

'No objections to that,' said Howard. 'It is not a bad idea at all. Then we'll all be afraid of the others spying out our hiding-places.'

'You must be a proper bad 'un, Howard,' said Dobbs, 'if you have such ideas always running in your head.'

'That doesn't worry me, my boy,' Howard replied. 'I know what men are and what pleasant things they can think and do when gold's in the question. At bottom all men are alike when there's gold to reckon with. One's as big a scoundrel as the rest. When there's a chance of being caught, they're more prudent and lying and hypocritical. But here there's no occasion for hypocrisy. It's all clear and above board. In the towns there are all kinds of obstacles and restraints. Here there's one obstacle – the life of the other man. And here there's only one thing to consider.'

'What?' asked Dobbs.

'I'd like to know what that is,' Curtin asked at the same moment.

'You need only to consider whether one day the memory won't weigh on you. Deeds don't trouble a man. It's always the memory that eats into you. But to come to business, we'll share out every evening and each man can look out a good hiding-place. When it comes to five kilos we shan't want to have it dangling round our necks any longer.'

Chapter Nine

Great care and ingenuity had been spent in concealing the diggings; and the camp where they cooked and slept was half a kilometre away. The diggings could only be approached from one direction, and here they were screened off so effectually by bushes and large stones that no one who passed by was likely to come across them. After a week the screen of bushes, the mounds of earth, the excavations and the blocks of stone were so entirely overgrown that even natives out hunting would have noticed nothing to suggest that work was in progress there.

They had no intention, however, of concealing their camp. It lay open to view, and in order to explain their presence there they stretched the skins of animals and birds on wooden frames. That showed at once that they were hunters who were collecting skins and rare birds. Not the least suspicion would be aroused, as hundreds of people carry on this profitable trade.

A secret path led from the camp to the diggings. To reach the path they had to crawl for the first ten metres. When they were through, the way they had come was screened by green prickly scrub. On their return to the camp, they first observed it carefully to see if there was anyone in the neighbourhood. If that had ever been the case, they would have made a wide circle and approached the camp from another direction, as though they had come in from hunting.

But they had never seen a soul, white or native, all the time they had been there. It was very unlikely that anyone would ever be wandering about in this wild spot. But they were too knowing and too prudent to leave it to chance. Even wounded game followed by a hunter would never have sought refuge where they were working. It would have smelt them and taken another course. Dogs, too, are nervous in the bush and never leave their masters to hunt on their own.

The life these three live here was more wretched than that of a Lithuanian factory-hand in Detroit. It was the most miserable existence you can imagine.

Dobbs said one evening that he had felt more of a human being in the worst trenches in France than during these weeks. Curtin and Howard could say nothing about that, because they had not had the honour of defending tender and innocent babes at the breasts of American mothers from the bayonets of the Huns. But every day they spent here made their life more intolerable. The monotony of their food, which they were too tired to cook properly, sickened them. The dreary sameness of their work made the labour of it even heavier than it was in any case. Digging, sifting, rocking, hand-picking, water-carrying, slabbing. One hour like another, every day like the last. And it had gone on now for months.

Perhaps they could have stood the labour. Hundreds of thousands of men spend their whole lives labouring in the same way and feel none the worse for it. But here there were other influences at work.

They had spent the first few weeks without realizing what they were in for. They never suspected for a moment that influences, of which they had had no experience, would sap their endurance. Each day at first brought something new. There was something to plan and carry out. Each of them, too, had a few jokes to tell, or some experience of life unknown to the others. Each was a study for the others, and had some peculiarity which interested or repelled, and at least occupied the attention of his fellows.

But now they had nothing more to tell. There was not a word in their vocabularies with which each was not familiar, even to the gesture and intonation which accompanied it.

Dobbs had a habit of half closing his left eye now and again as he spoke. At first Curtin and Howard found this very amusing and chaffed him about it. Then one evening, Curtin said: 'If you don't leave off winking that left eye of yours, you son of a bitch, you'll get an ounce of lead in your belly. You know it annoys me, you jail-bird.'

Dobbs leapt to his feet and pulled out his revolver. If Curtin had got his out as quickly, there would have been a shooting match. But he knew that if he put his hand to his hip he would get six bullets in his belly.

'I know what you are,' Dobbs shouted, balancing the revolver from his wrist. 'You were flogged in Georgia for rape. You are not here in Mexico for your health, I know.'

Dobbs knew as little whether Curtin had ever been in Georgia as Curtin knew whether Dobbs had ever been in jail. They had drawn these conclusions from their pipes and chewed them out of their bacon, and came out with them now merely to excite each other to the highest pitch of rage.

Howard took no notice of them. He puffed out thick clouds of smoke and stared at the fire. When the two were silent for lack of further abuse, he said: 'Now, boys, leave shooting out of it. We've no time here for hospital work.'

After a while Dobbs put up his revolver and lay down to sleep. Curtin sat with Howard by the fire and lit another pipe.

One morning, not long after, Curtin prodded Dobbs in the ribs with the muzzle of his gun. 'Say a word, you toad, and I'll shoot.'

It happened in this way. Dobbs said to Curtin: 'Don't munch like a hog with acorns when you eat. What sort of a reformatory were you brought up in?'

'It doesn't concern you any more than a dog's turd whether I smack my lips or run at the nose. Anyway, I don't suck a hollow tooth like a whistling rat.'

Whereupon Dobbs replied:

'Have the rats in Sing Sing hollow teeth?'

Sing Sing, for those who don't know it, is the residence of all New Yorkers who get caught. The rest have offices in Wall Street.

This friendly joke was more than Curtin could stand, and he pushed his revolver between Dobbs's ribs.

'Damn you,' Howard shouted, losing patience, 'you

behave as if we were all married to each other. Put that gun away, Curtin.'

'Who spoke to you?' Curtin shouted back in a rage. He let the muzzle fall and turned on the old man. 'What do you want to give orders for, you cripple?'

'Orders?' Howard replied. 'I'm not giving orders. But I came here to dig for gold, not to scrap around with two young fools. Each of us needs the others, and if one is shot to hell the two that are left can pack up, for two could do nothing, or no more than would amount to a fair day's wage.'

Curtin had now shoved his gun back in his hip pocket.

'And I may as well tell you,' Howard went on, 'I've had enough of your carry on. I don't want to be left here with either of you, and I'm going. What I've got will do for me.'

'But it won't do for us,' Dobbs shouted in a fury. 'It may be enough for the six months you have to live. But not for us. And if you sneak off before we've puddled the lot – we'll soon find a way of keeping you here.'

'Stow that, you old bag of bones,' Curtin said, joining in. 'We'll get you within four hours if you try that on. Do you know what we'd do with you then?'

'I can imagine it, you stiff,' Howard sneered.

'No, you can't,' Curtin replied with a grin. 'We'd take your belt off and tie you to a tree, tight and proper, and then we'd go and leave you there. Perhaps you thought we'd do you in? No, that's not the game.'

'Not a bit of it. You're too pious and I might be on your innocent consciences. Tie me up and leave me – you're not worth spitting on. And yet you weren't too bad when I met you down there in the town.'

All three were silent for a bit. Then Dobbs said:

''Tis is a lot of bullsh. But, damn it, when you never see a fresh face month after month, it's more than you can stand. It must be the same with married people. At first they can't be apart for half an hour, and as soon as they have to live together and haven't another word to say that the other hasn't heard a hundred times already, all they want is to poison each other. I know that from my sister. At first she wanted to drown herself because she couldn't get the man, and then when she'd got him she wanted to drown herself to get away from him. Now she's divorced and wants to try it on with someone else.'

'How much do you think we've got now, Howard?' Curtin asked unexpectedly.

The old man thought it over for a moment. Then he said: 'I can't say offhand. We don't get it all washed out clean. There's bound to be other metal along with it now and then. But I should say we'd got from fourteen to sixteen thousand dollars apiece.'

'Then,' said Dobbs, 'what about putting in another six weeks at it and then shutting down and quitting?'

'That'll suit me,' Curtin threw in.

'We shall have got all there is by then, anyway,' Howard said. 'By what I see of it, we shall be so far through even in four weeks that it won't pay for the labour. Have you noticed that, ten paces higher up in the direction we're digging now, the soil alters? There's no more sand. Either the stream must have fallen over the cliff at this spot, or else taken its rise at the foot of it. You can't tell which at this distance of time. No doubt there's been a landslip at some time or other and after that the stream took another course, or else the spring found another outlet.'

Peace was now restored to the camp. There were no more quarrels like the last one. They now had a fixed aim, and the day on which they would abandon their camp was settled. This so entirely altered their mood and their attitude to life that they could hardly understand how they had come to quarrel so bitterly. They were now preoccupied with plans for the future. There was the question of getting away unnoticed and conveying their dust into safety, and where, when that was done, to settle down, and what use to make of it when they had turned it into money. All this gave them something fresh to talk about. They looked forward already to living in a town among all the resources of civilization.

And knowing that it wouldn't be long now, they found it easy to put up with each other's peculiarities; instead of being exasperated, they were tolerant of each other. If Curtain perseveringly scratched his head and then absent-mindedly surveyed his finger-nails with satisfaction, Dobbs, who also had bad habits of his own, did not tell him off. He said with a laugh: 'Are they biting, Curtin? Well, wait a bit, the meat's just roasted, and you'll have something else to worry at.'

And Curtin replied with a laugh: 'I'll have to break myself of this cursed habit, or they'll throw me out of the hotel.'

They got on better and better as the day drew nearer. Howard and Dobbs even spoke of going into partnership and opening a cinema together at Monterey or Tampico. Dobbs was to take charge of the artistic side, selecting the films, taking charge of the performances, writing the programmes and seeing to the music, while Howard was to be responsible for the business side, the café, the payments and receipts, the printing, the repairs and decoration of the building.

Curtin was in some perplexity. He couldn't decide whether to stay in Mexico or return to the States. He let fall once that he had a girl in San Antonio. It did not seem to worry him, however, though perhaps he gave that impression to avoid being chaffed.

Women were seldom mentioned among them, unless with contempt. Why should they bother about them? One always speaks contemptuously of what cannot be had. It would have been difficult for these three to imagine themselves with a woman or a girl in their arms. It could only have been the runaway wife of a bandit. A decent girl would rather have drowned in a bog than trusted herself to any one of them, at least in their present situation and looking and behaving and expressing themselves as they did.

The gold that a beautiful and elegant woman wears on her finger, or a king in his crown, has been in strange company and washed in blood as often as in soap and water. A chaplet of flowers, a wreath of the leaves of a tree has a nobler origin, and though gold may be more durable this advantage is merely relative.

Chapter Ten

The day came when Curtin went to the village tienda to bring the last stock of provisions they would need before their departure.

'Where the devil have you been all this time?' Howard asked him when he dismounted and set to work unloading the pack-donkey.

'I was just going to saddle my donkey and go and look for you,' Dobbs put in. 'We thought something must have happened to you. You ought to have got back by two at latest.'

Curtin went on unloading the donkey without a word. Then he sat down and lit his pipe and handed out tobacco from the saddle-bags.

'I've had to come the devil of a way round,' he said at last. 'There's a guy down there in the village – says he's from Arizona.'

'What does he want here?' asked Dobbs.

'That's what I want to know,' Curtin replied. 'But the Indians only said he'd been hanging around there the last few days. He asked the villagers whether there were any gold or silver mines in the neighbourhood. The Indians told him there weren't any, and no gold nor silver either, or anything else; and that they had a job to keep themselves by weaving mats and making pots. But then that half-wit at the tienda told him that there was an American somewhere in the mountains after game. He doesn't know that you are here too, he only knows about me. At least, I think so. And then he told the fellow that I came along now and again to buy provisions, and that I would probably be coming this week. So then the guy from Arizona said he'd wait for me.'

'And so he waited, did he, the dirty swine?'

'He did. As soon as I got down there he was on to me, and what was I after here, and was there anything doing, and he'd heard there was plenty of gold about and a lot more of the kind. I was pretty short with him and scarcely answered.'

'Didn't you put him right off it?'

'Sure. When I made any answer at all, I told him a lot of bunk. But that was no use. He was dead keen to come back to the camp with me. He said he was certain there must be gold in these parts, he could tell from the course of the dried-up streams, from the sand they had brought down, and bits of rock which had split off and come down from the cliff.'

'He's a great man,' said Howard, 'if he needs no more than that to tell him there must be gold here.'

'He knows nothing about it,' Dobbs broke in. 'He's a spy. Either a government spy or a spy of bandits who mean to hold us up when we start back. Even if they don't think of gold, there are the donkeys and tools and clothing, knives, revolvers and skins, as they think. All worth something. Enough to make it worth the while.'

'I don't think he's a spy,' Curtin said. 'I believe he's really after gold.'

'Then he has the outfit?' asked Howard.

'Not that I saw. He has a mule he rides on, a blanket, a coffee pot, a pan and a sack, with a few rags in it, I daresay, that's all.'

'He can't start washing out gold with his bare hands,' said Dobbs.

'Perhaps he's had his tools stolen, or had to sell them. But what do we want with him nosing round?'

Curtin scratched his head and was just going to look at his nails. But when he saw that Howard and Dobbs had their eyes on him, he let his hand drop and decided once more to break himself of the habit. Howard and Dobbs however were not this time thinking of reminding him that in a few days he would be on his way to civilization. It was in their absence of mind that they followed Curtin's movements with their eyes. Their thoughts were busy with this mystery man from Arizona and they watched Curtin with the vague idea that it might help them to unravel the secret.

Curtin stared into the fire. Then he said:

'I couldn't make him out. He doesn't look as if he had anything to do with the government or bandits either. He looks innocent enough and speaks as though he means what he says. And whatever Dobbs says we have to do with him already. He followed me. At first he asked whether he could come back with me to my camp. I said no he couldn't. Then he rode after me. I stopped and waited for him and when he came up I told him to go to the devil and not bother me any more. He said he wouldn't be any bother to me only wanted company for a day or two as he was half crazed here in the mountains seeing nobody but these Indians. All he wanted was to sit by the fire for an evening or two with a white man and have a talk. Then he'd go. So I told him to look for another pal as I didn't want to have anything to do with him. I couldn't call him a hobo very well. He could have said the same of me, the way we both looked.'

'Where is the man?' asked Howard.

'He's not here by any chance?' Dobbs said, turning round.

'I hardly think that,' Curtin replied. 'I went all round-about through the bush. But whenever I had him in view he was making straight here. If I'd been on foot I could have taken him right off the track. But try that with two donkeys. He only needs to know that there's somebody camping here in the mountains, and then if he has the direction roughly, he's bound to come on us today or tomorrow or the day after. And so he will. The only question is – what to do with him when he turns up? As long as he's here we can't go to the diggings.'

'It's a bad business,' said Howard. 'If it was an Indian I wouldn't mind so much. He wouldn't stay long. He'd be off home to the village. But this guy'll stick to us like a pitch plaster. He won't need telling either, to know that we've got something on here. For what should three white men be lying low here for – here in the mountains? We can only say we're robbers and murderers who are here in hiding. But then as soon as he's down in the village again we shall have a regiment of soldiers along, and that'll be the end of all our nice plans for the future. And if there's an officer and he believes the story of our being here because of robbery and murder, he'll perhaps have us shot on the spot to be sure we don't escape.'

'It's simple enough,' said Dobbs. 'We'll soon be even with the fellow. As soon as he comes we'll tell him to quit the neighbourhood, unless he wants a few ounces of lead in his carcase.'

'We'd look the fools then,' said Howard. 'Back he'd go and talk a lot of bunk and perhaps run across some mounted police, and then we'd be properly in the soup up here. You might as well tell him right off that we're escaped convicts from Santa Maria.'

'Well, there's still the straight way with him,' and Dobbs looked resolute. 'As soon as he comes, snipe him and be done with it. Or else hang him from that tree yonder, and strip the bark of it. Then we'll have peace.'

For a time nothing was said to this proposal.

Howard got up and looked at the potatoes (a rare treat), and after poking about among them sat down again.

'There's no sense in shooting the man down at sight. For all we know, he's a poor devil of a tramp who'd rather walk the wide world than rack his guts for a bare wage in the oil-fields or the mines. It'd be a crime to snipe a harmless hobo.'

'But how do we know he's harmless?' Dobbs protested.

'We shall find out,' said Howard.

'How?' Dobbs was only the more convinced that his plan was the best one. 'We'll bury him out of sight. If anyone down there says he saw the man come up here, it's easy enough to say we saw nothing of him. We can tip him down the gully there. And the might have fallen down there by accident.'

'Will you do it, then?' asked Howard.

'Why should I do it? We can draw lots who does it.'

The old man grinned. 'Yes, and the one of us who does it will have to crawl on his knees to the other two all his life long because they saw him do it. It's all right enough if you're by yourself. But as things are, for myself I say: No.'

'And I say no, too. It's too risky and too little sense in it. We must think of some other way.' Curtin now took his part in the discussion again.

'Are you downright sure he followed you and'll come here at all?' Howard asked.

Curtin looked down on the ground in front of him and said with resignation: 'I know he'll come and I know he'll find us. The impression he made on me was . . .' here Curtin raised his eyes and looked towards the narrow opening in the scrub. 'There he is,' he said in a weary voice.

Neither the old man nor Dobbs asked where. They were so astonished that they even forgot to curse. They followed the direction of Curtin's eyes and there in the dusk, fitfully lit up by the camp fire, stood the stranger, holding the bridle of his mule.

He stood quite still and did not even utter the customary Hallo. He did not say good evening. He simply stood there and waited, like a hungry man who is too proud to beg.

When Curtin was describing his encounter with the man in the village, each of his listeners formed a distinct idea of his appearance; but each had formed quite a wrong one. Dobbs had imagined a man with the coarse and bestial features of a vagabond in the tropics who ekes out a living by robbing travellers, thinking nothing of murder if it pays him or if his own safety requires it. Howard, on the other hand, had imagined the stranger as a regular gold-digger, impervious to any weather, with a face like tanned hide and hands like gnarled roots, afraid of no danger and undeterred by any difficulty, never at a loss, whose mind and body are undeviatingly fixed on the single aim of finding gold and working his find to the last ounce. He had imagined a gold-digger of the real honest sort, who will never be guilty of a crime and will commit murder for nothing short of defending his find or his share of the colour.

And now they were both taken by surprise. The stranger

fitted neither Dobb's conception of him nor Howard's. If neither of them spoke nor uttered an exclamation of surprise, it was partly because he looked so different from what they had imagined, and partly because he had made his appearance so suddenly and so much more speedily than they had expected.

The stranger still stood motionless in the small opening which led to the camp. He seemed to be just as much surprised as the three who sat round the fire. He had expected to find only one man, Curtin, and there, to his astonishment, he saw three. His mule nuzzled the bushes. Then it scented the donkeys and began to whinny. But in the middle it stopped abruptly, as though the silence of the human beings made it afraid.

Still the three men did not utter a word. They paid no heed to the fire, nor to their supper simmering over it. They kept their eyes fixed on the stranger as though they waited for him to say or do something. But he did not stir.

Then Dobbs got to his feet and strode with long strides up to the intruder. It was in his mind to ask him roughly what he wanted and how he had come there, and who he was. But when he was up to him all he said was Hallo, and the stranger likewise said Hallo.

Dobbs's hands were in his pockets. He had no idea what to say next. Finally he said: 'Come over to the fire.'

'Thanks,' the stranger said shortly.

He came nearer, but first lifted the old saddle with its two-saddle-bags off the back of his mule, and after hobbling one of its forefeet gave it a clap on the hind-quarters. It ambled slowly away in the direction where the donkeys were grazing.

Then he said good evening and sat down by the fire.

Only Howard replied. 'How's things?' he asked.

'Hm!' the stranger answered.

Curtin stirred the beans and shook up the potatoes. Howard turned the meat, and Dobbs, who had not yet sat down again, chopped wood and threw it on the fire.

'I know I'm not welcome here,' the stranger said.

'I made that clear enough when I saw you down yonder.' Curtin did not look up as he spoke.

'I can't be for ever hanging around with no one but Indians. I want to see what Christians look like for a change.'

'Then go somewhere else and see for yourself.' Howard did not trouble to be polite. 'We don't know any more than you do.'

'It doesn't interest us either,' Dobbs put in sourly. 'We've something else to think about. If you want to know, it's you we're worried about. We've no use for you here, not to light the fire for us or anything else. You'd best make yourself scarce as soon as it's daylight. Otherwise you may not find us too pleasant.'

The stranger said nothing to this. He sat still and watched the preparations for supper. When it was ready Curtin said: 'Help yourself. For tonight it'll go round. As for tomorrow, that's another thing.'

The meal was eaten in silence, or if anything was said it was only about the food – that the meat was not up to much, or the beans too hard, or the potatoes watery. The stranger did not join in, and he ate little.

When they had done, the other three lit their pipes.

'Got any tobacco?' asked Dobbs.

'Yes,' he replied quietly and began to roll a cigarette.

The others, for the sake of saying something and also of putting the stranger further off the track, spoke of hunting. But what they said did not sound very convincing, because it was not their real job. They felt, too, that the stranger knew more of hunting and of skins and the rest of it than they did. This made them uneasy and they began to talk of breaking camp and going to another district where there might be more game.

'It's no place for game here,' the stranger said, joining abruptly in the discussion. 'But it's a fine place for gold. There's gold here. I saw that some days back from the old dried-up water-courses which come down from the mountains here.'

'There's no gold,' Dobbs replied. 'We've been here long enough to know that. Do you think we'd hunt if there was dirt to wash? You must be bughouse,' he added, laughing derisively. 'We weren't born yesterday and we can tell a lump of gold from a pebblestone as well as you. We don't need your advice.'

He got up and went to the tent to turn in.

No one said any more and the stranger appeared to take Dobb's ill-mannered remark in good part. Perhaps he was accustomed to that style of conversation.

Howard stretched himself and yawned. Curtin knocked out his pipe. Then they got up, one after the other, and went slowly over to the tent. They neither bade the stranger good night nor invited him into the tent.

The stranger got up too. He whistled, and after a moment his mule came hobbling up. He went up to it and patted its neck and spoke to it and then sent it away with clap of his hand.

Next he put more wood on the fire and sat down and hummed to himself. Finally he got up and went to his saddle. He brought one of the saddle-bags over to the fire, pulled out a blanket and, rolling himself up in it, settled down to sleep with his head on the bag and his feet to the fire.

Talk went on in the tent. It was too far from the fire for the stranger to hear what was said. They spoke in low tones, too, but very emphatically all the same.

'I said it before and I say it again,' said Dobbs. 'Get rid of him. It doesn't matter how.'

'We don't know yet what sort of a guy he is,' the old man said it in a conciliatory tone. 'He seems harmless enough. I don't believe he's a spy either. He hasn't the look of one. He wouldn't be alone and he wouldn't be so hungry. I believe he has something on his conscience. They're after him for something or other.'

'We could start an argument with him,' Curtin said, 'and then lay him out once and for all.'

'That sounds amusing,' said Howard, 'but it isn't very commendable. It's a dirty trick.'

'Dirty or not,' Dobbs said in a rage, 'we've got to be quit of him, that's all. He's had his warning.'

They talked on, but always came back to the same thing – that the man had to get out of it, but that there were various objections to doing him in. At last they fell asleep on it.

Chapter Eleven

Next morning they all assembled round the fire in a very bad humour. The stranger had already fetched wood and made the fire up. He had filled his kettle and put it on to boil. Dobbs greeted him at once: 'Where did you get the water, my good friend?'

'Out of the bucket.'

'Oh – out of the bucket. Very kind of you. But don't kid yourself we're going to carry water for you.'

'I don't. I'm going to fill the bucket again.'

As he spoke Curtin came up to the fire, in a worse temper if possible than Dobbs. He too said at once: 'Pilfering wood and water, eh? That's the notion, is it? If you lay a finger on anything of ours again, we'll put a bullet through you, see?'

'I took you for decent fellows who wouldn't grudge a drink of water.'

Dobbs went for him at once: 'What's that, you vermin? We're not decent fellows – bandits, I suppose?' And he gave him a well-directed punch in the face.

The man dropped and lay full length. Slowly he got up again.

'I might do the same for you now. But what's the use against the three of you? You're only waiting for the excuse to do me in. But I'm not such a fool. The time will come, perhaps.'

Howard meanwhile came to the fire and asked the man quietly whether he had anything to eat.

'I've got a tin of tea and some beans and rice and two tins of milk.'

'You can have some coffee with us. Some grub too – for today. Tomorrow you must look after yourself.'

'Thanks,' the man replied.

'Tomorrow?' Dobbs questioned. His temper was noticeably improved by the success of his knock-out,

'Tomorrow? Look here, do you think you're settling here for good?'

'That's the notion,' the man replied quietly.

At this Curtin shouted: 'Settling down here? Not without our leave.'

'The bush and the mountains are open to all comers.'

'Not so fast, young man,' said Howard. 'The mountains and the bush are free and the jungle below and the desert beyond. It's all free. But we're the first here and the first-comers have the right as settlers.'

'That's good enough. But how do you know you're the first here? Perhaps I was here before you ever thought of squatting here.'

'Have you registered a claim?'

'You've no claim either.'

'It's up to you, as we're in possession If it's true you were ever here before, you didn't stake any claim and you gave the place up again, so you've lost any rights you had.'

The stranger made no reply. The three others began to get breakfast ready. They didn't hurry because they didn't know what there was to do when it was over. They couldn't go and work, because then the stranger would have discovered their diggings. They couldn't go hunting and so deceive the stranger about their real occupation, because one of them would have had to stay behind to prevent him nosing around and perhaps coming on the mine by accident; and he might be a match for the one of them who stayed behind. There was only one way out of it. Two of them might reach the mine by the secret approach and work there, while one stayed behind to keep a watch on the stranger. But he wasn't likely to sit doing nothing. He would scout around. And as soon as he was told not to, he would know for sure that there was more going on than met the eye.

Curtin at last came to a conclusion.

'We'll go hunting, you and I, after breakfast,' he said to the stranger. 'We could do with some fresh meat.'

The stranger looked up at them to see if he could read the meaning of this proposal in their faces. If he went after game alone with one of them, he might easily meet with an accident; and that would be one way of getting rid of him. But then he said to himself that if they meant to put him out of the way they would do so in any case. Excuses are never lacking.

'I can go with you today,' he said, 'and then we'll be supplied. But tomorrow I shan't have much time.'

'Why not?' they all asked at once, and looked at him with astonishment.

'Well, I'm starting to look for gold here tomorrow. There's gold here. And if you haven't found any it only shows what dam' fools you are.'

This got the old man's goat and he blabbed out: 'Perhaps we aren't such dam' fools as you think. Perhaps we have found gold.'

'That wouldn't surprise me,' said the stranger. 'But you haven't found any. Or, if you have, it's just a few handfuls you've scratched up from the surface of the ground. But there's more than that here, close here somewhere. There's a good million.'

'A million?' Howard asked, opening his eyes wide.

Dobbs and Curtin could not speak for excitement.

'You haven't come on the placer, I know,' the stranger went on with composure. 'I know you've been a year here. The Indians down there told me a man had been up here that long. If you had struck the placer, you'd have been gone long since. For you could never have hoped to get away with all the lot without attracting attention. Or else you'd have opened a regular mine, with a licence and machinery and two or three dozen men.'

'We've nothing, not a cent,' said Dobbs.

'Call me what you like. But I'm not an infant. And if you three have been up here all these months, it isn't for your health. What I say is, let's be open and put our cards on the table. What's the good of this hole-and-corner business? I'm not a crook. To say the least, I'm as straight as any of you. I won't say I'm any better. We're all on the make, whether out here in the bush or back in the towns. Of course, you can put me out of the way, I know that. But that may happen any day. I have to risk that. So why can't we be open with one another?'

'Spit it out, then,' said Howard.

'You're right, Howard,' Dobbs answered to this. 'What I say is, let him have the chance to prove he's not a spy and isn't keeping anything else back that doesn't suit our book.'

He then turned to the stranger.

'We can't tell by looking whether you're a crook or not. It's true we've done a few months' hard labour here, honest work though, you can take our word for it. If we let you into it, you might easily make yourself a nuisance, and that might cost us all we've got for our hardships and privations. But I tell you this – we'd have you, even though you went as far as Hudson Bay first. We'd have you, and we'd show no mercy. So out with it. What d'you want and what's your game?'

The stranger drank up his coffee and then he said: 'I've been honest with you from the start. I've told you there's gold here and that I've come to dig it.'

'What else?' asked Curtin.

'Nothing else,' the stranger replied.

'Good enough,' Howard put in. 'But what if we've found the muck? You don't suppose we're going to account to you for it. We've done our bit without you. So there you have it. We've found it and we're pretty well through.'

'So far so good,' the stranger replied without hesitation. 'You've been straight with me and I'll be straight with you, and we'll see if we can work together. For a start, then, I've a claim on this place. Wait now before you chew the fat. Of course I've no registered claim and no licence or anything of the sort. My claim lies in the fact that I know something that you don't. That is better than any licence, stamp and all. You've found nothing. A few grains, I dare say. You can keep them.'

'So we shall, don't you worry,' said Curtin.

'That's how it stands,' the stranger went on, speaking very

slowly. 'I can't carry on alone. I want men, and it seems to me that you're the best men for the job. It's as much to your interest as mine to keep it dark; and you have tools and I haven't. I might sell my secret to a company. But it'd be a job to get more than a hundred dollars for it. They'd want it under their eyes and that they could only have here on the spot. Besides, I've good reasons not to shout about it, for then someone might come along with mining rights. I put it up to you. What you have, you keep. Of what you get after today through working on my plan, I take two-fifths.'

The three looked at each other and laughed. Then Howard said: 'We don't need you to tell us the tale, my boy. We can do that for ourselves. What do you say?' And he turned to the other two.

Dobbs said: 'What does it matter? We're as good as through and done with it. We've nothing to lose by giving him a day or two.'

'That's what I say. We lose nothing. We may as well see what there is in it now we're here,' said Curtin.

'I'm not on for it,' the old man said. 'It's a try-on and I've had enough of the wilds. I want to be in a proper bed again. I've got all I need. But of course if you're for it, then I've nothing to say. I can't trek two weeks through the bush on my own.'

'Listen to me, old cock,' said Curtin. 'I'm not out for overtime any more than you are. I've someone waiting for me. We'll give him a week. If in a week we come on the business this fellow's talking about, well and good, and then we can see if it's worth it. If in a week we've come on nothing, then I'll go with you. Is that agreed?'

They all agreed, and now it was for the stranger to lay his plans before them.

'What's your name, for a start?' asked Howard.

'Lacaud' he said. 'Robert Lacaud from Arizona.

'Any relation to the Lacauds in Los Angeles, furnishing store?'

'Yes, on my grandfather's side. But I don't have any truck with them. We wouldn't be seen dead with them, and if we thought they were going to heaven we'd burn half a dozen churches to a cinder just to be sure of going to hell. But there's no need to worry. They'll never get to heaven.'

'Then you'll have to make it a dead cert that you do.' Dobbs said laughing. 'As you're shaping at present you'll hardly keep out of the way of those relations of yours.'

'I don't know,' said Curtin. 'If I'm not misinformed, there are different boiling departments down there, and he'll be able to put in a word at the right moment, so as not to be popped into the same cauldron as the other worthy members of his distinguished family. That can always be arranged, for Satan has a good heart. If he hadn't, how could he be up to so much fun and mischief?'

Howard had gone to see that the donkeys didn't stray too far, and in order to get a better view he had climbed on to a shoulder of the mountain side.

'Hallo!' he shouted.

'What's up?' Dobbs and Curtin shouted back. 'Have the donkeys gone?'

'Come here, quick. Quick as you like.'

The two of them jumped up and ran across to Howard. Lacaud too hurried after them.

'What's that over there coming this way?' the old man shouted. 'Perhaps you can tell better than I can.'

'Soldiers or mounted police,' Dobbs said. Then he whipped round on Lacaud. 'So now we have it, you skunk. So this was your secret.'

In a second he had him covered, but Howard, who was standing behind, knocked his arm up.

'You're wrong,' said Lacaud. Dobbs's sudden action had sent the blood from his face. 'I've nothing to do with them – police or soldiers.'

'Listen, my lad,' Howard said to him. 'We don't want any of that here. If they're after you, clear out of it – quick. And let them see you. We don't want any police up here. So down you go, quick march and where you like. Otherwise we'll take good care they get you. We can't do with you up here.'

90

Curtin had climbed higher up for a long and careful scrutiny.

'Not so fast,' he said. 'I don't think they're soldiers. Nor police either. They're not clothed alike and their firearms are all sorts and sizes. One of them, as well as I can see, has a great blunderbuss that must be a hundred years old at least. I know what they are – bandits.'

'Damn!' Howard shouted. 'Then it's out of the rain into the sump. We could do with mounted police ten times better than bandits. The police would tie us up and if there was no more in it than escaping taxes we could come to terms. But bandits – that's another story.'

Then a new idea struck him and he turned to Lacaud. 'Now then, cough it up. It's you we've got to thank. You're a spy of theirs. That's what I thought a time back.'

'I have nothing to do with bandits either,' Lacaud said. 'Let me have a look.'

He climbed up beside Curtin and took a careful look at the figures far below.

'They're bandits, and I know what bandits, too. I heard of them at Señor Gomez's Hacienda. And there was the account in a newspaper there. I can see one with a bronzed straw hat that was mentioned in the description of them. He's a good plucked one not to have changed it for another. But he won't know it was mentioned. They never see a paper and couldn't read one if they did. That's the very last band I'd choose to run across.'

And now, while all four watched the movements of the bandits, waiting to see whether the leader would turn into the track which in all probability would bring them up to their part of the mountains, Lacaud told them all he had read in the paper, and all that the people in the Hacienda had been able to tell him. For though few Indians and Indian workers on the Haciendas can read, the news of such events as these spreads through the length and the breadth of the land with the speed of a prairie fire.

Chapter Twelve

At a small station, where the night express stops for two minutes to drop and collect the mail, and to pick up or set down a couple of passengers, twenty or twenty-five men got into the train. It was between seven and eight o'clock and already pitch dark.

It never happened that so many people got in at this little station, but neither the station-master nor the officials on the train thought anything about it. They might be men going to market somewhere, or men on strike from one of the mines or on their way to another mining district to look for work.

They were all Mestizos, wearing their large straw hats, trousers and shirts, and sandals or boots on the feet. All were wrapped in blankets, as the night was chilly. No tickets are issued in small stations after nightfall, but they could get them on the train. The station was unlighted and quite dark. Only the station-master and the officials who got out, and ran hastily along the train had lanterns. No one, then, had a sight of the men's faces, which in any case were shrouded up to the eyes by their blankets; and this, being the usual thing, caused no remark.

They all got into the first coach of second-class compartments, in front of which was the luggage van. In this coach as usual were the twelve soldiers and an officer, all with loaded rifles, to protect the train against bandits.

Most of the men remained in the first coach, but some, after the train had started, passed along into the next one, apparently to look for better seats. Both these second-class coaches were pretty full. There were peasants, tradespeople and Indians taking their wares to the next town. Behind these two coaches came a coach of first-class compartments which was also fairly full, and behind this, at the end of the train, was the Pullman sleeping-car.

The train quickly got up speed. It was twenty minutes or a

little more to the next station. And now the train was in full career and the attendants were busy with the tickets for the passengers who had just got in, and who were blocking all the doors on to the corridor, where they had been standing from the start as though they were not going to sit down until they had found themselves good seats.

The next moment, without a word or any warning, they pulled rifles and revolvers from under their blankets and opened rapid fire. It was directed particularly on the soldiers, whose rifles were between their knees or leaning against the sides of the carriage, while they studied spelling-books in order to learn to read and write, or munched their supper or dozed.

The firing lasted only about ten seconds; by that time the coach was a shambles and all the soldiers were either dead or at the point of death. The train attendants too were either shot dead or mortally wounded and lay about on the floor or the seats. Twenty passengers were hit. Many were dead; others bleeding to death of their wounds. Babies at their mothers' breasts, women and children were bleeding and dying in a scene of wild confusion. Men and women begged on their knees for mercy, mothers held up their weeping children in the hope of arousing the bandits' pity, while others offered their wretched belongings to pay for their lives. But the bandits went on shooting until no one stirred any more.

Then they turned to plunder, and took all that seemed to them of any value. Part of the band went to the first class and plundered without shooting. Watches and purses, rings, ear-rings, necklaces and bracelets – and if the booty did not come up to their hopes, a prod from a rifle or revolver quickly reminded their prey of a gold coin or two in a trouser pocket or a diamond ring in a dressing-case.

Next the lights were switched on in the Pullman, the passengers turned out of their beds and stripped of all they had with them.

All this while the train sped on its way. Perhaps the driver had not heard the shots, or else he hoped to reach the next station at such speed that the bandits would be unable to jump from the train.

But now the bandits returned to the front of the train, passing through the two second-class coaches, where the panic of the passengers, when they saw them coming back, rose to an indescribable pitch of terror. The bandits didn't turn their heads or move an eyelid. They went on into the luggage van where they broke open the trunks or else threw them overboard, to sort out at their leisure later on. They murdered the guard and climbed along into the mail van, where they shot down the two men in charge and ransacked the mail bags.

Meanwhile the driver realized that something was wrong or else saw some of the bandits clambering from the mail van on to the tender. The station was still far away and there was no hope now of reaching it. He put on the brakes and the train came to a sudden stop with the violence of a collision.

The fireman jumped clear and tried to reach the bush at the foot of the embankment. But he was hit by half a dozen bullets and rolled to the bottom. Four men climbed into the cab of the engine before the driver had time to jump and grabbed him. The bandits had found a large number of tins of petrol and gasolene on the train which were being sent express to the owner of a tienda. They poured it over the coaches and in at the broken windows and then threw lighted brands after it. Instantaneously, like an explosion, the flames shot up into the darkness of night.

The passengers trapped in the burning train uttered heart-rending cries and surged against the windows in a frenzied effort to escape. If they succeeded, they fell burnt and singed from the height of the windows to the track and broke or sprained their limbs. Those who were too severely wounded, and could not in the panic find anyone to help them, were burnt to death.

In front, two of the bandits had the engine-driver covered with their revolvers; they forced him to uncouple the engine and drive off, with the whole band crowded on the tender, until they told him to stop. The burning train and its occupants were left to their fate. The wildly leaping flames shed a ghastly light upon the scene, while the victims ran backwards and forwards, crazed with horror and pain and fright, gesticulating and crying aloud and praying, and making last frantic efforts to rescue those who had been left behind in the raging furnace. Less than seven minutes all told had elapsed and the station towards which the engine was now racing was still far away. Suddenly one of the men told the driver to stop. The engine stopped and the men jumped down. The last shot the driver and pushed him with a kick down the embankment. Then he followed his comrades.

After a time the driver came to, and though on the verge of death he crept up the embankment and pulled himself into his engine. In spite of the pain he was in and the fear that he would collapse at any moment, he managed to get the engine started and reach the station. The station-master, who was already surprised by the delay – for the train had long ago been signalled from the last station – was amazed now to see an engine arrive by itself, and running up to it he found the driver wounded and bleeding. Passengers waiting for the night train helped him to carry the man into the station building and here the dying man was just able to give a bare outline of the disaster before he died.

The station-master telegraphed immediately to the stations on both sides of him. He got them both and heard that a relief train would be sent immediately. There was a goods train on a siding in the station waiting to let the passenger train through. Two empty wagons were shunted and coupled to the engine, and the first relief train was ready.

But who was to drive it and go in it? The bandits were undoubtedly still on the line, collecting all that they had thrown out of the train. They would attack the relief train at once, if only to make sure of their booty. Probably they had torn up the rails or blocked the line.

'Better wait for the other train,' the station-master said. 'There's sure to be soldiers on it.'

But the driver of the goods-train engine broke in at once. 'I'll drive it,' he said. 'There are women and children bleeding there, and comrades of mine, and some of them may not be past help. I'll drive the train. What do you say, mate?' he asked the fireman.

The railwaymen of Mexico are all without exception members of a first-class union, radical to the backbone and never averse from a strike; and they hang together to a man. Their organization and the spirit prevailing in it make self-respecting men of them, who are eager to improve themselves as citizens of their country. Courteous and helpful, always laughing and joking, they bear no resemblance at all to the growling and snarling N.C.O.s who, disguised as railwaymen, make travelling in Central Europe such a disagreeable experience. They are not the subordinates of arrogant superior officers, for all share as comrades in the pride of their organization. The fireman may be president and spokesman of the group at whose meetings the chief of the line sits modestly on the same bench as shunters, pointsmen and wheel-greasers and listens quietly and attentively to the proposals the fireman has to make, as chairman, for improving the conditions of the railway worker. And in the event of a strike, the chief of the line, whose pay is ten times that of a wheel-greaser or shunter, does not organize the technical staff as an emergency gang. On the contrary, he gets out the bills and posters which inform the public of the reason and the necessity for the railways strike, because he is better at writing than the fireman, though the fireman is chairman and spokesman. The chief of the line and the shunter eat from the same spoon, so to speak; by virtue of their organization the dirty wheel-greaser is more to the chief of the line than the state can be, or the interests of trade and industry, or the common weal, all of which come second to the aim of securing the necessities of existence for the pointsman, his comrade. For this reason the engine-driver need not have asked his fireman what he had to say; for he might have known what answer he would make; and what answer all the other railwaymen who were standing about waiting for the goods train to start, would make also.

It was a question first of all of their own union members; but even if they had all been safe and sound, still they would have gone, because there were the passengers in desperate straits. Even though they put the members of their union first, the passengers came second. Indeed the railwayman feels a greater responsibility for the welfare of the passengers than for the welfare of his own family. For that is what his union teaches him. And his union is never wrong whatever anyone, the archbishop included, may say.

So the fireman spoke up: 'I'll take the passenger engine along first to see if all's clear. You follow at five hundred metres, and that'll give you time to stop if I come to grief through the rails being up.'

The engine was started, a wheel-greaser jumped in as fireman, and then they went backwards out of the station.

The small relief train meanwhile got up steam, and all the railwaymen, though they all had wives and children, jumped on board. So did some of the other people standing round; and then the train forged ahead into the darkness.

The scouting engine found the rails in order. The line was clear. But when it approached the scene of the disaster rapid fire was opened on it.

The bandits had had their horses concealed near the spot where they had made the engine-driver stop and they were still collecting their plunder. Those of them who were standing by with the horses, opened fire at once on the engine, hoping to bring it to a standstill, so that the rest of the band could carry on with the looting.

The driver was was hit in the leg and his fireman grazed on the ear. But they went full speed ahead, signalling the all-clear by lantern to the train behind. It too was fired on. But some of the railwaymen had revolvers and returned the fire. The bandits could not be sure in the darkness whether there were soldiers in the unlighted wagons. Apparently they thought so; for they made their mounts in a hurry and left everything lying that they had not had the time to sort out.

They mounted and rode away into the depths of the jungle, making for the hills.

With the help of the passengers who had escaped serious injury, the dead and wounded were lifted into the wagons, and the train returned to the station with its pitiful load.

A telegram had come to say that a hospital train was on the way. It could not, however, be on the spot before dawn. There were telegrams also from the government and the nearest garrison. All the detachments of mounted police of the neighbouring district were on the march, and four regiments of cavalry of the Federal Army were mobilized and would be dispatched by special trains to the scene of the outrage before daybreak, in order to pursue the bandits.

It is not easy to find a needle in a haystack. But if it has to be found it can be done, whatever the size of the haystack. Its eventual discovery is a mathematical certainty. But to find a bandit who has a good start of his pursuers along jungle tracks which he knows well and his pursuer does not know at all, and who, after traversing the jungle has the mountains, the high mountains of Mexico, before him is incomparably more difficult than finding a needle in a haystack.

But the soldiers are for the most part Indians themselves. That means a lot. Also they knew that the bandits at a given time had been at a given spot on the line between those two stations. And it was not very long before the officers ascertained that the bandits had split up into small parties each of which had taken its own way. The needle in the haystack had, in fact, been broken into small pieces.

A superficial description of the bandits had been telegraphed in all directions. But even though one of them rode through an Indian village, and even encountered soldiers there and roused their suspicions, the description would be worthless unless in his pockets or on his person there was something to connect him with the hold-up of the train. He could always advance an alibi and say that he was sleeping on that night twenty kilometres away from the scene of the hold-up under a tree on the road to Chalchihuites. No one could disprove it.

98

However, a troop of Federal Cavalry was riding through Quazamota. Two Mestizos were squatting in front of a hut, wrapped in their blankets and smoking. The troopers rode quietly past. One of the men got up to go behind the hut. But at a wink from the other he turned back and squatted down again.

The troop had already gone by when the officer turned and halted it. He was thirsty and he rode up to one of the huts. After drinking he rode across to the other side and dismounted just where the two men sat smoking.

'Do you live here?' the officer asked.

'No, señor, we don't live here.'

'Where are you from, then?'

'Our home is in Comitala.'

'Right,' said the officer, and put his foot in the stirrup. He was going to mount and ride off with his troop.

He was tired and the horse danced round. He could not get his foot into the stirrup. One of the two Mestizos got to his feet because the horse was almost on top of him. He came up and took hold of the stirrup to help the officer. His blanket fell from his shoulders.

The officer put his foot to the ground again.

'What's that in your trouser pocket?' he asked the Mestizo.

The man looked down at the bulge in his pocket. He turned half round as though to enter the hut or to seek some way of escape. Then his eyes wandered to the troopers and back to the officer, and drawing at his cigarette and taking it from his lips again he blew out a small puff of smoke and smiled.

In an instant the officer had him by the open neck of his shirt, while with his left he made a grab for his pocket.

The other Mestizo by this time was on his feet too. He shrugged his shoulders, as though annoyed by the disturbance, and looked about for another spot where he could squat and smoke in peace. But a sergeant and two troopers had dismounted, and neither of the men could escape.

The officer let go of the man's shirt collar and looked at

what he had pulled out of his pocket. It was a nice plump, handsome leather purse. The officer laughed and the Mestizo laughed too. Opening the purse, the officer shook the contents into the palm of his hand. Not a great deal – a little gold, some big silver pieces. About twenty-five pesos all told.

'Is this money yours?'

'Of course it's mine.'

'It's a lot of money. You might have bought yourself a new shirt.'

'So I shall tomorrow. I'm going to the town.'

But there was also a first-class ticket to Torreon in the purse. Mestizos never travel first. Moreover the date was the day of the hold-up.

They searched the other man. He had money on him too, but loose in his pocket. But there was a diamond ring in the watch pocket of his trousers.

At a wink from the sergeant the rest of the troop had dismounted.

'Where have you got your horses?'

'Behind there,' said the first Mestizo, shaking tobacco on to a cigarette paper. Then he drew the string of his pouch tight with his teeth and rolled his cigarette. He was not nervous at all and not a flake of tobacco was spilt. Smiling calmly, he lit his cigarette and smoked, while another N.C.O. went through all his pockets.

The horses of the two were brought along and searched. Wretched saddles and bridles and a worn lasso.

'Where are your revolvers?' asked the officer.

'Where the horses were standing.'

The sergeant went there and kicked up a revolver and an old pistol out of the ground.

'What are your names?'

They gave their names and the officer wrote them down with an entry of what he had found.

People of the village had now come round. 'Where's your cemetery here?' the officer asked one of them.

The officer, and the troopers with the two Mestizos

among them, followed the villagers along the road to the cemetery. The rest of the villagers followed on behind, men and children and women with babies in their arms.

A spade was brought, and while the Mestizos dug their graves the soldiers stood at the corner of the cemetery.

The officer smoked, the troopers smoked and chatted with the villagers. When the holes were deep enough, the two Mestizos sat down and rested and rolled themselves another cigarette. After a while, the officer said: 'You can say your prayers now if you want to.'

He then told off six men and they fell in.

The two Mestizos showed not the faintest concern or alarm. They crossed themselves, muttered a few words and crossed themselves again. Then lit one more cigarette, and without waiting to be told, stood up side by side.

As the officer gave the order to fire, the two bandits smoked another puff or two and threw their cigarettes away.

When the grave had been filled in the officer and troopers took their caps off and stood in silence for a moment. Then they put on their caps again, left the cemetery, mounted and rode away.

Why should the state go to further trouble when the ultimate aim is the same?

Another troop of cavalry caught sight of eight men on horseback among the foothills in front of them. Apparently the men saw the soldiers, for they abruptly broke into a trot and vanished. The officer pursued them with his troop, but he could not make out in what direction they had gone. There were so many hoof marks on the sandy track, leading in so many different directions, that the officer was at a loss which of them all to follow. He chose those that seemed to be the freshest.

After some hours the troop reached a lonely Hacienda. They rode into the spacious farmyard and dismounted in order to rest themselves for a bit. The owner of the Hacienda came out and the officer asked whether he had seen anything of a party of mounted men. The man declared that no one could have ridden past the place without his knowing it. Whereupon the officer informed him that he would have to search the Hacienda, and the owner replied that he might do as he liked, and went back into the house. The troopers were about to follow him when they were met by a volley from different parts of the house. By the time they had retreated through the yard gates they had four wounded and one dead.

A Hacienda is a large farm, and being enclosed by a stout high wall it stands up like a small fortress in the country round.

The soldiers were no sooner outside, carrying the dead and wounded with them, than the gates were shut and the defenders continued firing over the top of the wall.

A desperate fight now began, which, as both sides knew, could end only with the total annihilation of one side or the other, unless the ammunition gave out. The besieged had nothing to lose. They would be shot in any case, and their only hope of altering the situation lay in defending themselves to the last.

The first thing was to take the horses back out of range, and the bandits, having no ammunition to spare, wasted none on the horses during this operation.

The soldiers were up against it. The Hacienda stood in open country with arable and pasture round it. They could not hope to starve the bandits out, and to wait for artillery would have been too great an indignity for either the officer or his men to stomach. There was nothing for it, then, but to take the place by storm.

The Hacienda was attacked from all four sides at once in a thoroughly professional style. Each detachment in turn made short rushes and then lay down and opened fire while another made a jump forward. They could not scale the walls; the objectives were the two gates, one in the front and one in the rear. After a three hours' engagement the officer contrived to concentrate the defence on the one in front, while he himself climbed the one in the rear, which was only defended by three men, and broke it open.

The bandits, however, did not give up the fight. It was

102

continued in the yard and then the battle raged from the house itself. It was late in the afternoon before the soldiers were undisputed masters of the Hacienda. They had four dead, and eleven wounded, two seriously. In the yards and the house there were not only the eight men they had caught sight of, but several others of the train bandits as well.

Seven were dead and five wounded. These were immediately shot. The owner of the Hacienda was among the dead, and it was not known whether he was a bandit or whether he had been forced to harbour them under threat of death. The farm hands had kept out of harm's way and they now crept out again. It was certain they at least had nothing to do with the business. The farmer's family was away on a visit in the town. A search of the men's clothing brought to light a number of objects which could have come only from the plunder of the train.

In this way more and more of the bandits were taken, singly and in bands. But it is not easy in such cases to bag the lot in a short time, and the difficulties increase as time passes; and those who finally escape are not likely to spend the remainder of their days in the calm of contemplation.

'And you,' said Lacaud when he came to an end, 'you seriously believe that I could have anything to do with bandits who committed such a horrible crime as that?'

'It'll be no tea party if they come up here. That's one thing we can be sure of,' said Howard.

'Then those fellows must be the last of the gang,' said Dobbs.

'That's what I think. It was mentioned in the report that one of them was wearing a bronzed straw hat, and they take him to be the ringleader, and the bloodthirstiest of the lot.'

'Then it won't be any tea party if they come up here,' Curtin put in. 'But I don't see them any longer.'

'You can't see them, they're in the bend,' said Dobbs. 'When they come out of it we'll be able to see whether they turn up hill or down the valley.'

Chapter Thirteen

They sat up there on the cliff, keeping a watch to see when the men on horseback came out of the bend.

'How many did you count?' asked Howard.

'Ten or twelve,' said Curtin.

'There can't be that many of the bandits left according to your tale,' Howard said to Lacaud.

'No fear. They've caught most of them. But the four or five who were left will have come on some others and formed a new band with something else in view.'

'Bob's right, I dare say. And if that's so and they come up here, we're for it. They're after revolvers and ammunition. You know the village and the people down there,' Howard went on, turning to Curtin. 'Perhaps they searched the village for revolvers, and the Indians, to get rid of them, said that you were up here with a rifle because you were hunting here.'

'Damn it, you're right. That's how it will be. They'll be up here for sure after the rifle.'

'Then we don't want to lose any more time,' said Dobbs. 'Curtin, you can stay here as you've good eyesight and keep a look-out to see if they're coming. We'll go and get everything under hatches.'

They caught the donkeys and took them into a thicket on the other side of the cliff and tied them up securely. Then they got their firearms and two buckets of water and the bags of biscuits, and took them to a dry gully close up against the perpendicular face of the cliff. This gully was well fitted for defence, for they could neither be taken in the the rear nor outflanked, and in front there was open ground, where any movement of an attacker could be seen and every man would offer a clear target.

'There'd be the time,' said Curtin during their preparations, 'to climb up the cliff and creep into a cleft and wait till they'd gone.'

'Oh, you fathead,' said Dobbs, 'then they'd come on the mine and we'd never get back there again to lift the colour we've got hidden there.'

'I've seen no mine here,' said Lacaud.

'We know that,' replied Dobbs. 'We must make a clean breast of it now, however. Of course we have a mine here, and as long as we're in possession they won't get to it. But if we slink off, then they'll look for Curtin and his rifle and come on the mine today or tomorrow. There's no time to shift our stuff now, and anyway we could never get away with it once there was anyone at the mine. No – we've got to watch out here and not give way to them. There's nothing else for it. Even if they don't know we have the fine stuff here, by the sackful too, they'll strip us to the soles of our feet and leave us to die.'

'That's so,' Howard agreed. 'If there was any other way out of it, I wouldn't come to grips with them. But we've no choice.'

'They've turned this way,' Curtin shouted. 'They're coming up!' He sprang down from the ledge. 'We've no time to lose.'

'How long will it be before they're here?' Howard asked. 'You know that better than we do.'

'Fifty minutes and they're here. If they came on foot and knew the short cuts, it might be ten minutes under.'

'You're quite sure they're coming up?' asked Dobbs.

'Once they've taken the turn up hill they can't go anywhere else. They've got to come up. There's nowhere they can turn aside.'

'They might turn back again.'

'They could do that, of course. But we'd best not wait to see.'

'We'll take down the tent,' Dobbs advised. 'Then they won't see at once that there's more than one of us here. Besides, it looks too prosperous.'

The tent was taken into a gully. Then they made openings to fire through, so as to have a clear field of vision without needing to raise their heads above their cover. They were discussing plans of action when they heard voices at the last bend of the path, and their hearts stood still.

A minute or two later the men emerged from the bush on the edge of the clearing. They had left their horses behind, no doubt at the last bend, for after that the path was too steep for horses. But perhaps there was another reason as well for leaving their horses behind. There were seven of the men; the remaining three were presumably with the horses, or posted where they could keep a look-out. All were armed. Every man had a revolver, and some rifles as well. They all wore their large straw hats and brightly coloured neckcloths, but apart from this they were a ragged crew. Two had sandals on and two were barefoot; one had a legging and a yellow lace boot on one leg, and a gumboot on the other. Not one had a whole shirt; but several had leather jackets and three wore long tight brown leather trousers reaching to the ankle. All were provided with one or more cartridge belts, and some had blankets thrown over their shoulders. Probably the blankets of the others, as well as the knapsacks containing provisions, were with the horses.

The open space they stepped on to was bounded on the further side by the perpendicular cliff and on the two other sides by thick and apparently impenetrable bush and thorny scrub, out of which rose an occasional tree. They looked about them with curiosity; and what they saw was apparently not quite what they had expected. It was obvious, however, that the clearing had very recently been a camping-place. There was wood lying about, the places where fires had been were still fresh, and the ash not yet dispersed; empty tins, broken crockery and bits of paper were scattered here and there; and then the patch where the tent had been was still clearly defined. The whole clearing was an irregular square of about sixty paces. It had been gradually enlarged by the daily wood-cutting and felling of trees for firing. The fresh stumps of felled trees showed that the camp had been recently occupied.

The men stood in a group and began to smoke. Some squatted down, while the others talked. The man with the bronzed straw hat seemed to be the leader, for they all looked towards him whenever he spoke.

They came forward a few steps and then stood still again and talked. It was easy to see that they did not know what to do next. One or two were clearly of the opinion that they were too late. The gringo had gone. Finally the leader too, whom they called Ramirez, came to the same conclusion.

The talk grew louder as they separated and addressed each other from a greater distance; and the four in the gully were able to gather what their plans were and to take counsel accordingly. Perhaps the bandits after a few hours' rest would go their way and leave them in peace.

Although some of the bandits as they wandered here and there went close to the sides of the clearing, there was not much fear of them finding the path to the diggings; for Dobbs and Curtin had occupied the last hour in screening it, and as long as the scrub they had stuck into the ground did not wither the secret was safe.

At last after a lengthy pow-wow the bandits appeared to have come to some conclusion. They spoke so loud and with such emphatic gestures that the beleaguered men quickly learned what it was they thought of doing. They had decided to make this their headquarters until the hue and cry over the train robbery had died down and the soldiers had carried the pursuit further afield. The place seemed to them exceptionally favourable. There was water not far below, grazing for the horses near at hand, and food could be stolen from the cultivated lands in the valley if they tired of eating game. A little way down there was a point from which they could have an open view of the track in the valley below, and if soldiers were seen actually approaching, they could still escape, as long as in the meantime they could discover a bolt hole; for there was no way on into the mountains, and once the soldiers were on the way up they would be caught in a trap.

They had already made a thorough reconnaissance, and all they wanted was another way out, and this they were sure to come upon, if not there at the top, anyway lower down – perhaps near the spring.

'I was just thinking,' Howard whispered to Curtin, 'that we'd been fatheads not to hide ourselves at the mine. But I see now it would have been the silliest thing we could have done. If they're going to settle down here, they'd soon have come upon us at the mine. We couldn't have done better than we have.'

'Darned if I know, all the same, what we're to do if they make this their headquarters,' Dobbs whispered back. 'Not one of us thought of that. I thought myself they'd have a look round and then clear out again.'

'Wait a bit,' Lacaud put in. 'Perhaps they'll change their minds and go.'

'It wouldn't be a bad idea,' Howard suggested, 'if we scattered along the length of the gully. If they did happen to come nosing round they needn't find us all in a bunch and shoot us down like rabbits. They don't know there's more than one of us up here, and if we let them have it from several places at once they may get the wind up and quit.'

Howard and Lacaud took the two ends of the gully. Each had a good rifle. Curtin and Dobbs took the middle and placed themselves so that anyone approaching the gully would be unable to see both of them at once.

The bandits squatted here and there in the open not far from the narrow path out of which they had just emerged. They smoked and talked and laughed; two lay full length, asleep or dozing. One had gone to the horses to tell the men in charge of them that they were going to stay where they were and that they were to look out a place lower down where the horses could graze. Another had been sent to join the man on look-out, so that the two of them could watch the valley. And now the same thought came to all of them in the gully – here was their chance to draw a bead on those five devils who were still in the clearing, and loose off. Then when the five others came to their help, they could give them a warm reception from the safety of their ambush. In this way they might hope to be rid of the lot. Each of the four cursed himself for not having advised this plan of action while there was time. It could hardly be called murder, they thought: for the bandits were not men. They were vermin.

Dobbs kept thinking it over, until at last he could not keep it to himself any longer. He crept along to Howard, who was nearest him.

'That's just what I was thinking,' the old man replied. 'But then we'd have their carcasses lying all about.'

'We can bury them, though,' Dobbs whispered.

'Course we can. But I don't want to turn the place into a cemetery. We may have to stay on here a week or two yet. Cemeteries are all right, but you don't want them in front of your windows day and night. Otherwise, I'm all for it; that fellow with the pock-marked face has such a villainous look that a grown man would be afraid to sit with him in church.'

'You won't meet him in church.'

'Won't you, though? Him and all this bloodthirsty lot. I take my oath it is just these fellows who hang up the most silver legs and arms at the feet of the Holy Virgin of Guadalupe and St. Anthony. They crawl on their knees from the door to the altar and three times round the four walls. Go and look. You'll find each man with his little picture or medal hanging round his neck. The government here in Mexico knows what it's about when it takes the Church in hand so roughly. These people are ten times as superstitious as the blackest heathen of Central Africa. They're – but what's that fellow up to? He's coming straight across. Back to your post.'

Dobbs crept back as nimbly as a cat. One of the men was, in fact, strolling across towards the gully and making straight for the spot where Curtin sat. He was not looking at the gully in front of him, for his head was thrown back in order to survey the whole extent of the cliff above it. He seemed to be searching for their means of escape. Perhaps, too, he had an idea that the gringo they were after might be hidden there somewhere, or had made his way along the cliff and down into the valley. They had seen nothing of him on the way up.

He saw, however, that there was no foothold there. It was like a wall. He whistled to himself and turned to go back. Looking down, as he did so, he noticed the gully. For sure, he thought, there was the path they might yet have need of. He went nearer, almost to the edge of the gully, and there he saw Curtin.

Curtin had had his eyes on him all the time, so it was no surprise when he saw the man almost on top of him.

'Caramba!' the bandit called out. 'Come here. Here's the bird on its nest, sitting on its eggs.' He laughed loudly.

The rest of them jumped up and started forward in astonishment. But when they were half-way across, Curtin shouted: 'Halt, you bandits, or I'll shoot.'

The bandits stopped at once. They did not dare put a hand to their revolvers. They didn't know what might be coming.

The man who had discovered Curtin held his hands up at once and went back, still with his hands up, to the middle of the clearing where the others were.

Not a word was spoken for some time, and then they all began to talk at once in great excitement.

At last the leader stepped forward.

'We're not bandits, we belong to the police and it's the bandits we're after.'

Curtin raised his head a little. 'Where are your badges, then? If you belong to the police, one of you at least must have a badge. Let me have a good look at it.'

'A badge?' the leader replied. 'I haven't any badge. I don't need one and don't need to show one either. Come out of it, we've something to say to you.'

'You can say it where you are. I can hear you all right.'

'We'll arrest you. You're hunting here and have no licence. We are going to arrest you and take away your revolver and rifle.'

Curtin laughed. 'Where's your badge? You've no right to carry arms yourself. You've no badge, and you don't belong to the Federal Police or the State Police either. You've no power to arrest me.'

'Listen, ' the spokesman said, coming a step nearer. 'We shan't arrest you. Only give us your revolver. Your rifle you can keep. We want your revolver and the ammunition for it.'

He came forward one more step, and the rest followed him.

'Not another step', Curtin called out, 'or I'll fire.'

'Why not be a little more polite, señor? We shan't hurt you. We only want the revolver.'

'I need it myself.'

'Throw the thing over to us, then we'll go away and not bother you any more,' one of the others called out.

'You'll get nothing here, so clear out.'

Curtin had raised himself a little higher, to have a better view of the ground.

The men consulted again. They saw that the gringo had the advantage of them for the time in the ditch; he had good cover. The moment they drew their revolvers, he would drop his head, and before they could reach the cover of the bush he could shoot six times and shoot the lot if he shot straight. So they retreated and sat down on the ground. It was ten o'clock and their next thought was for warming up their tortillas and tamales and whatever else they had brought with them. They made a small fire and crouched round it to prepare their scanty meal.

They had naturally convinced themselves that the gringo was bound to fall into their hands in the long run. He could not get away and as they were going to make their camp there it could only be a matter of two days at longest before he gave himself up. Besides, he would fall asleep some time or other, and then they would have him.

After they had eaten they lay down for the midday sleep. It was two hours before they came to life again and began talking. They wanted something to do, and their need of occupation prompted the notion of capturing Curtin by a trick and passing a pleasant afternoon at his expense. The victim does not find this way of passing the time so pleasant. Sometimes he does not survive this game of forfeits. You

111

see, in the churches these people look at so many images and pictures of the most bloodthirsty tortures: figures of saints and martyrs standing up there lacerated and stuck about with spears and arrows, mouths gaping to show the stump of a tongue, hearts torn out and dripping with blood and emitting red flames, nailed and gory hands and feet, broken knees and crushed knee-caps, backs flogged with fish-hooks, and heads on which crowns of thorns are planted with blows of a heavy wooden mallet. These images and wooden statues are so realistic that the sight of them is unspeakably terrible. They are a waking nightmare and before them for hours together the faithful and pious kneel on their knees with arms extended and open palms, weeping and groaning and praying and droning their Ave Marias by hundreds and five hundreds. And when the time comes and they want to have a pleasant hour with a victim, they have no need to exercise their powers of invention. They only need to copy what they have seen from their tenderest years in church. And they make a careful and faithful copy of the originals, for all the imagination they have has its origin in religion, in a religion which influences them only through material and realistic representations and ceremonial magic. It is here, in this country, that the whole hideous crucifixion story is acted during Easter week in all its minutest details, with life-sized figures and a shocking truth to nature, before the eyes of credulous multitudes. It is no passion play; the representation is taken in all its literal crudity by these wretched people, who have been left for centuries in ignorance and superstition by the powers of darkness in pursuance of their narrow aims and selfish interests. And a government which strives in a progressive spirit to lift the curse from this tormented land, and is forced, therefore, to wage war against these unholy powers, must also send cavalry regiments to capture and treat as criminals men who do nothing but copy what they see. Is it possible that the incredible cruelties of that train robbery could be committed by normal men? The heathen Indians of the Sierra Madre of Oaxaca, Chiapas and Yucatan are incapable of such bestialities. But the Mestizos and Mexicans, who before undertaking a crime pray to the Mother of God and kneel for an hour to St. Anthony, begging for his help in it, and who after the crime again throw themselves on their knees before the Mother of God and promise her candles if she will see that they are not caught, these men do not know a crime of a cruelty which they are not capable of executing. Their consciences can never be troubled, for they lay the burden of their sins on the backs of these images, which in their scheme of things were fashioned for that very purpose.

So now the bandits began to think of a pleasant afternoon's entertainment, with the innocent diversion of forcing glowing embers into their victim's mouth as the first item. They talked about it, too, quite openly, and so clearly and circumstantially that Curtin was able to understand what awaited him.

One of them pulled out his revolver and put it under his open leather jacket in such a way that no one would notice that he had it there ready to fire; and Curtin could not see the movement from where he was. But Lacaud saw it.

The men got up one after another, stretched, and went to the middle of the clearing.

'Listen, señor,' the man with the bronzed straw hat called out, 'we'll do a deal. We wanted to get off now. We have nothing to eat and we want to be at market early tomorrow. Give us the revolver. I've a gold watch and chain here. You can have it for your revolver. It's worth a hundred and fifty pesos. Good business for you.'

He pulled the watch from his trousers pocket and swung it about by the chain.

Curtin was on his feet again. He called out: 'Keep your watch and I'll keep my revolver. Please yourselves about going to market. But you won't get the revolver. And that's the end of it.'

He was just going to drop down again when the man with the revolver under his jacket took aim at him. He stood behind one of the others and even if Curtin had seen him he could not have seen that the gun was levelled at him. But before the bandit pulled the trigger a shot rang out and the revolver fell from his grasp. He threw up his arm and shouted out that he was hit.

When the shot rang out all the men turned in astonishment to the gully. They saw a small puff of smoke ascending into the air. But it came from the left-hand corner, not from where Curtin had been seen. Yet they could see nothing of the marksman or his revolver.

They were so astounded that not a sound came from them. They retreated warily to the edge of the clearing and as soon as they got there they sat down and began talking again. The men besieged in the gully could not hear what they said, but they could see that they were in the utmost confusion. Could it be the police in ambush there?

And now the three who were posted as look-outs came up in a hurry. They had heard the shot and thought they might be wanted. But the leader sent them back again, because everything pointed to the need of having their horses ready.

After they had talked together for some time they suddenly laughed aloud. They got up and came back to the middle of the clearing, laughing uncontrollably.

'Listen, señor, you can't play your tricks on us,' the leader called out. 'We saw your game. You've got a fixed rifle in the corner there and you fired it with a string. But you don't come it over us like that.'

They all laughed at the joke and in an instant each man had his revolver in his hand.

'Come out of it, you fool, before we pull you out,' the leader called. 'You've no time to lose. One, two, three! Now then!'

'I'll see you to hell first,' Curtin shouted. 'One step and I'll shoot.'

'We'll soon show you.'

With one accord they all dropped to the ground and with their revolvers in their hands they began to stalk Curtin's hiding-place from different directions. But they did not get far. Four shots rang out along the gully, and two of the men shouted that they were hit. They only had flesh wounds, certainly; for they all turned and crept back into the bush.

There they discussed what to do next. It was obvious now that the gully was held by more than one man, and perhaps by four or five. And what else could they be but a detachment of police? And in that case there would be more of them posted on the track to bar their retreat. There was nothing for it, then, but fighting it out. Nevertheless, they showed no disposition to begin the battle. Apparently they wanted to see what the party in the ditch were going to do. And when no attack followed and not a sound was to be heard, they became once more uncertain and wondered whether it might only be the gringo playing another trick on them. For if there were soldiers there, they would not wait. They would attack and drive them into the arms of the police ambushed below.

But the men on look-out had reported nothing, and when one of them came up he shook his head and maintained that there were no soldiers lower down. The track was clear.

Next, one of the men apparently urged a regular siege of the gully, for whether the garrison were soldiers or hunters it was now clear that there was more in it than they had thought at first. If there were several of them, they must all have arms, as well as provisions and a lot else, all of which would come in handy. At the same time, there could only be a few of them – otherwise they would have followed up their advantage and come to grips at the moment when their fire had thrown their opponents into confusion.

The four men in the gully now found time for a council of war, for they could see that the bandits were not going to take any action just yet. They all crept to the corner where Howard was and discussed what to do. They had something to eat, drank some water and took their ease and smoked as the bandits had done for hours past.

'If we only knew what they'll be up to next,' Curtin said.

'It comes to the same whether we know it or not,' said Howard. 'We can't do anything until they begin.'

'We could get out and go for them,' Dobbs suggested.

'Then they'd have us.' Howard shook his head as he filled his pipe. 'They don't know how many of us there are. But then they could split up. We can command the clearing, but we can't reach the track – they'd have us ambushed. And we can command the clearing only by staying quietly in the gully here. We don't know either whether there isn't another gang on the way up.'

'That's my advice – stay quietly where we are,' said Lacaud. 'They won't be here for ever.'

'But how long will the water and bacon biscuits last us?' asked Curtin.

'Three days if we're careful.'

At this moment the donkeys began to bray. The bandits listened, but took no further notice. Perhaps it convinced them that they had not got soldiers to reckon with, for soldiers would not have come on donkeys. Even if they thought of taking the donkeys away with them, they would have to get possession of the open space before they could get to them.

Howard now said: 'We've got the night to think of. They've the chance to stalk us.'

'Not tonight nor tomorrow night,' said Lacaud. 'It's full moon and as light as day. I know that from last night.'

'That's true,' Howard agreed. 'We're in luck there. We'd best hold the two corners, two and two together for the night. Then one can sleep and the other watch out. If both sleep, then not one of us will ever wake again.'

Nothing more was seen of the bandits in the open. They kept in the bush, where they could be heard talking and occasionally seen moving to and fro in the undergrowth.

'Now's the time for two of us to get in a little sleep,' said Howard half an hour later. 'They won't come any more today. We can be sure of that. But I don't mind betting they come before dawn.'

They now took turns to sleep, and the night passed without incident except for a stealthy approach at nightfall. But before more than two of them were out of the bush a shot barked out and they gave it up. A little later the moon was so bright that a cat could not have crossed the open without being seen.

But at three in the morning Lacaud gave Curtin a nudge, and Howard prodded Dobbs.

'Are you awake?' Howard asked.

'Sure.'

'They're stirring. They're crawling out from four sides.'

'Seems to be all ten of them,' said Dobbs after looking out for a moment.

'Yes, they mean business this time. Let's hope the other two are on their guard at the other end. I tell you what, Dobbs – as soon as they're half-way, we'll fire. Pick a man and shoot straight, so they get it hot straight away. Then if the other two are nodding – that Curtin's a glutton for sleep – they'll wake up when we fire. And they'll still have time.'

But before the enemy reached the middle of the clearing, two shots came from the corner where Curtin and Lacaud were. For it had occurred to them too that it might be as well to rouse Dobbs and the old boy before the bandits got too close.

The attackers, however, were not to be scared off. They crawled on. None of them had been hit – at least not seriously. Not a curse nor a cry escaped them.

Dobbs and the old man now loosed off and one of the bandits cursed; so he no doubt had got one.

Apparently they thought the fixed rifles had now all been fired off – but whatever they may have thought they decided anyway to make a quick end of it, for after crawling a little way farther they jumped up and made for the gully in open order, crouching as they ran.

Now, naturally, they offered a far better target. Three were hit at once. Two of them clasped a wounded arm and the third limped back with a bullet in the leg. Fire was kept up without a pause from the gully, while the attackers could make no use of their weapons because they could see nobody to shoot at.

They dropped to the ground again and passing the word along began creeping back to the bush.

After this it was soon daybreak. Experience had taught them that a daylight attack was not to be thought of.

When the four assembled in one corner for breakfast, Howard said: 'They'll come back tonight. And they'll have some other plan of attack. There's no chance now of their giving it up. We've shown what a good fort this ditch makes. They couldn't find a better place for their headquarters. Then there's our firearms and the rest of our traps. We must think out what we're to do.'

But four against ten who could retreat when they liked, four, whose drinking water had to be eked out, against ten who had water in their rear as well as provisions and even fresh forces – what plans were they to make? And the attackers had the further advantage of being able to sleep or not as they chose.

Curtin, who was standing sentry while the rest ate, suddenly called out: 'Come here. What are they up to? This looks bad.'

The other three went at once to the openings they had scooped out for firing through, and they all saw at once the danger they were in.

The bandits were very busy. They were breaking off branches and pulling down young trees and beginning to construct a movable palisade after the fashion of the Indians. Concealed behind it they would be able to stalk the ditch at their leisure and rout out the besieged without further trouble. A shot or two might be exchanged at close quarters in the ditch, but the end was certain.

Even Howard could think of nothing to counter this manoeuvre. They could do nothing but sell their lives as dearly as possible in the hand-to-hand fight at the finish. Any one of them who was taken alive would have little to rejoice about.

'The only thing that surprises me is why they haven't done it before this,' said Curtin. 'It's an old Indian trick.'

'Too much trouble,' Howard replied.

They talked it over, but they could think of no way out of the plight they were in. They might hack a way through the

118

bush, but they'd be seen at once. They thought, too, of the mine. But that would not delay their fate very long. At last they came back to the idea of making an attack, in spite of the hopelessness of it – considering that they would attack across the open while the others would be in cover and in command, of the track. Finally they dropped this idea too, for even Dobbs, who had urged it more eagerly than any of them, saw that it was sheer folly.

If only the cliff gave a foothold – but it was too steep, and even if they made the attempt in the hope of finding foothold higher up above the projecting shoulder, there would be nothing gained. The attempt could not be made in the night, and by day they would be shot down without trouble and without the chance of putting up a fight.

They could do nothing but sit and watch the enemy at their work. It would be completed by four in the afternoon, and then they might expect the attack, unless the night were thought a better time for it.

It was getting on for eleven. The bandits sat eating their midday meal near the entrance to the clearing. They were in good spirits and laughing. The four in the gully were clearly the objects of their mirth, for whenever they thought they had made a good joke they looked across at the ditch. Then there was suddenly a shout:

'Ramirez, Ramirez, pronto, muy pronto, quick here!'

One of the look-outs came running up the path and rushed up to the leader. All jumped up and disappeared down the path. They could be heard talking excitedly as they went farther and farther away.

Then no more could be heard and the besieged men wondered what to make of it.

'It's a trick,' Dobbs said. 'They want us to think they've gone – to fetch us out. Then they'll be lying in wait for us farther down.'

'I don't think so,' Howard put in. 'Didn't you see how excited the look-out was when he ran up?'

'That's part of the ruse, so as we'll think they've cleared out in a hurry.'

But Howard shook his head. 'They don't need any ruse once they'd hit on that Indian trick.'

Dobbs, however, was not to be persuaded. 'That Indian trick's all right. But it might cost them a few men, dead and wounded, and perhaps they're short of ammunition. If they can catch us without needing to fire a shot, and without our firing off our ammunition, which they regard as their own now, they'd be fools not to try it on. If it doesn't succeed, they still have their screens in reserve.'

'You may be right,' Howard admitted. 'It may be they want to spare our ammunition; for if they come for us, naturally we loose off all we've got.'

Curtin had not joined in the discussion. He had crawled cautiously farther along the gully and then climbed up the projecting shoulder of the cliff. As there was nothing to be seen of the bandits and their voices came from a distance, he ventured to make use of it as a look-out.

He crouched on the shoulder of the cliff and looked down into the valley. He sat there for a good while. Then suddenly he called out: 'Hallo – out with you. There's a squadron of cavalry down below there. They're after our friends here.' The other three crept forward and all climbed up to the look-out; and a lively scene greeted their eyes. The troopers, in six detachments, were sweeping the plain in all directions. No doubt they had heard that the bandits were somewhere in the neighbourhood; and as they knew that the bandits had horses, they would not be thinking of the mountains where it was scarcely possible for a horse to go.

Lacaud, however, was of another opinion. 'Seems to me they know already where they're hiding. But they have more sense than to run into an ambush. Once they started climbing, shut in by thick bush and sheer rock, they couldn't do much – or only with heavy losses. Either they're going to bottle them up in the mountains or else they have some wheeze – and I think it's that.'

The soldiers swept on – five or six kilometres out into the valley. Till then the bandits had been sure their hiding-place was discovered. But now when they saw the soldiers riding farther away they began to think they were safe where they were. A stretch of the track up the mountain could be seen and Curtin observed that the bandits came riding back to resume possession of their headquarters.

But the officer of the Federal Troops was by a long way more wily than they.

When the detachments were far enough off they began, as could easily be made out even at that distance, to pick up a trail. With wide circling movements and a vigorous riding to and fro, they let it be seen that they had at last discovered for sure that the bandits were among the crags. They reformed in column, without great haste, and made for the mountains and the track leading up into them. This was a feint. They knew that the bandits would do anything rather than allow themselves to be shut up in their mountain fastness, as long as the least chance was left of reaching other ground. Once their retreat was cut off, they would never extricate themselves from the wilderness of rock, and the troops had only to hold the approaches without needing to attack or expose themselves on the mountain paths to the bullets of the bandits ambushed in the thickets and rocky clefts.

Every movement of the troops was carefully noted by the bandits' look-outs. As soon as they realized that their hiding-place was discovered, they decided to take advantage of the start without a moment's delay and break away into the open country under the perfect cover afforded by the bush. Once there they could make themselves scarce, and even if they were discovered it would not be until their well-rested horses had so increased their start that the soldiers would perhaps lose the trail again.

But a small detachment of mounted troops lay concealed in the bush towards that side of the country which the bandits made for. This detachment had taken up its position the night before, when it was impossible for the bandits, who were in any case occupied with their night attack up above, to know anything about it. Shots had been heard in the night, echoing far down the valley from the face of the cliff, and this had convinced the ambushed soldiers that they were on the right track. They had no idea, of course, what the shooting was about, but they supposed either that the bandits were drunk or that they had accounts to settle among themselves.

The four men sat up there and waited for the fight; they reckoned that it would be an hour before the curtain went up. Once the show was over, they would be able to go back in peace to their interrupted labours.

Now the first shots were heard, and the main body, after enticing the bandits from their lair, wheeled and went for them at the gallop. The bandits were now cut off from the mountains, and uttering wild cries and waving their arms they raced for the open, urging their horses on by brutally goring their sides with their long spurs; and the horses fled down the valley at headlong speed.

Behind them followed the troopers who had been lying hidden in the bush. They had first had to mount after being disappointed in their hope that the bandits would pass close enough to give a good target. Thus the bandits got the start here too. On they rode, and as they rode they shot at their pursuers.

'All the better if they get a good start,' Howard said.

'Why?' Dobbs asked in surprise.

'We'll be quit of the soldiers too. They might pay us a visit to see if any more bandits were in hiding up here. They've got us out of a tight corner, but we don't want them here all the same. I'd rather keep our thanks until we're well on the way home.'

On and on they rode; the sounds of firing grew fainter; and soon the watchers on the cliff could no longer see how the race would end, for the riders disappeared into the quivering horizon.

Chapter Fourteen

The camp was once more in going order; they had cooked and eaten a meal and lain for a long time round the fire. There were still several hours of daylight, but not one of them suggested doing any work that day.

When it grew dark they were still round the fire, drinking coffee and smoking.

'Howard's right,' said Curtin. 'We'd best give up and shut down the mine. We might perhaps get another thousand, but we'd do better to be content with what we have. Some more uninvited guests may blow in and we may not come out of it so well next time.'

At first nobody answered. Then after a pause Dobbs gave his opinion:

'That'll suit me, for one. Tomorrow we'll shut down the mine, and next day early we'll sort things out and pack up and get the donkeys in, and early the day after we'll get off. I've had my bellyful too.'

Lacaud listened and made no remark. He smoked and looked with apparent indifference into the fire. Now and then he got up and broke a branch across his knee, and those he could not break he threw whole on the fire.

'Do you know the story of the Cienega Mine?' he asked abruptly.

'We know so many stories of mines,' Howard said wearily. He was absorbed in dreaming over his plans for employing his share of the takings to the best advantage, so as to have an easy life of it while his money doubled of its own accord, and then increased by stages to a hundredfold. Lacaud's question disturbed the computations by which he was arriving at the hundredfold. He was afraid he had made a mistake in his figures, and as he was too tired to go over the rows and columns again in his mind, he said: 'Sure – we'd forgotten all about you.'

At this Dobbs and Curtin looked up too, and Curtin

laughed. 'That only shows what a damned lot you mean here. You'd dropped right out, although you fought with us and sit here now with us over our food and drink. Fact is, we've our own affairs to think about, and you don't come in there.'

'Weren't you saying something about some plan?' Dobbs asked. 'You can keep it. I don't give a damn for it – not if there's another ten thousand in it. I don't want them. I want the towns and to see some girls and to sit at a table with a cloth and a waiter to put the food down on it. I want to see how other people cook, for a change, and slave for a starvation wage.'

'There's more than ten thousand,' said Lacaud.

'Where?' asked Curtin.

'In my plan.'

'Oh – in your plan,' Curtin replied, and yawned.

'The stuff's there to see.' Lacaud tried to get them interested, but without success, for Dobbs said: 'If it's there to see, then pick it up. Don't leave it lying. Otherwise you may be sorry later. You're just the man who's always regretting something and always has something to regret. Well, I'm going to turn in.'

Howard and Curtin too got heavily to their feet, stretched and yawned, and went over to the tent. Curtin stopped on the way there, lost in reflection; then turned round, and stretched himself again as he looked up at the moon.

A thought struck him and he called into the tent: 'Howard, did you block the path when you let the donkeys loose this afternoon?'

'Sure,' Howard called back. 'At the bend beyond the grass patch, where we always do, near the pool.'

Lacaud meanwhile brought his bags along and lay down by the fire.

Curtin went up to him.

'You can come into the tent, man. There's room for a little one.'

But Lacaud replied that he was all right where he was. 'I'd always rather sleep by the fire than under cover. But say –

won't you come in on it? Trust my word, there's something in it?'

'Come in on what? Oh yes – your plan. No, I'm too keen to be gone. I can't stand any more of it. We've got all there is to find here, and I won't do another hand's turn.'

Curtin went across to the tent and crept in.

'What did the guy want from you?' asked Dobbs.

'On about his plan, but I put him off.'

'I don't know what to make of him,' said Howard. 'I shouldn't be surprised if he had a screw or two loose. If I knew what he's been up to the last six months, I could tell you whether he's the wandering digger or just bush crazy. Perhaps both.'

'The wandering digger?' Curtin asked curiously.

'Yes, one of those who're always prospecting for gold, and know fairy tales by the dozen of lost and buried gold-mines, and has plans and drawings by the dozen too in his pocket or in his head, which show him the way to a forgotten mine, and dozens of silly yarns told him by Indians and Mestizos about places where gold and diamonds are to be found. He looks and looks, and the more wild and untrodden the mountains and the greater the danger, the more convinced he is that he's on the track of a lode as thick as your arm. But he never comes on a grain though he knows for sure that he's right on top of it and must strike it next day. It's a kind of lunacy which can make a man as dangerous to his fellows as any other kind. And the victims are more to be pitied than other loonies, because they're always roaming without rest and without end. They're nearly dead of hunger one day, and of thirst the next; one time they have to defend themselves against mountain lions, rattlesnakes and other poisonous beasts and reptiles, another time against Indians; then again they fall and break their bones, and there they lie till they're found by some Indian or by bandits who take the trouble to fix them up again. But nothing stops them. They always know they're sure to find a gold-mine tomorrow.'

'That's not how he strikes me,' said Dobbs. 'There's something else in him besides that.'

'Maybe so,' Howard agreed. 'He can be what he likes for all I care. All I worry about is what to do with him if he tries to hang on to us when we go. We can't have that.'

'He'll see the mine tomorrow,' said Curtin.

'Doesn't matter now if he does,' Howard replied. 'We'll shut it down and if he likes to stay and open it up again, that's his own affair.'

Next morning, after breakfast, Howard, Dobbs and Curtin got to work in earnest. To their surprise Lacaud showed no disposition to crawl along with them to the mine. Certainly they hadn't asked him to, but they took it for granted that such a thing as a gold-mine would not be beneath his notice. He did not even ask a question about it. As soon as he had drunk up his coffee, he got up and went down the path.

Curtin followed him because he thought he might be going down to the village to let them know there that the time had come to rob the nest before it was too late. Lacaud did not know that Curtin was following him. He went his way unsuspectingly, stopping only to note the bigger trees and every rock, as though he were looking for some landmark. Now and then he bent down to examine the ground. At last he came to the grassy patch where the donkeys were. He crossed it to the pool. After inspecting it carefully he looked up at the face of the cliff. He went to the foot of it and, stooping down, began to poke about there.

Convinced now that Lacaud had other designs and was not proposing to cook their broth for them, Curtin went back to the other two and told them what he had seen.

'What did I tell you?' said Howard. 'The wandering gold-digger. We don't want to have any truck with him.'

He and Dobbs were busy breaking up the plant, and Dobbs had scratched his hand. Losing his temper, he said: 'What are we taking it down at all for? Why not leave it standing and clear out?'

'We agreed at the outset that if we found the fine stuff,

we'd take our plant to pieces and fill in the trenches.'

'It's only delaying us and I don't know what's the good of it,' Dobbs growled.

'Well, boy, for a start I think the least we can do is to show some gratitude to the ground which has been so generous to us. We can close the wounds we've inflicted on it and not leave it disfigured. It's not decent to leave it cluttered up with our gear and turn its garden into a builder's yard. The mountain has earned of us the right to have its beauty respected. I'd rather remember the place as it was when we came than have it always before my eyes as the rubbish shoot we've made of it. It's bad enough that we can do no more than show our good intentions. This spot will still be an eyesore when we're gone.'

'It's a bit far-fetched what you say about the mountain,' said Curtin, 'but all the same I agree that you should sweep out the room that was clean when you came, even though there's no one there to praise you for it.'

'There's another reason, too,' the old man continued. 'It might be that someone came up here while we were on our way back. He'd see in a flash what we'd been up to and he'd be on our heels with half a dozen more. If we make things as shipshape as we can, it'll only look as if we'd been camping here a long time for some reason or another – not that it was for washing dirt and nothing else. So lend a hand, Dobbs; we worked many a day for nothing till the mountain opened its hand, and the day's work is worth it even though it brings nothing in. When you make a garden for your home, it isn't with the idea of a cash return.'

The midday meal in the course of months had become short and simple. They made a tin of tea and ate a bit of leathery pancake, cooked early in the day. As soon as the tea was drunk and each had smoked a pipe, they went back refreshed to their labours. Not a moment of daylight could be wasted; breakfast had to be over by the time the sun rose and supper begun only when it had set. Otherwise they could never have got through all they had. The length of the days was pretty well the same all the year through, and what difference there was they scarcely noticed. Nor had the rainy season had much effect on their labours. Now and then the rain had poured down in regular cloudbursts; but there was always something else they could turn their hands to. The rain, in any case, was of some help, for it filled the tank they had dug out so as to have enough water for washing the sand, and saved them the labour of carrying water.

'It's been a dog's life,' said Curtin, sitting down a moment to rest.

'You're right,' the old man agreed. 'But when you look at it, none of us has ever worked for higher wages than we've earned here.'

Dobbs too had put his spade aside and sat down to fill a pipe. 'It strikes me,' he said slowly, 'that there's not much to shout about yet. I don't mean as regards what we've got, but until we have the whole box of tricks safely stowed away in a town and sit quietly in a hotel bedroom with it all in front of our eyes, we can't say it's actually ours.'

'That's what I've been thinking too these last weeks,' the old man said. 'It'll be touch and go getting back with it, what with bandits, and accidents on the road, and the police who may be inquisitive and want to know what we have with us. And if they catch sight of the yellow stuff, then either we've stolen it, or killed and robbed somebody, or we've dug it without a licence and evaded paying the tax. All that needs thinking about. Yes, you can turn it over in your minds, how we're to come to port with our cargo of pepper.'

The two younger partners were silent. Then they wrinkled up their foreheads in the effort of thought and groaned, for it cost them more than the hardest navvy work; and finally with deep sighs they got up and went on levelling the heaps of earth.

Late in the afternoon they collected all the dismembered equipment into a heap and burnt it. Next day the charred patch was to be strewn with soil. Then a few shrubs, young trees and turf were to be planted here and there.

'It might happen, you see,' the old man remarked, 'that one of us didn't get home with it, or else blued it all in a few weeks, or came to grief one way or another. Then he could come back here and puddle again. There'd be something left for him to get. That's another reason for leaving no traces behind us, which might put someone else up to having a look round here.'

Dobbs and Curtin understood this better than the old man's notion of showing gratitude to the mountain and not leaving the face of Nature disfigured. Dobbs was of the opinion that Nature could look after herself. She had more time and patience than he had; and he was not night watchman of the lonely mountain landscape. But they had promised the old fellow, and so they did it; he was old, and even after all these months he still seemed to them a bit of a freak.

By the time they downed tools, no one would have supposed from a casual glance that there had ever been a mine there. There was only the bonfire still glowing and smoking. Next day the last signs of it would disappear.

Lacaud had not been by the fire at midday, and none of them knew whether he had been in the camp either before or afterwards. They had forgotten all about him. They were too much occupied with their own affairs to think of him. It was not until they came creeping out from their concealed track and saw him crouching over the fire and making it up that they remembered he was still there.

'Have you found your gold-mine yet?' Dobbs asked him as he came up to the fire with the kettle of water.

'Not yet,' Lacaud replied. 'But I don't know when I've been so close to it as I've been today.'

'Then I wish you the best,' Curtin laughed, bringing the frying-pan.

Lacaud had a pot of his own rice on the fire.

'You needn't make yourself any coffee,' Howard said good-humouredly. 'You can share ours. We don't put any more coffee in, only more water, and we needn't go easy with the water any more now.'

'Thanks,' Lacaud said shortly.

They washed and ate and sat by the fire. Howard, Dobbs and Curtin felt like factory hands on a Saturday night. They knew that they had nothing worse in front of them than a pleasant hour's work first thing in the morning, planting up the vacant space where the mine had been, followed by the even more pleasing job of packing up; and after that there was only getting the donkeys ready for the journey. It was all light and welcome labour over which they could smoke and sing and chat.

And so for the first time for months past they sat in comfort and good humour round the fire.

The thought that they were soon to separate, after sharing for nearly a year the anxieties and labours and privations of their life together, made them more tolerant of one another than they had ever been. They felt for the first time that they were bound together by a bond of friendship, comradeship and brotherhood. They felt that they would stand by each other even at the cost of their lives. They felt closer to each other than actual brothers. Without saying so, they were sorry for all the petty and yet very contemptible malice and spite they had so often been guilty of towards each other.

Lacaud was excluded from this brotherhood. He could not read and understand their feelings as they, who knew each other off by heart, could. They could make no secret of what went on inside them; but they could keep it a secret from Lacaud if they wanted to, and even deceive him and lead him astray. This they could never do among themselves. Each during the past months had had no study but the study of each other. Neither books nor newspapers nor change of scene or faces had distracted them from this common study. It often happens that as soon as one of them began a sentence, the others knew how it would conclude, even the exact words and their exact sequence. Hence a remarkable habit had arisen of never concluding a remark at all; there was no need, for the other replied as soon as three or four words had been spoken. That was one reason for their getting so much on each other's nerves that they could have committed murder just to be spared the irritation of being forced to know beforehand what the other man was going to say. But what was there to enrich their vocabulary or enlarge their ideas? They were concerned always with the same circumstances and the same tasks, and without knowing it they had evolved a method of communication entirely their own which left an outsider stranded.

They had constructed a paddle-wheel, and this was set in motion by means of a primitive capstan to which a donkey was harnessed. This contrivance scooped up the water into the gutter which conveyed it to the washing-troughs where the dirt was paddled. Howard used to take charge of the capstan, as it was lighter work. Originally, they shouted: 'Howard, pump the water along. We're ready for it.' This had been abbreviated to: 'Pump.' And this word, pump, had finally come to mean water, because it was shorter and easier to say pump than water. When they meant water for making coffee or for drinking, they said simply: 'Pump a fire?' which meant: 'Is there water on the fire?' A spade, for reasons which none of them could explain later, was a cat, a pickaxe a shrike, and a dynamite cartridge a Mary. When a Mary was to be detonated, two words were used. One was Mary; the other cannot, for reasons of politeness and also on other grounds, be given here, although in a certain context and in certain conditions it can well apply to any Mary. The same word was used in reference to lighting a pipe or the fire. Eat, besides referring to meal times, acquired a meaning almost the opposite and stood for a word seldom employed by polite persons and not even alluded to without great caution.

Howard was never called by his name. He was called Olb, and this had been evolved from old boy. Curtin was Cow and Dobbs Pamp. Why, none of them could have said.

It was the same with all the words and phrases they used. They could talk for ten minutes without Lacaud's understanding a word they said; and of course it never occurred to them that he couldn't follow them and sometimes felt he was among foreigners. They were so used to talking as they did that it would have seemed to them ridiculous to talk in any other way.

Chapter Fifteen

'Yes, as for getting back ...' Howard picked up the discussion where they had left it at midday. Instead of getting back he said kipping, but their talk must be put into a form which can be understood by those who are not of the brotherhood.

'Yes, as for getting back, it's the devil. We'll get back all right, I don't doubt. But even when you think you've got home with it, you're a long way from having opened a bank account. Did you ever hear the story of Donna Catalina Maria de Rodriguez? I'm sure you didn't. With her too it wasn't just a question of the gold and silver, but of getting away with it and putting it somewhere safe. At Guadalupe there's the miraculous image of Our Lady of Guadalupe, the patron saint of Mexico. You can go there by train from Mexico City. Every Mexican and Indian who has anything on his mind makes a pilgrimage to this wonder-working image in the certain hope that his desire will be granted, whether a man wants an acre of his neighbour's land, or a girl has lost her lover, or a wife is in fear of its coming out she's poisoned her husband to get another one instead of him.'

'It's all eyewash and superstition,' Dobbs put in.

'Not a bit of it,' replied the old man. 'It's no eyewash as long as you believe in it. If a man believes in a God, for him there is a God; and if he doesn't, then for him there's no such thing. But there's no need to argue about that. I'm not saying what I think. I'm telling you the sober truth.

'It was about a hundred and fifty years ago, just about the time of the American Revolution. There was a prosperous Indian living near Huacal, a descendant of the chiefs of the Chiracahuas. He had all the land he wanted and took no part in the raids and murders of the neighbouring tribes. His own tribe was settled on the land there and found more pleasure and profit in cultivating it than in everlastingly scrapping with the Spaniards. This chieftain had only one sorrow in the world: his only son and heir was blind. In earlier days the child would have been killed: but now that he and his tribe had settled down and all the tribes been converted to Christianity, their ideas were more humane. Added to that, the child was strong and shapely and unusually beautiful.

'A wandering monk, who wanted to exploit the liberality of the chief to the last inch, advised the father to make a pilgrimage with the boy and his mother to the miraculous Virgin of Guadalupe, and not to be sparing of his offerings; for the Mother of God was greatly pleased by generosity and well able to appreciate the worth of what was given her.

'The chief left his estate in his uncle's charge and set out on his pilgrimage. He was not allowed to employ horse, donkey or wagon and had to make his long trek of nearly two thousand kilometres on foot with his wife and child. He had to say three hundred Ave Marias in every church he passed by and offer large numbers of candles and silver eyes.

'At last he reached Mexico and after offering up prayers and petitions in the cathedral, for several hours he prepared for the last stage of his painful ordeal. It is five kilometres from the cathedral to the miraculous image of Guadalupe. He and his wife with their little boy had to go on their knees for these five kilometres, each of them holding a lighted candle which had to be kept alight in spite of wind and rain. When one candle came to an end, another had to be lighted from it, and as they were consecrated candles they cost more than ordinary ones. It took all night to get there. The boy fell asleep, and even in his sleep he cried for a little piece of maize cake and a drink of water. But they were forbidden to eat or drink. They waited until the child was quieter and then the procession went on. All who met them, Spaniards and Indians, got out of their way and crossed themselves, for they thought the family must be guilty of some unusually discreditable sin if they had to expiate it by such a terrible pilgrimage.

'They were utterly exhausted when they got to the foot of

the Cerrito de Tepeyacac, the hill on which in the year 1532 the Mother of God appeared three times to the Quauhtla-tohua Indian, Juan Diego, and printed her picture on his ayate, or outer garment. Here they spent three days and nights on their knees, praying and imploring. The chief had promised the Church his cattle and his whole harvest if the Mother of God came to his help. But the miracle did not happen. At last, following the monk's advice, he promised his land and all he had, if the Virgin gave sight to his son.

'But even now there was no sign of the miracle he awaited and had been so confidently promised. The child was so exhausted with his long fast and the fatigue of the journey that it took all his mother's care to keep him alive.

'The chief, not knowing what more he could do, began to doubt the power of the Mother of God and of the Christian religion in general, and he said that he would now go to the medicine men of his race who had often enough proved to his forefathers that the old Indian gods had power to work miracles. The monk forbade him to speak in so blasphemous a manner, and threatened him that more disaster would fall on his family if he gave utterance to his doubts. And they told him that the fault was his own. The miraculous Virgin knew very well, what no one else might know, that he had done wrong on his journey – passed over a church here; purposely miscounted his Ave Marias there, to be quicker done; eaten when he ought not and on various occasions drunk water in the morning without first keeling down and praying. The chief was forced to confess that he might now and then have said two hundred and eighty instead of three hundred Ave Marias, because of the difficulty of keeping count. And, said another monk, he had no doubt omitted to confess various sins, when he confessed in the cathedral; for to all who deserved it the miraculous Mother always granted help in their need. Therefore he had better repeat the pilgrimage in six months.

'Perhaps this was too much for the chief, or else – and this seems more probable – he had lost his faith in the miraculous power of the image. In any case, he returned to

Mexico, ate heartily and took his young wife in his arms again, as, in obedience to the task he had been set, he had not done during the whole journey. Then he made inquiries in the town and was recommended to go to the house of a certain Don Manuel Rodriguez. Don Manuel was a famous Spanish doctor, but avaricious and greedy of power. He examined the boy and told the chief that probably he would be able to give him his sight. What would the Indian pay?

'The chief said he had a farm and many cattle. But that, said Don Manuel, was not money. "I want money, a lot of money." The chief then told him that he would make him the richest man in all New Spain if he gave his son his sight. How, asked Don Manuel, could he do that out of his farm? The chief replied that he knew of a rich gold- and silver-mine, and he would take him to it when his son could see. And they made the terrible contract that Don Manuel should have the right to put out the eyes of his son, if the mine either did not exist or by this time belonged to someone else.

'Don Manuel gave his whole attention to the boy for two whole months, working on him and performing operations, and neglecting all his other patients, even the Viceroy's private secretary. And after two months the child could see like an eagle. Don Manuel told the chief that the cure was permanent. And so it was.

'The chief was overjoyed and his gratitude knew no bounds. "Now I will prove, Don Manuel, that I did not lie to you," he replied when Don Manuel asked about the payment. "The mine belongs to my family. When the Spaniards came my ancestor covered it up, because we wanted no Spaniards in our country. We hated them and knew that the white men loved gold and silver more than their Son of God. The existence of the mine was betrayed to the Spaniards, and they came and tore out the tongues of my ancestor and his wife to make them say where the mine was. But though his mouth was full of blood and he was nearly frantic with agony, my ancestor laughed in their faces and they never got hold of the mine. And my ancestor wrote the words down, and after his death they went by word of mouth from father to son, until they came to me, and these are the words: If some great service is done to you or your family or your race, greater than the feather-crowned god of our people or the blood-crowned god of the white people was able or willing to perform, then give the treasure to the man who performs it and let it be his.' You, Don Manuel, have, in the person of my son, done to me, my family and my race that service which the god of the white people was too weak to do, in spite of all my pains and prayers and offerings, and therefore the mine is yours. Follow after me, on the road I will tell you, in three months' time, and speak to no one of what you know, and I will make you the richest man in all New Spain."

'The Indians,' Howard said, continuing his tale, 'don't know of many more mines than we do. At one time they knew the exact position of all the hidden mines of which, after the conquest of Mexico, the Indians obliterated every trace in revenge for the cruelties inflicted on them. But the Indians have not been stationary since the days of the conquest. Thousands of them were carried into other districts by the Spaniards as workpeople and slaves; others in the course of rebellions and wars were driven from their homes into the hills and the jungle; others perished of the poxes and epidemics which the white men introduced into their country in the cause of civilization; the families of chiefs died out or were murdered before they could hand on their knowledge to those who followed them. Hence it is very seldom now that an Indian knows of a buried mine. Sometimes he thinks he knows of one, but what is known in his family about this mine or the other has become so legendary, so mixed up with mines already discovered and known, that the actual site can never be identified, all the more as the site is described by words and landmarks and directions which in the course of time have lost their original meaning and are bound to put you on a false track. This story I am telling you goes back to a time when the traditional memory of the Indians was fresher and less influenced by the trade and commerce brought by the railways. These have caused the Indians to move about much more freely. They leave their homes and go wherever there are better opportunities of making their living.

'As soon as Don Manuel had wound up his affairs in Mexico he and his wife Maria made the long and difficult journey to Huacal. He found the chief and was welcomed by him like a brother. "It occurred to me on the journey," Don Manuel said to his host, "that it's a very strange thing you didn't work the mine yourself, Aguila. You could have given me a hundred thousand gold gulden, and for that I'd have done whatever you asked.

'The Chief laughed.

' "I want no gold and I want no silver. I have enough to eat, I have a good and beautiful wife and a son whom I love and who is strong and well formed. What is gold to me? The earth brings a blessing; the fruits of it and my herds of cattle bring blessings. Gold brings no blessing and silver brings no blessing. Does it bring a blessing to you white Spaniards? You murder each other for gold. You hate each other for gold. You spoil the beauty of your lives for gold. We have never made gold our master, we were never its slaves. We said: Gold is beautiful. And so we made rings of it and other adornments, and we adorned ourselves and our wives and our gods with it, because it has beauty. But we did not make it into money. We could look at it and rejoice in it, but we could not eat it. Our people and also the peoples of the valleys have never fought or made wars for gold. But we have fought much for land and fields and rivers and lakes and towns and salt and herds. But for gold? Or silver? They are only good to look at. I can't put them into my belly when I am hungry, and so they have no value. They are only beautiful like a flower that blooms, or a bird that sings. But if you put the flower in your belly, it is no longer beautiful, and if you cook the bird it sings no longer."

'Don Manuel laughed.

' "I shan't put the gold in my belly, Aguila. Trust me for that."

137

'The chief laughed too.

' "I believe you. I can work for the earth, but I cannot work for gold, because then I should have nothing to eat, no tortillas and no camotes. You don't understand what I say, and I don't understand what you say. You have another heart. But all the same I am your friend."

'For three days they searched about in the mountains and the bush, scratching about and digging. Don Manuel was inclined to be suspicious of this long search and to believe that the Indian had cheated him of his reward. But then again, when he saw how cleverly and methodically the chief examined the neighbourhood, how accurately he noted the position of the sun and also the shadows which were thrown by the mountain tops, he was forced to recognize that he was not taking his course at random. "It is not as simple as you thought," said the chief. "There have been earthquakes, and a few hundred years of rainy seasons and cloudbursts and landslides; rivers have changed their beds, streams have vanished and new ones risen. Little trees have grown into big ones, and big ones which were landmarks have died. It may take a week longer, Don Manuel, you must have patience."

'It took longer than a week before the chief said one evening: "I can give you the mine tomorrow; for tomorrow I have it under my eyes."

'Don Manuel wanted to know why he should not have gone straight home with the chief when he left Mexico.

' "We should still have had to wait till tomorrow, because the sun was not in the right line. Now it is right. I have known for some days where the place is, but tomorrow I shall have the mine and I can give it you."

'Sure enough, on the next day they found the mine in a gully. "There has been a bit broken off from the mountain here, as you can see. That is why it was so hard to find the place. There is the mine and it is yours. But now you must leave my house."

' "Why? I would leave it in any case, because I shall build myself a home near the mine."

' "Yes, my home is no more good to you. You have the rich mine and you bring no blessing."

'The chief held out his hand, but Don Manuel said: "Wait, Aguila, I want to ask you one more question. If I had asked you for a hundred thousand gold gulden to heal your son, would you not have opened up the mine?"

' "Certainly I would have done so. But as soon as I had got the sum you asked I should have buried it again because gold is not good. For what could I have done? The Spaniards would have heard of it and murdered me and my wife and my son to get possession of it. According to your customs, murder is always committed for gold. So be careful, Don Manuel, that you are not murdered, when your people know that you have a mine. When they know that you have nothing but bread and tortillas, you are never murdered. I shall always remain your friend, but now we must part."

'Don Manuel began at once to make a camp there, and Aguila returned to his home, which was a day's journey away. Before he set out Don Manuel had procured the Certificados from the government which entitled him to search for precious metals and gave him mining rights over the places where he found them. He had left his wife in the last town they had passed through and he went back to fetch her, and also engaged workmen and bought the necessary machinery and tools and explosives for blasting. And now he got to work opening up the mine. It exceeded his wildest hopes. It was rich in silver that it surpassed all mines of which there was any knowledge. Its chief product was silver, but there was gold too, as a by-product.

'He knew enough of what went on to know that a man should never say too much about his mine, or put too high a value on it. Not only ordinary persons but even officials of the Crown and the highest dignitaries of the Church were very ready to cheat a man of his mine if he had not enough power behind him to defend his possession. The owner suddenly vanished and no one knew where he had gone, and the mine, having no owner, came into the hands of the Crown or the Church. The Inquisition, which kept its unholy power much longer in Mexico than anywhere else on earth and only disappeared at last when the Revolution triumphed and the country became a free and independent republic, was then in full and untrammelled vigour. It was enough for a bishop to hear of a wealthy mine for the discoverer and possessor of that mine to be dragged before the Inquisition on a charge of blasphemy, heresy, sorcery, or lack of reverence for the miraculous powers of an image. The Viceroy himself, the most powerful man in the country, trembled before the tribunal. If he was bidden to attend it, he went with a heavily armed bodyguard and made the announcement that his troops and the artillery had orders to open fire on the building of the Inquisition at once if he was not in his palace again within a given time and had shown himself to the soldiers. What then could an ordinary citizen do? Ten or twenty witnesses got up and took their oath that he had not kneeled down before the Pyx, or had said he found it hard to believe that a son could be his own father, or that the Pope could never be in error. And once this was sworn to, the miscreant was burnt and might take it as a special favour if he was strangled first instead of being burnt alive. But whatever his punishment, as long as his guilt was sworn to, all his possessions went to the Church. So it is not at all surprising that the wealthy who declined to make a voluntary offering of their land and their mines to the Church and the monasteries were summarily accused and found guilty of heresy, while poor Indians were usually treated by the Inquisition with far greater indulgence; for who, in their case, was to pay the high costs of the complicated judicial inquiry? The costs of the tribunal were by no means light. It proceeded against no one for nothing, as the documents prove; and the witnesses were the last people to make themselves cheap out of regard for the holiness of the end in view. But the power of every religion has its limits, and no religion can defy them without dying out. A religion which becomes too rigid to adapt itself to changing conditions and the passing of time, dies. Nations whose religion forbids them to draw the sword and enjoins on them to do no murder cannot go on waging wars for ever with impunity.

'Don Manuel had been made wise by the experiences which had so frequently befallen others. He sent away no silver or gold. He hoarded it up and bided his time. In spite of the rich yield of the mine, he treated his Indian workmen as shabbily as possible, paid them wages on which they could scarcely live and made them work till they dropped or died; if they did not work hard enough, he encouraged them with the lash. With niggers this method may answer for a long time, but not with Indians. During the three hundred years of Spanish rule in Mexico, the Spaniards never at any time had undisputed possession of the whole country. There was always rebellion somewhere. And if in one place it was stamped out with inhuman brutality, it blazed out somewhere else. If it was so in large, so it was in little; and one day there was a mutiny at Don Manuel's mine. His wife, Donna Maria, was able to fly in time, but he was killed. His treasure was not plundered. As soon as Don Manuel was dead, the Indian workers left the place and went back to their villages.

'When Donna Maria heard that the mine was safe again, she went back to it to carry on. She found all the treasure safe and undisturbed where it had been buried; and what she already possessed would have been enough to keep her in comfort for the rest of her days.

'But she had got it into her head to return to Spain, and to figure there as the richest woman in the land. As she was still young, and beautiful besides, she cherished the ambition of buying a castle and a nobleman's estate and appearing at court as the wife of a marquis. Grandees of Spain had married the daughters of Aztec, Tezcuc and other Indian princes of Mexico and Peru solely for their wealth. Why should not she, who came of a good Spanish family, get a marquis for her husband much more easily than they with the assistance of her boundless fortune?

'She was even better at figures than her deceased husband. She reckoned up how much a castle and a princely estate

141

would cost in Spain, how much it would cost to keep up and the cost of servants, carriages, horses and travelling; how much the marquis would need and how much she would need herself day by day in order to make a brilliant appearance at court. But still she found that there was much she had not thought of. There would be disbursements to the government, and a church to build, in order to put the lofty personages of the Inquisition in good humour and stay their avarice. And then she still carried on until the sum total she had reckoned could be doubled, and thus insured herself against any possible error in her calculations. They were hard years she had to battle through. She was far from civilization and deprived of even the barest comforts; she was on the alert night and day, keeping a vigilant eye on the workmen to see that their wages were not too high, and on the other hand not so low that they gave out and mutinied. She had to think, too, of raids and the armed bands of criminals and deserters and escaped convicts and the dregs of the towns, which went about marauding and spreading terror among Indian and white people alike.'

'Even envy itself could not grudge Donna Maria the credit of being a better match for her formidable task than her deceased husband had been. She feared neither death nor the devil, neither marauding bandits nor mutinous Indians, and she would assuredly have been a match in one way or another for the Inquisition itself, if she had been summoned before it. She was robust, indefatigable and energetic; but if she met with a check, she fell back on her gift for diplomacy and triumphed all the more certainly. She could laugh when it suited her book; she could weep if that seemed more profitable; she could curse like a footpad and she could pray more devoutly than a Franciscan monk. She could do the work of six Indians, and when things did not go as she wished she went at it with her own hands, and the Indians, who were not used to seeing a woman do heavy labour as if it were child's play, were so dazed with astonishment that they had to do whatever Donna Maria required of them. So it went on for years. But at last she felt such a longing for Spain, for a clean house, for a good kitchen, a soft bed and a husband to fondle and caress that one day she decided to pack up and go. When she surveyed her hoard she found that it was enough for even the most fantastic luxury.

'She had got together an armed guard which watched over and defended the mine and her treasure. It consisted of Indians and a few Mestizos and two Spanish soldiers who had either deserted or been dismissed. One of the two Spaniards took command by day, and the other by night.

'The metal, of which about one-sixth was gold and all the rest pure silver, she had run off into rough bars and ingots, so that it would be easier to transport. These bars were securely packed in boxes. How great the riches were which she had got from the mine may be judged from the fact that sixty mules, each one laden to the limit of its strength, were required for the transport of her treasure.

'The caravan with its escort of twenty armed men set off on the journey of two thousand kilometres to the capital city of Mexico. There was no proper road and their way led over deserts and steep mountains, through rivers and gullies and defiles, through primeval bush and forest and stretches of jungle; now in the ice-cold winds of the sierra and high snow-covered plateaux, then again in the blazing heat of belts of fever-haunted jungle.

'And then one evening after they had camped for the night it seemed to her that something unusual was going on. She went to see and found that one of the Spaniards had made an attempt to arrange matters to suit himself. He came up to her and asked: "Will you, or will you not marry me, Donna Maria?"

' "I marry you, a common thief who only escaped hanging because the hangman used a bit of rotten rope instead of a good new one?"

'Whereupon the fellow replied: "I'm quite ready to take it without you. I'll find a prettier girl than you."

' "What will you take without me?"

' "What's in the boxes."

' "Not as long as I'm here, you bastard."

'The man pointed across to where the men were encamped and said with a grin:

' "If you take a look over there you may change your mind. I can wait an hour."

' "You can wait your whole life or until you're hanged."

'However, she went across to the men and found that the fellow had done a fine bit of business for himself. The other Spaniard and the Indians were bound, and the Mestizos had joined the mutiny, hoping to go shares. There they stood with pistols in their belts and looked at her with impudent grins on their faces.

' "Very fine," Donna Maria remarked to the fellow.

' "That's so," he replied. "And now perhaps you'll make up your mind and say yes nicely."

' "You're right that I'll make up my mind, you hound."

she said, and at the same moment she seized hold of a whip lying with the saddles on the ground, and before the man saw what she was up to she blinded him with a merciless cut across the face. He staggered and like lighting she followed it up with a half dozen more. He fell in a faint and lay motionless. But she had only begun. The Mestizos were so astonished that it did not enter their heads either to make off or to shoot. And as soon as they realized what had happened to their leader the whip was already being slashed across their faces. Some fell, others began to run, putting up their arms to shield their faces. Donna Maria sprang to the other Spaniard and cut his cords with a few rapid jerks. He at once released the Indians, and in a moment they had jumped on to their horses and lassoed the Mestizos.

' "Hang the bastard," Donna Maria called out, pointing to the Spaniard who had designed to marry her and now got heavily to his feet. Half a minute later he was hanging.

' "What did I tell you?" she called out to him as the Indians hoisted him up. "I told you you'd hang first. And as for you," she turned to the Mestizos, "I ought to hang you too. But I'll let you off. You all have the hangman's noose round your necks, and I don't want to spoil his trade. But I warn you that if you try it on again I shall flog you myself until the flesh hangs in strips from your carcasses, then I shall roast you and then hang you. There is no need for you to stay, you can go if you like. You will get no wages and you will give up your arms. But if you choose to stay on, I will give you your pistols, your saddles and the horses you are riding on when we get to Mexico. Listen, you – what is your name?" she went up to the Spaniard who had taken her part. "Rügo, yes. When we get to Mexico, you shall have—' she was about to say a mule and its load, but she checked herself in time "—you shall have the right-hand load of that mule there, and the Indians half of the left-hand one between them." With this the mutiny was at an end.

'But there were still the marauding bands against whom the caravan had to be defended at all costs. These bands cared nothing for life or death. They fought to the last, for they had everything to gain; and the lives they staked they had already forfeited as criminals long ago. Not once but many times over.

'Then one animal fell with its load into a cleft and its load had to be salvaged. Another sank in a bog with all its treasure. A third disappeared while fording a river.

'It was a question whether it was easier to get the metal out of the mine or to transport it in safety to Mexico without Donna Maria's laying down her life in the attempt.

'The journey was a gruelling experience for her, and when she looked back to the long hard years at the mine, could she say they had been any better? She had never had a moment's joy since the mine came into her possession; and she could not recall a single hour when she had felt quite sure of her life or her treasure. In fact, taking it day by day and reckoning up all she had been through, her life had been wretched beyond words, more wretched than the life of a beast. Fear and anxiety had never left her. Dread pursued her into her dreams and there was no respite from the tormenting thoughts which harried her all day. There was one, and only one, ray of light in the misery of her dreary existence – the thought of the moment when she handed over her treasure to the safe keeping of His Majesty's Government in Mexico. This moment, the moment for which she had lived such a pitiful life for years past, came. She reached Mexico City without having lost very much of her precious load. She was received by the Viceroy in person, and he paid her the high honour of a private audience and talked to her for a long time. Her joy and gratitude exceeded all bounds when the mighty personage said that the fortune she had won at the cost of such arduous toil and severe privations should be received into the vaults which were exclusively reserved for the royal treasure.

'This was more than Donna Maria had ever dared to hope. Nowhere in all the Spanish dominions, not in the crypt of the Cathedral or in a monastery, could her treasure be so safely lodged, and from nowhere else could it be so certainly recovered. It was in the vaults of the government itself, and the Viceroy, the greatest power in the land, was personally answerable for its safety. Here her treasure was lodged in security at last, until she could convey it under military escort to a ship and carry it with her to the land of her longings. For his forethought and the gracious condescension he had shown her, she begged the Viceroy to accept a share which was large enough to seem a princely one even to a Viceroy of the Spanish dominions.

'Next she paid her men off and discharged them; and then retired to her Inn, the best in the town.

'And now at last after so many years she could lie down without a care and sleep. For the first time for years she could draw her breath in peace, eat in peace and allow her thoughts to wander. At last she could dismiss the cares which had ceaselessly revolved all these years in her brain, and welcome other and more delightful ones.

'But then something happened, something she had never expected. Her treasure did not disappear. It was not stolen from the vaults under cover of night and mist. Something else disappeared. Donna Maria lay down to sleep, safe in a beautiful white bed; but no one ever saw her get up. No one has ever seen Donna Maria again. Nothing has ever been heard of her. She vanished and not a soul knew where she had gone.

'That is easily explained,' Howard said, as he concluded his tale. 'Donna Maria had forgotten one thing only – that gold often makes a person invisible. And the only reason why I wanted to tell you the story was to prove to you that the difficulty of transport is just as great as the difficulty of the finding and digging. And even when you think you have got the loot safely home, even then it is not certain whether you will be able to buy yourself so much as a cup of coffee with it. It all goes to show why gold is so dear.'

'Is there no chance of finding where the mine was?' Curtin asked. 'The woman can't have exhausted it. There must be plenty left.'

'You can find the mine very easily,' Howard replied. 'But you'll come too late. It is worked by a big company, and it

147

has yielded the company ten times the amount the vanished señora got out of it. It seems it is inexhaustible. You can easily find it. It is called the Donna Maria Mine, and it is not far from Huacal. You can work there for a weekly wage if it would give you any satisfaction.'

The men sat on round the dying embers, and then got to their feet. They stretched, stamped their feet on the ground and thought of turning in.

'That story is over a hundred years old,' Lacaud said.

'Nobody said it wasn't,' said Dobbs.

'But I know a story that is only two years old, and just as good, or perhaps better.'

'Oh, shut your mouth,' Dobbs said with a yawn. 'We don't want to hear your story, not if it's only a week old. We know it already and it doesn't interest us any more than you do. You'll do best to say nothing at all. You're only a wandering . . .'

'What?' asked Lacaud.

'A hobo,' said Dobbs and went after the two who had gone across to the tent.

Next morning, the last but one they were to spend there, the three of them were so excited that they could scarcely stop to have breakfast. They slunk off to their secret hiding-places and brought out the fruits of their labour – grains of gold and sand and dust, carefully wrapped in old canvas tied with cord. Each possessed a good heap of these packets. The task now was to pack them up safely and in a manner not to arouse suspicion. They put dried skins round them and tied them up in bundles which looked as though they consisted of skins and nothing else. The bundles were then put into sacks ready to load on the pack animals.

Dobbs and Curtin then went off to shoot some game for the journey. Howard made wooden pack saddles for the donkeys and looked the straps and ropes over, so as to avoid delays on their journey owing to packs giving way. Lacaud again went off on his own, pottering about in the bush in the neighbourhood of the level grassy patch. But he did not say what he was looking for and none of the three asked him.

148

They showed neither pity nor contempt for his occupation. Pity was not in their line, and he did not interest them sufficiently to earn their contempt. It was a matter of complete indifference to them now what he did, so long as he did nothing to hinder them. Even if he had found a mountain of solid gold they would have hesitated to put off their departure by a day. They were so set on getting off that nothing could have stopped them. They were suddenly so sick of the drudgery, the privations and the solitude; and if Lacaud had tried to persuade them that he was on the track of something good and that they ought to stay a week longer, they would have fallen on him and beaten him half to death. When Howard let fall the remark that Lacaud seemed to know too well what he was after to be the wandering gold-digger, Curtin said: 'Nothing can make me alter my mind. If he brought me a lump of gold as big as my fist I wouldn't have it.'

'Not have it? Why not?' said Dobbs. 'I'd have it all right. But we can hardly get what we have away as it is. Let him bring it me in Durango. Then I'll have it. But now – I'm off.'

That evening they sat round the fire saying little. Each was too much preoccupied with his own thoughts and plans to tell a yarn or disturb the others' meditations. It was still dark when they struck camp and got ready to move off.

'You stay here, then?' Curtin asked Lacaud.

'Yes, I'm not done here yet,' he said.

'Good luck then, my boy. Perhaps another time we'll have time to listen to your fine story,' Dobbs said laughing. 'Then perhaps you'll have proofs to show us.'

Lacaud put his hands in his pockets. 'Proofs? Proofs, do you say? I can give them now. But you've no time.'

'We have not,' Dobbs replied. 'That's why we have to get off. We're in a hurry to get under cover.'

Howard shook Lacaud's hand.

'I've left you some salt, pepper and one or two other things that would only be in our way. They'll come in handy perhaps. There's a bit of tent cloth as well. You can have it. It's good for a wet night.'

'Thanks,' Lacaud said.

Dobbs and Curtin shook hands with him too. Dobbs gave him some tobacco, and Curtin a handful of cartridges. Now that they were parting they felt friendly of a sudden. It was on the tip of Curtin's tongue to ask him to accompany them instead of leaving him there alone in the bush, where he had not a hope of finding anything; they had been there long enough and turned every stone over and they knew what was to be found and what wasn't. But instead he only said: 'Good-bye.'

Howard felt the same desire. He wanted to urge him to come with them, and thought of giving him a job in the Cinema, as operator or manager. Then he kept it to himself and only said: 'Good luck.'

And Dobbs thought that a man more for the journey would do no harm. It would be an added defence against bandits, and their loads would excite less suspicion if they were divided among four. But he only shook his hand heartily and said: 'So long.'

Lacaud was as brief as they were, and then he stood and looked after them for a time. When they were out of sight, he turned to the fire and stirred the embers with the toe of his boot. 'Pity,' he said aloud.

Chapter Seventeen

They had to make a long detour with their train of pack animals in order to avoid the village where Curtin used to go for provisions; for as long as they were not seen, the inhabitants would think that he was still up there in the mountains. Even after leaving the village behind they still kept away from the roads and followed paths on which they were unlikely to meet anybody. The farther they got from this district the better hopes they had of reaching the town unobserved. Once there, they and all they possessed were in safety. They would go to an hotel, and continue their journey by train after packing their stuff in cases such as any traveller might have.

For the time they had scarcely any ready money in their pockets, a few pesos only, and these had to last until they reached the town. There they could sell the donkeys and whatever else they had no longer any need for, and the proceeds would buy their tickets. But first they had to reach the town. This distance was not very formidable. But they did not want to travel by the roads, where bandits and police were more likely to be encountered than on the hidden and winding paths. The fewer people they met the better.

But the paths did not always lead in the direction they wished. All paths led to villages or some human habitation. Sometimes they suddenly ran into a village when they least expected or wished to. And they could not very well turn back once they were in sight of it. It would look suspicious.

That was how they got into an Indian village on the second day. They had been unable to avoid it. It is not very unusual for a donkey caravan to pass through a place. To see it driven only by white men is unusual, certainly; but no one thought much about it, because white men have so many extraordinary ideas. But when they reached the middle of the village they saw four Mexicans standing in front of a hut. Three of them had bandoliers buckled round them and revolvers at their hips.

'That's police,' Dobbs said to Howard. 'We're for it.'

'Does look like police,' the old man replied.

Dobbs stopped the donkeys, but Howard gave him a push. 'Don't be a fool,' he said. 'If we stop all of a sudden like that, or even turn round, we're finished. That'll tell them at once there's something wrong. Keep going ahead as if we had a clear conscience. So we have, too. It's only the taxes and not having taken out a licence.'

'May cost us the whole bag of tricks all the same,' Dobbs cursed.

Meanwhile Curtin came up.

'Who's the guy with spectacles?' he asked with a jerk of his head towards the fourth man, who was armed and stood in the door of the hut apparently talking to some of the villagers.

'Probably he is a government inspector,' said Dobbs. 'The devil knows what's up here. Let's go quietly on.'

The Mexicans had not seen them approaching. It was not until they got to the village square where the hut stood that one of the police turned and looked after them. Then he spoke to the others and they too turned their heads and looked after the caravan which was quietly jogging on. When it had nearly crossed the square, one of the police suddenly called out:

'Hallo, señores, one moment!'

'That's done it,' Dobbs said in a low voice.

'I'll go across alone,' Howard proposed. 'You two stay with the donkeys. I'll find out what they want.'

Howard went across and politely asked what he could do for them.

'Have you come down from the mountains?' one of them asked.

'Yes, we've been hunting.'

'Have you all been vaccinated?' he asked next.

'Have we what? Been vaccinated?' Howard said it with obvious relief. He knew now what they were up to.

152

'Sure, we've all been vaccinated as children. That's obligatory with us. I've been vaccinated ten times at least all told.'

'When was the last time?'

'Two years ago.'

'Have you got the certificate on you?'

Howard laughed.

'I don't carry that about in my pocket.'

'I should say not,' the man said. 'But in that case you must be vaccinated right now. We are the vaccination commission and we have to vaccinate everyone we come across in the villages.'

The man with the spectacles went into the hut and came out again with his case. He opened it. Howard bared his arm and the man scratched it with the needle.

'We have an easier job of it with you than with the people here,' he said with a laugh. 'We have to lie in wait for them. They run off to the mountains and into the bush. They think we want to cut their heads off.'

'Yes,' said one of the police, 'it takes more to vaccinate the people here than catching a whole gang of bandits. But if we don't get them all done the smallpox will get the upper hand. It's the worst with the children. The women make an uproar as if we were going to murder the brats, and fight like wild cats as soon as we touch them with the needle. Look at my face, how they've scratched me. And my mate here has a great bruise on his head where a woman hit him with a stone. We've had four days here. They've all slunk off and we'll have to starve them out before they'll come back. But they're coming back by ones and twos when they find that the children who've been vaccinated haven't died of it. But how are we to explain to them that we only do it for the good of them and their children?'

While he spoke he turned the leaves of a book till he came to the first empty page.

'Write your name here, in both places.'

Howard wrote it and gave the book back.

'Your age?'

The official entered it, wrote his signature and tore off half the page along the dotted line and gave it to Howard.

'That's your certificate. The other half we keep in the book. Now send the other two across. It'll do them no harm even if they've been done ten times already.'

'What do I pay?' the old man asked. 'We're a bit short of money.'

'There's nothing to pay. It costs nothing. It's the government pays.'

'Then it's a cheap do,' Howard said laughing, and pulled down his sleeve.

'We know you've all been vaccinated,' said one of the other officials, 'or at least we take it you have. But we're only too glad to have a shot at you. The inhabitants watch every movement we make from their hidden places. That's why we chose this hut in the open here. When they see that we make no difference between Indians and white men and that you hold out your arms as if you did it every day, it'll give them confidence. They see it won't cost them their lives.'

Howard went back and sent Dobbs and Curtin to be vaccinated too.

'That's the best news I ever heard,' Curtin said laughing. 'I thought every moment they'd come and ask a lot of dam' fool questions.'

'If you like you can tell them all you've been doing for months past,' said Howard. 'It won't interest them any more than your family tree. They are the vaccination commission, and anything that hasn't got to do with vaccination leaves them cold. They'd vaccinate a bandit if he came by and let him go again. It's not any part of their job to catch bandits.'

'Now then,' Dobbs broke in, 'stop that blather. We'll be vaccinated and then get on quick.'

'Did I say we were going to spend the night here?'

'No, but you talk as though we had to fall on their necks over there,' Dobbs said, and hastened across to the hut.

Howard shook his head with a rueful expression and turned to Curtin.

154

'That Dobbs has no sense of humour, as I've said more than once. I'd rather fall on the necks of a vaccination commission than into the hands of a police detachment going their rounds on a mining control. Now off with you, Curtin, and get your certificate so as we can go on again.'

In the evening they camped near Amapuli. They had to stop there, because they were told they would not find water again before night.

While they were preparing their meal, four Indians came to their camp from the village, and after a polite greeting asked whether they might sit down.

'Como no? Why not?' Howard replied. 'You won't be in our way at all.'

The four Indians sat for some time watching how the strangers roasted their meat and cooked their rice.

'You've come a long way, no doubt,' one of them said at last, 'and no doubt you have a long way still to go. You are very clever men, that's sure.'

'We can read books,' Curtin replied, 'and we can write letters, and we can reckon with figures.'

'With figures?' another of the four asked. 'Figures? We don't know that.'

'Ten is a figure,' Curtin explain. 'And five is a figure.'

'Oh,' said another of their guests. 'That's only half of it. Ten is nothing, and five is nothing. You mean ten fingers or five beans or three hens. Is that it?'

'That's so,' Howard put in.

The Indians laughed, because they had understood, and one of them said: 'You can't say ten. You must always say ten what. Ten trees or ten men or ten birds. If you say ten or five or three without saying what you mean, there's a hole and it's empty.'

Then they laughed again. After they had been silent again for a good time, one of them said: 'My son has fallen into the water. We pulled him out again at once. I do not believe, though, that he is dead. But he does not wake up. You have read books and know what to do.'

155

'When did your son fall into the water? Yesterday?' asked Howard.

'No, this afternoon. But he does not wake up.'

'I will go with you and have a look at your son. I will see if he is dead.'

The men got up and Howard went with them. They took him to a house built of sun-dried bricks. There was a mat on the table and on the mat lay the boy.

Howard examined him carefully. He raised his eyelids and put his ear to his chest and felt his hands and feet. Then he said: 'I'll just see if I can bring him round.'

For a quarter of an hour he worked the boy's arms up and down, and then had hot poultices put on his stomach and chafed his hands and feet; and when he put his ear to the boy's chest again he found that his heart was beginning to beat. After an hour the boy began to breathe by himself and a few minutes later he opened his eyes.

The men and women who were in the hut had been watching what the stranger did without uttering a sound. The women who heated the poultices communicated with each other by gestures or in low whispers. Even now, when the boy was fully awake, not one of them dared speak.

Howard got his hat and putting it on went to the door. No one stopped him and no one spoke. Only the father of the boy went after him and held out his hand and said: 'Señor, I thank you.' Then he went back into the house.

It was now quite dark and Howard had difficulty in finding his way back to the camp. But finally the light of the fire put him on the right road.

'Did you manage to do anything?' Dobbs asked.

'Nothing much,' said Howard. 'Artificial respiration, and he came to. He'd just had a shock. He'd have come round by himself in a few hours without help. It was just a mouthful of water. Have you left me a bit of meat?'

Before sunrise they were on their way again. They were in a hurry to reach Tomini, and from there they hoped to find their way over the mountain range. After they had had their midday rest, they loaded up the donkeys again and were just getting them on to the path when Curtin said: 'What's this? Looks as if we had something on the line.'

'Where?' asked Dobbs. 'Yes, you're right. Indians on horseback. But it doesn't mean we've hooked them. They may be out riding or going to market.'

It was not long before the Indians came up with them, and they were the same four who had paid them a visit the evening before, and with them were two others whom Howard had seen in the house.

The Indians greeted them and then one of them said: 'But, señores, why have you run away from us?'

Howard laughed. 'We didn't run away, but we have to get on. We have to go to the town. We have important business there which cannot wait.'

'Oh,' said the father of the boy whose life had been in danger, 'business can always wait. Business is never in a hurry. There are days after today and days after tomorrow and days after that. But first you must be my guests. I cannot let you go. You have given his life back to my son. In return you must be my guests – for two weeks. No, that is too little. You must be my guests for six weeks. I have land and plenty of maize. I have cows. I have many goats. I will give you every day a good turkey cock to eat and eggs and milk. Every day my wife will make you tamales.'

'We thank you with all our hearts,' said Howard, 'but if we do not reach the town in time, our business is lost.'

'Business does not run away,' one of the other Indians replied to this. 'Business is tough, like the flesh of an old goat. Business makes trouble. Why do you want to make trouble for yourselves when you can have all you want with us? You will have no troubles, and we have music and dancing as well.'

'No, we have to go. We must get to the town,' Dobbs said, beginning to show annoyance.

'We have taken your gift,' the father said, 'and you must take our gift.'

When the Indians saw that the strangers made more difficulties than they expected over the invitation to be their guests, one of them said: 'The two young men can go if they like, but you—' and he pointed to Howard '—you may not go. My brother's son would die for certain, if we did not have you for our guest. We must pay for your medicine, because you were good to the boy.'

All their annoyance and all their protestations went for nothing. There was no escape. They were surrounded by the six men and in their power.

Finally Dobbs had an idea.

'There's no undoing last night's foolery. If you stay, they're content. It's only you they want to keep back. We'll go on and you can follow later. There's no other way out of it.'

'It's all very well to talk – but what about my packs?'

'They can stay with you,' said Curtin.

Dobbs was against this.

'I don't advise it. They'll rummage through them and take the stuff from you, or they'll start talking and it'll get about, and if they don't kill you, bandits will get to know and lie up for you.'

'Then what am I to do?' asked Howard.

'We'll take your lot and bank it in your name. Or perhaps you don't trust us.'

It was Dobbs said this.

'Trust you? Why not trust you?'

Howard laughed and looked from one to the other. 'We have lived together getting on for a year and worked together all that time. That's meant trusting each other, I should say.'

And since there was nothing else for it, they had to take the only decision with which the Indians could be satisfied. They were concerned only in showing Howard their gratitude. So the only thing to do seemed to be for Howard to hand over his share to the other two. They both made themselves answerable and both gave chits on which they acknowledged the receipt of so many packages, each of about the same weight in grams of washed sand.

'And where will you hand it in?' Howard asked.

'We'll put it in a safe with the Banking Company of Tampico in your name,' Curtin said.

'Right then,' Howard agreed, and then they had to part.

'It's only a few weeks, old boy,' said Curtin. 'Whatever comes, I'll wait for you in Tampico. You'll find me at the Southern, or the Imperial, I'd stay with you, but there's the waste of time, and, as you know, I have someone waiting for me.'

Howard was given one of the horses, and the Indian whose horse it was got up behind one of the others. Then they returned laughing and talking to their village, carrying Howard along with them in triumph.

Chapter Eighteen

This delay meant the loss of half a day; for the Indians were in no hurry at all to end the discussion, however pertinaciously they stuck to their guns. They had made it quite clear that they were not particularly eager to rope in Howard's two companions. If Howard had wished, they would have been ready to include them, and they would have offered them the same hospitality. But they did not seem to take to them. Perhaps they did not like their expression. Indians take more stock of a man's expression than of anything else about him.

It was owing to this delay that Curtin and Dobbs did not get as far even as the Indian hamlet, Cienaga, and so they had another day's journey before they could reach the pass by which they meant to cross the range. The whole affair had annoyed them, and they were so bad-tempered that they scarcely spoke a word. If they had to say anything they spoke in a growl. They were furious at having Howard's load on their hands and his donkeys to drive, loading and unloading them at every stop. He had failed them and shirked his share of the job. It was just his donkeys that broke away from the caravan, and just his packs that were not properly roped and shifted on the pack saddles during a journey. With curses they made them fast again, and meanwhile the other donkeys scattered and had to be rounded up. When there were three of them none of this happened. All they could do was to curse and revile Howard from afar. They soon saw how ridiculous this was; he could not hear them, and it was a mere waste of energy to curse at him. So then they cursed the donkeys – who could not understand and paid no attention. They trotted on, snatching a bite of grass here or a twig from a branch there, if ever there was a second's space in which to reach out their tongues without the beast behind rudely barging into them.

Finally there was nothing left but to grouse at one

another, blaming each other senselessly for the most remote and trivial matters merely in order to produce a reply and to find in it further cause of aggravation. It is always the replies that made the quarrel. But whoever has the philosophic composure to refrain from replying to reproaches, accusations and ridiculous assertions?

Curtin took the head of the caravan and Dobbs the rear, and they directed their amiable and well-meant remarks at each other over the backs of the donkeys in between them. The donkeys twitched their ears forwards to pick up a flaming oath from Curtin, then backwards to hear how Dobbs would take it and how violent his retort would be. The donkeys which were next to each other put their noses together and snuffled and whispered something and grinned with open mouths. If the path was too narrow to go two by two, then the one behind snuffled at the rear of the one in front, and he in turn looked round and nodded and grinned, and make it very clear that he understood and had come to the same conclusion. And so, snuffling and looking back and nodding and grinning and wagging and twirling their long ears, they passed the word along the line. If Dobbs and Curtin had only spared a moment to observe what the donkeys thought about it, they would certainly have acquired the rudiments of true philosophy. But who would sink so low as to learn from a donkey?

'I'm stopping here,' Dobbs said suddenly. 'I'm not plodding on like an ox all day.'

'It's only three o'clock, man,' Curtin answered.

Dobbs got into a temper at once. 'I didn't tell you, did I, to camp here?' he shouted over the donkeys' backs. 'You can go on till morning and bust yourself for all I care.'

'Tell?' Curtin roared back. 'You've nothing to tell me about. You are not the boss yet.'

'Perhaps it's you, then. I've just been waiting to hear you say it.'

Dobbs went purple in the face.

'All right,' Curtin said more quietly, in spite of his annoyance, 'if you're beat . . .'

'Beat?' Dobbs shouted. 'I can see you beat any time.'

'Well, anyway – if you don't want to go any farther, we can unload and camp here. I don't mind.'

'There's water here, for one thing,' said Dobbs, calming down also. 'Who knows whether we'll find water again before night?'

Eating generally mends the temper, unless there's a discussion about what it's costing. And so it was here, although it was no feast. There was even a toast proposed, a toast to the absent member. Dobbs was toast-master.

'What'll the old fellow be doing now?' he said, and as he said it he thought of himself and his own interests, not of Howard's at all. At first he thought of Howard, but even before the words were out of his mouth he realized that there was something nearer to him than Howard. He looked across at the packs, and his eyes rested for a moment on the old man's.

Curtin too looked across at the packs, but he misinterpreted the toast-maker's look. For he said: 'We'll get home all right with the whole cargo. We are far enough from the mountains. There's nothing suspicious about us now whatever. In two days, if we get a clear view from the top, we'll see the smoke of the trains.'

Dobbs said nothing to this. He stared into the fire and then looked away at the dark shadows of the grazing donkeys, and as he didn't want to go on watching them nor to stare any more into the fire, his eyes went back to the packs and fastened upon Howard's.

Suddenly he gave Curtin a dig with his fist and laughed out loud. His laugh was tumultuous and unsteady.

Curtin looked at him in astonishment; and, though he had no idea what the joke was, he caught the infection and laughed a little, looking round at the same time to see what had suddenly made Dobbs so merry.

'What makes you laugh like that?' he asked.

Dobbs burst out louder than ever.

'It's so damned comical.'

'What is?'

162

'That fool of a man giving us all his bronze. Out here in the wilds. What's easier? He can whistle for us. He'll never find us, the old bag of bones.'

Curtin had stopped laughing. 'I don't understand what you're talking about, Dobbs.'

Dobbs laughed and gave him another dig. 'Don't understand, you poop? Where were you brought up?'

'I'm damned if I do understand,' Curtin said, shaking his head.

'What's there to understand? Don't be so thick-headed. We clear out. That's all.'

Curtin showed no sign of understanding what was expected of him.

'We clear out,' Dobbs explained. 'Land home with it, share out and each go his way.'

'Now I begin to see what you are after.'

'You've taken your time about it,' said Dobbs, and slapped him on the shoulder.

Curtin stood up, walked about and came back to the fire. He did not sit down, but stood there looking up at the sky. Then he said dryly: 'If you mean we're to jockey Howard out of what he's got by his labour . . .'

'Of course I do. What else do I mean? And I mean it good and proper.'

'Yes. Well, if that's what you mean,' Curtin went on, as though Dobbs had not interrupted him, 'then I'll have nothing to do with it. I'll take no hand in that game.'

'If it comes to that,' Dobbs now said, getting up and planting himself in front of Curtin, 'I don't need your permission. It's none of your business. If you don't come in on it, it's your own look out. Then I take the lot, and if you don't like it you can lump it. Do you understand now?'

'Yes, I understand you now.'

Curtin shoved his hands in his pockets and took a step back out of Dobbs's way.

'And?' asked Dobbs sharply. 'And what?'

'As long as I'm here you won't touch a bean of the old fellow's. I signed his chit. . . .'

163

'So did I and spit on his chit. He's got to find us first. Then I'll tell him bandits robbed us. It's clear as daylight.'

'I signed the chit,' Curtin went on undeterred, 'and I gave him my word, apart from you altogether, that I'd bank his share. It's not just the chit and the signature, or the promise either. There's a lot you promise and put your name to that it'd take you all your life and longer to carry out. It's not that. It's another thing altogether. It isn't as if he stole it or picked it up, or won it in a lottery or in the money market or at Monte Carlo. He got it out of the ground by honest labour, and hard labour too. There's not much I respect. But I have some respect for what a man has got by the toil of his own hands.'

Dobbs made a contemptuous gesture.

'You can keep your Bolshie notions for someone else. They don't go down here. I know them off by heart.'

'It's nothing to do with Bolshies,' Curtin replied. 'It may be true that it's the object of the Bolshevists or Communists to put some respect for the earnings of labour into the heads of those who don't need to work and have money already and to give the worker the full benefit of his labour instead of cheating him of it on all kinds of pretexts, and applying it to schemes that don't interest him at all. But that's another story. Whatever you think about it, that's not what I'm talking about. But I tell you straight, as long as I'm with this caravan or anywhere near it, you don't lay a finger on anything that belongs to the old man. You don't go near his bronze as long as I stand upon my two feet. So now you know.'

Curtin sat down and, taking out his pipe, began to fill it. He did his best to seem unconcerned.

Dobbs remained standing and looked steadily at Curtin. Then he laughed derisively.

'You're right, my boy. Now I do know. I know now what you're up to. And I've known it for some time.'

'What have you known for some time?' Curtin asked without looking up.

'That you've had it in mind yourself to put a bullet

through me tonight or tomorrow night, and bury me like a dead dog, and then make off with Howard's lot and mine too, and laugh at us for a couple of fatheads.'

Curtin lowered his pipe, which he was just lighting, and looked up. His eyes were wide and vacant. This accusation robbed him of all power to give them any expression. He had never for a moment thought of acting the part that was foisted on to him. He did not call himself a pattern of integrity. He could help himself with the best, if it came to that, and he was not the victim of his conscience. The oil magnates and steel kings and railway lords could never get where they do if they were troubled by consciences. Why should an insignificant creature like him have more exalted views and a more sensitive conscience than those who are pointed to as the great ones of the earth and extolled in newspapers, magazines and story books as the highest examples of energy, will-power and achievement? But, nevertheless, what Dobbs now attributed to him was more than he could stomach. Perhaps if he had thought of it himself he might not have thought so hardly of it. But thrown at him in this rancorous and disgusting way, he thought it the dirtiest action he had ever heard of. And if Dobbs thought him capable of it, it showed what Dobbs himself could sink to. How could he have thought it of anyone, unless it had been in his own mind? And in that case, Curtin was a dead man; for Dobbs would not think twice about destroying him in order to get the whole lot for himself. It was the consciousness of the peril he was in that deprived his eyes of all expression. He saw that from this peril there was no escape. He was helpless – about as helpless as a man can ever be. For what defence had he against Dobbs? They had four or five days' journey before them. And even if they met anybody it would be no help. Dobbs had only to hint at the reward and he would have anyone they met on his side. And if they met no one, so much the better for Dobbs. Curtin could keep awake for one night and save his skin. But the next night he would only sleep the sounder. There would be no occasion for Dobbs to waste a bullet. He could tie him up and knock him on the head and bury him. He could even spare the knock on the head.

There was only one way out. Curtin had to do with Dobbs what Dobbs meant to do with him. Slay or be slain. There is no other law.

I won't have his bronze, thought Curtin, but I must put him out of the way. The old man shall have his share and I shall have mine, and that swine's I'll bury with him. I won't be the richer for him, but my life is worth as much as his.

His left hand with his pipe in it was on one knee, and his right hand on the other. Now his right began to travel slowly to his hip pocket. But in the same moment Dobbs whipped out his revolver.

'You stir, my boy, and I shoot,' he shouted.

Curtin kept his hands still.

'Up with 'em!'

Curtin stretched his arms above his sead.

'I wasn't far out,' Dobbs jeered. 'Your fine talk was only a smoke-screen. But you don't get past me like that. Stand up!' he said, coming nearer.

Curtin did not utter a word. His face had gone white. Dobbs went up to him and reached round to his hip pocket to disarm him. Curtin whipped round. Dobbs shot. But owing to Curtin's sudden movement the bullet missed him; and before Dobbs could fire again Curtin laid him out with a powerful punch to the chin, and flinging himself on top took away his revolver. Then he jumped up and retreated a few steps.

'The boot's on the other foot, Dobbs,' he said.

'So I see,' Dobbs replied. He sat up, but stayed where he was.

'I don't mind telling you now that you're altogether mistaken,' Curtin told him. 'It never so much as entered my head to take a thing off you or to put you out of the way.'

'That's easy said. But if you're such a good boy you can give me my gun back.'

Curtin laughed. 'It had better stay where it is. It's no toy for you.'

'That's the game, is it?' Dobbs said, and went to the fire.

Curtin took the cartridges out of Dobbs's revolver and put them in his pocket. He thought of handing it back to Dobbs and Dobbs held his hand out for it. But thinking better of it, Curtin put both revolvers in his trouser pockets. Then he sat down by the fire, taking care to give himself room in case of an unexpected attack.

And now he lit his short pipe. Dobbs said nothing and Curtin had ample leisure to pursue his thoughts.

He was no better off than he had been half an hour before. He could not keep a watch over Dobbs for four days and nights. He would have to fall asleep some time and then Dobbs would overpower him. And he would show no mercy, for he was now convinced that his suspicions of Curtin were correct and that if he put him out of the way it would be in self-defence. There was only room for one of them. Fear and exhaustion would drive them both half crazy. Whoever first fell asleep would fall a victim to the other.

'What about separating first thing tomorrow – or tonight and each going his own way?' Curtin asked.

'It would suit you well.'

'Why me?'

Dobbs laughed rancorously.

'You'd get me from behind, eh? Or put bandits on my track?'

'If that's what you think,' said Curtin, 'then I don't know how we're to get quit of one another. I'll have to tie your arms together, day and night.'

'Yes, that's what you'll have to do. So come and do it. Here I am.'

Dobbs was right. It was not so easy to do. It might mean that the boot came on the other foot again. And it would be for the last time. Dobbs was the stronger and the more unscrupulous. He was the stronger owing to his robuster conscience. The unscrupulous man survives the man who hesitates. Those who put their trust in acting quickly rather than in carefully considering and weighing their actions are the winners. But the others conquer in the end and possess the land. Here, however, it was a question only of winning, because the life of each depended on overpowering or destroying the other. Curtin was in the stronger position, but he dared not make use of it. He was political by nature, but no doer. Dobbs on the other hand could waste, but he could not spend; he could destroy, but not overthrow. And therefore he too was no doer; for the doer can both spend and overthrow.

Chapter Nineteen

The night that now began was terrible for Curtin, but not for Dobbs. Now that he had discovered Curtin's weak side, he felt perfectly sure of himself. He could play with Curtin as he chose.

Curtin sat close enough to Dobbs to keep an eye on him, but not so close that he would not have time to lift his revolver if Dobbs thought of attacking him. He set himself with all his strength to the task of keeping awake. He was tired by the day's journey and he felt that to hold out all night would not be easy. He could not walk about because it would tire him more. For a time he sat upright, but that too was tiring. Then he came to the conclusion that it would be better to get under his blanket and lie down. It would rest his limbs. Also Dobbs would not be able to see so clearly if he dozed off for a moment.

After about an hour when Curtin had not stirred for a long while. Dobbs sat up and began to crawl. Instantly Curtin levelled his revolver. 'That'll do,' he shouted.

'You're a good night watchman,' Dobbs replied with a laugh.

Later, after midnight, Dobbs was wakened by the braying of one of the donkeys. He made another attempt to stalk Curtin, but Curtin held him up at once.

Dobbs knew now that he would win. By his two feints he had prevented Curtin from sleeping, and now he slept on himself. The next night would be his.

Next day Dobbs had the head of the caravan. So there was nothing he could do. Then came the evening; and then the night. Soon after midnight Dobbs got up quietly and went over to Curtin and took his revolver. Then he gave him a kick in the ribs.

'Up, you swine,' he said. 'The boot's on the other foot. And now it'll stay there.'

Curtin was dazed with sleep and asked: 'Boots? What about boots?'

Then he understood and began to get up.

'Sit where you are,' Dobbs said and sat down facing him. He pushed the burnt-out brands into the fire and the flames shot up.

'There's not a lot to say,' he went on. 'I'm not going to play the night nurse for you as you have for me tonight and last night. I'm going to make a clean end of it. I don't mean to live in fear of my life from now on.'

'Then it's murder you mean.' Curtin said it without a tremor. He was too tired to realize all that had happened.

'Murder?' Dobbs replied. 'Where's the murder? I've got to save my own skin, I suppose. I'm not your captive. I'm not bound to hang on your mercy for every day you leave me lingering.

'You won't get out of it like that,' Curtin said, slowly coming to his senses. 'The old man won't let you get away with it so easy.'

'Won't he, though? Why, it's simple. You tied me to a tree and went off with the whole cargo. Nothing simpler. You'll be the skunk of the two of us. You can leave it to me to see he never finds you. Get up and now and – quick march.'

'Where to?' Curtin asked.

'To your burial place. Did you think you were going to dance somewhere? You don't need to pray. There's no one to hear your prayers. You'll find the right place, don't worry. I'm only sending you there a little earlier than you thought. So up you get – quick march!'

'And suppose I won't?' Curtin asked. He was still tired out and dazed with sleep. He knew well enough now that it was deadly earnest. But he was too tired to think beyond the shot he was soon to hear, too sleepy to grasp with the shot his existence would be ended. It all seemed to him like a dream, a dream in which he never quite lost the consciousness of its being only a dream out of which he would wake in the morning with nothing but a faint recollection of what the dream had been about. And yet he tried to impress on his memory all that went on in his dream so as to be able to recall it clearly to his mind when he woke. He felt that it was important not to forget his dream because it gave such a clear insight into Dobbs's character, clearer than he had ever had, or thought possible. He remembered distinctly having heard once that sometimes you get to know a person better through a dream than in waking life, and he made up his mind to be more effectually on his guard against Dobbs, as soon as day dawned than he had been hitherto.

'I can just as well go on sitting here,' he said with closed eyes. 'What have I to get up and march anywhere for? I'm tired. I want to sleep.'

'You'll have time enough to have your sleep out. Up you get now – step out.'

The loud and harsh command tortured Curtin. Swaying and stumbling he got to his feet, merely to avoid hearing it again.

Dobbs drove him forward with blows of his fists for fifty or sixty paces into the bush. Then he shot him down.

Curtin collapsed and fell. Dobbs bent over him and when he heard neither a breath nor a sigh he put the revolver back into his pocket, and returned to the fire.

He sat there for a time and tried to think out what to do next. But not a thought would come. He felt quite vacant. He stared into the fire, heaping on more wood or pushing bits further into the glow with his feet. Then he lit a pipe.

After drawing a few puffs, suddenly a thought flitted across his brain. He thought that perhaps he had missed Curtin. Perhaps he had only stumbled and fallen at the very moment the shot was fired. He turned about towards the bush where Curtin lay. For a time he looked intently into the darkness as though he expected to see Curtin coming for him.

Next he found sitting uncomfortable and got up. He walked once or twice round the fire, kicking at the branch ends with his toes. He sat down and pulled his blanket round him; then rolled himself up in it and lay down. He drew a long breath in the hope of getting off to sleep, but he checked it in the middle. He was certain he had not hit Curtin and that suddenly he would see him standing over him with a revolver in his hand. The thought was intolerable. He could not sleep for it.

Snatching a stout and fiercely burning branch from the fire, he went with it into the bush. Curtin lay there on the same side as before. He did not breathe and his eyes were shut. Dobbs put the flaming brand to his face, but Curtin did not stir. His shirt over his chest was soaked in fresh blood.

Reassured now. Dobbs was about to go. But before he had gone three steps he turned and, drawing his revolver, he fired another shot into him. Then he went back to the camp.

He put the blanket round his shoulders and sat down by the fire.

'Damn it,' he said, laughing to himself, 'it gave me a prick of conscience to think that he might be alive still. But now I'm satisfied.'

The word conscience, however, stuck fast in his mind. It made itself at home there and any sentence that took shape in his mind hinged on this word, conscience. Not as a conception so much as a naked word.

Now I'll just see, he thought, whether conscience is playing a trick on me. Murder is the worst crime you can commit. So my conscience should be lively at present. But I never heard of a hangman who was troubled with his conscience. Mr. McDollin in Sing Sing has put a hundred and fifty in the electric chair, and he seems to enjoy it. He sleeps quietly in his bed every night without his conscience pricking him. Perhaps there may be four switches and four men to press a button each and none of them knows which button did the damage. But all the same, Mr. McDollin must clap the fellows in the chair. He has accounted for a hundred and fifty and perhaps more, and yet he is a respected man and an officer of the state.

And how many Germans did I kill in France? Fifteen? Twenty-three, I believe. 'Fine,' said the Colonel. And I've always slept well. Not one of those Germans ever appeared in my dreams and not one of them ever disturbed my conscience. Neither their mothers, nor their wives, nor their little children ever bothered me night or day. There was that time in the Argonne. A German machine-gun nest. Lord, how they stuck it! With two full companies we couldn't get near them. At last their losses were too heavy and they showed a rag of white. There were eleven of them still alive. As we went forward they put their hands up and laughed. They were true soldiers, and thought us the same. We bayoneted the lot like so many cattle. The worst of us was a fellow called Steinhofer. He went mad and wouldn't spare even the wounded. He had been born in Germany and only left it when he was seventeen. His parents and brothers and sisters are all in Germany to this day. And it was he who showed no mercy. There were one or two who begged for their lives because they had so many children. What did this fine Steinhofer say to these fathers? What was it? Anyway, it was a swinish thing to say and he followed it up with the bayonet. I believe he got a medal. But an English artillery officer came along just as the slaughter was over. And the Englishman said: 'You swine, you ought to be ashamed of yourselves.' If Steinhofer wasn't ashamed of himself and if so many more of his fellow-countrymen were not ashamed of themselves for crying murder on the Germans more lustily when war broke out than the most bloodthirsty Jingo, why should I be ashamed of myself? I've never felt a pang of remorse over those young Germans, let alone Steinhofer. Why should my conscience be upset over this skunk Curtin? As long as he's dead, my conscience is easy. Conscience is active only when the prison doors are open and the hangman is by. If you're acquitted, or if you've done your time, a murdered man will never worry you.

He worries you only if you're afraid it'll come out, or that you may be caught.

Soldiers and hangmen get their pay. That's why their consciences don't trouble them, however many they may do in. And what have I to be afraid of? I have the plunder and

Curtin will never be seen again. I'd better bury him first thing in the morning.

Dobbs laughed out loud. It amused him that his thoughts were suddenly so lively and chased each other so fast through his head. It struck him as remarkable that he had grown so wise and had such clever ideas. If they were written down, he thought, they'd take him for a very learned fellow. He was surprised that he had never known before what a clear-headed, open-minded fellow he was. He went on to think how easy it was to be a match for preachers who twaddled on about conscience without ever having come up against it in any matter of importance. He could soon show them that all the stuff they talked and wrote about it to keep people in fear all their lives was nothing but humbug.

If you believe in conscience, then it is there, and it acts when you tell it to; if you don't believe in it, then you haven't one and it can't ever bother you.

Dobbs stretched himself at full length by the fire, and as he fell asleep he felt he would sleep better than he had for days. And in fact he slept right on till daylight.

He drank some coffee left over from the night before and began to load the donkeys. It was only then it occurred to him that Curtin was dead. He regarded it as a fact, one which no longer concerned him any more than if Curtin had died of some sickness or than if someone else had killed him. He felt like an onlooker. Not for a moment did he feel any pity or even a pang of remorse. There was nothing to regret. Curtin had been put out of the way, and this was a matter only for satisfaction.

He wondered whether to take Curtin's stuff along with him or simply to leave it there. But he decided at once that it would be folly to leave the packs behind there. They would only fall a prey to bandits or marauding Indians. Curtin could never have any use for them now. On the other hand, what wouldn't it mean to himself to have the whole of the swag? He might, for example – but there was no good beginning to think of all he might do with it. It would be an exaggeration to say that the whole freight would make him stink of money. It would not even make a rich man of him. But it would put him beyond want. And he did not intend to sit and do nothing: no, he was going to start some enterprise, a factory or a ranch, or else speculate – but better not speculate perhaps. He might not be lucky. Why not, though? Because of his paltry life of want? Why, the most miserable specimens had most luck. It was just the most worthy and respectable people who always had bad luck, whatever they might touch or whatever they started on. Of course, if he left all the property of the other two behind, no one would be able to bring it up against him that he took to self-defence for the booty's sake. There were people, judges even, who could turn and twist things so that in the end it came out as downright murder. But then, suppose he left Curtin's share behind and someone else picked it up, not a soul would ever believe that he had taken nothing that belonged to Curtin. The best thing, all said and done, was to take it boldly and for the time think no more about it. If it came to light there would be plenty of time to say: 'What d'you mean? Here's the man's whole property. I stole nothing from him.' First, though, he would see how things went and how far he could go.

It was just the same thing with Howard's share. If Howard ever found him – well, there it all was just as it had been handed over. But first he'd have to find him. And if he did not find him until later, who could ever say? So many things happen. Bandits might have stripped him of all but his life and one sack which he had rescued with difficulty. There are so many bandits about. You can put anything down to them because they're capable of anything. It was they who shot Curtin too. Perhaps it would be better to say that they had quarrelled and fought, and then separated. Curtin had gone another way and he couldn't say what had become of him. But, after all, it would be best to tell the story of the bandits. What was the use of flogging his brains to decide what he should say and what story he should tell. Once safe in the town, there would be plenty of time to put it all in order. He might wait for the old man in Tampico quite openly and rush to meet him with such a hair-raising tale that he would never think of questioning the truth of it. The pack or two which he had rescued from the bandits' claws could be shared with the old fellow. He'd be so glad that anything at all was left that he would not say another word. Perhaps, again, something might happen to the old swine on his tramp to the rail. If only he had a couple of Mestizos handy. For twenty or twenty-five pesos, they'd lie up for the old man and put him out of sight; then no one at all would know a thing about the whole business.

Chapter Twenty

The donkeys were loaded. They stood there patiently, moved a few paces and then stood still again. Now and then they turned around. They waited to be told to go on, and didn't understand what the delay was for. They were used to their programme and it was getting on for midday. Loading up had given Dobbs more trouble than he had expected. It was not so easy without help to load the animals in such a way that the packs would not slip; for he could not be on both sides of them at once. It was impossible to get both loads on to the pack saddle at once, because the packs were too heavy and he could not lift them high enough to get them both on at the same time so that they balanced. If only donkeys would kneel down to be loaded like camels. But, just because they are not camels, donkeys will not do this. Besides, they could never get to their feet again under such loads, although they can travel with them for hours up mountains and down again without showing a sign of fatigue. Finally, however, Dobbs succeeded in getting the animals loaded.

He was just going to give the donkeys a shout and a blow, when he thought of Curtin. He had been thinking of him the whole morning and particularly while loaded up, but as of someone absent or gone away rather than dead. He had not yet so fully realized that Curtin was actually dead and done with as to be able to think of him only as a dead man.

Now, however, when the caravan was about to start, he thought of Curtin as a dead man. And then it occurred to him that he ought as a matter of prudence to have buried him before setting off. For a moment he was undecided whether after all to leave him lying where he was. The coyotes, mountain lions, vultures, ants and flies would dispose of the body quick enough. But then there would still be a few bones and rags left over. And it was not very advisable to leave them there as an advertisement of what had happened, or of what might have happened.

But these thoughts became entangled with another thought which until now had never come to him, and it made him irresolute. He thought that perhaps the sight of the corpse would make him lose his head. There was such an unearthly desolation and silence all around him. The scrub was so meagre that it looked as though the trees had never grown up. They seemed unable to decide whether they ought to grow a little larger or whether it was better to stay as they were. The droughts are so long and may cost them their lives if they need too much water. And since many of them from sheer cunning refuse to grow any bigger, the earth beneath them takes its revenge by making them grow crooked, stunted, askew and grotesque.

There was not a sound of beast or bird in the undergrowth. There was a wind. Dobbs felt it and saw the clouds moving overhead. But the trees did not stir. They stood as though turned to stone. They were not green, but grey-blue like brittle bits of lava. The air round them took on this same dead grey, and it seemed to Dobbs that the very air had turned to stone and could not be breathed.

The donkeys were now standing quite quietly as though they waited to be turned to stone like everything else around them. Sometimes with an unnatural slowness they turned their heads and gazed at Dobbs with their large black eyes. For a moment he was afraid of them, and to shake off his fear he went up to one of them and tightened its cords. Then, going up to another, he pulled at its load to see whether it was tight enough and wouldn't shift during the descent of the pass. But everything was fast enough. The puffing and blowing against the bodies of the animals and the feel of their hides calmed him, and he forgot the look from their great glassy eyes, shining, like flakes of coal.

Had he too, thought Dobbs, his eyes open, glassy, vacant and dim? Only natural, he told himself. Dead men's eyes are always open, and their eyes are always glassy and dim. But no, he thought again, they are not glassy and they do not shine like the donkeys' eyes; they are worn, dull glass. In fact, they are not glassy at all. They are glazed. It will be better to bury him. I might perhaps think of his eyes. Yes, I must certainly bury him.

He pulled out a spade from one of the packs. But as soon as he had it in his hand he thought again that burying the body was unnecessary and a mere waste of time. It might mean that he would just miss a train, and the sooner he left that neighbourhood behind him the better.

While he was pushing the spade back again through the cords he felt a curiosity to know whether the vultures had found Curtin out yet. If he were only sure of that, he thought, he would feel safe. Once more he pulled out the spade and walked away into the bush. He went straight for the spot where Curtin was lying. He could have hit on the direction, perhaps even the very spot, blindfold. But when he came to the place there was nothing there. He had made some mistake. The darkness of the night before and the uncertain light of the flaming branch must, he supposed, have made him mistake the direction. He began to look about, creeping through the undergrowth and pushing his way through the scrub. Suddenly he felt bad. He was afraid of coming on the corpse when he least expected it. He did not want that. It might even happen, he thought, that groping round he might unawares touch the corpse on the face. The thought gave him an eerie sensation. He now decided to give up the search.

All the same, when he was half-way back he said to himself that he would never have peace until he had seen the corpse lying there under his eyes and could be convinced that Curtin was really dead and past troubling him any more.

He began his search over again. He quartered the bush in all directions, then ran back to the camp to take up his direction again from there. Suddenly he found he could not any longer remember for certain in which direction he had driven Curtin out on the night before. Time after time he took his direction afresh. It was no good. The corpse was not to be found. Could he possibly have so completely mistaken the direction?

His excitement rose to fever-pitch. The sun was now straight above and blazed without mercy. He panted and broke out in a sweat. He was parched with thirst. But instead of drinking he poured water without thinking straight down his throat.

When he went back to grope through the bush he kept glancing nervously about. For a second he wondered whether it was fright. But he persuaded himself it was nothing but his nerves. Certainly it was not his conscience, he was sure of that. It was only excitement.

The donkeys had become impatient. The ones in front had begun to get underway. And soon the rest of the caravan followed as a matter of course. With a curse he was after them. This frightened the donkeys and upset them. They began to trot and he had to overtake the leaders before he could bring the carvan to a halt. Quite out of breath, he chased them back to the camp, where they stood quietly nibbling at the sparse grass. Now and again one of them turned and looked at him with large and wondering eyes. This terrified Dobbs and he decided to blindfold them.

Nevertheless, he began again on his search, and when for the hundredth time he had convinced himself that he was on the spot where he had shot Curtin down, he saw a piece of a charred branch. And now he knew that he was at the right place. It was a piece broken off from the branch which he had used to light his way the night before.

The ground looked disturbed. But that might just as well have been caused by his own trampling and groping about. He saw no blood. In any case it could scarcely have been seen on ground like that. Had Curtin been dragged away by some animal? Or had somebody found him and carried him away? He could not have crept away by himself because he was dead. Dobbs had convinced himself of this. It must have been an animal that had dragged him away.

All the better, thought Dobbs, because soon there would be nothing left of the corpse. And now, feeling calmer, he

began to think of making a start. All the same, he kept turning round, and first he thought he caught sight of Curtin
between the trees and then had as bad a shock when he
decided that it was another man he had seen. Next he started
up because he was convinced he heard voices. And if a twig
snapped or a stone was dislodged he thought some beast was
stalking him, the same one that had dragged Curtin away,
and which, once having tasted blood, would spring on him
from behind.

He shouted to the donkeys and they started off. But the
journey was far more difficult than Dobbs expected, for if he
went to the head, the tail of the caravan began to string out
and even to take side paths and look for grass in the bush.
Time after time he had to halt the caravan in order to round
up donkeys which had been left behind.

So then he took the tail of the caravan, and now the
donkeys in front went astray and the whole caravan went to
pieces. He got out rope and tied each donkey to the pack
saddle of the one in front to keep them together, and once
more he took the head. But as soon as a donkey pulled on
the pack saddle of the one in front, the one in front came to
a standstill and the whole caravan halted.

He began now to give all his attention to the leading
donkey, whipping him on and so forcing him to drag the
others after him. This succeeded for fifty yards or so, but
then the donkey thought better of it. He came to a stop,
planted his forefeet firmly in front of him and putting back
his long ears stood as fast as a rock. Dobbs might whip him
or kick him in his tenderest spots, the donkey would not stir;
for he had no idea what was up. He was supposed to go and
at the same time he was dragged back from behind. Once
more Dobbs changed his tactics and, getting in front, he
dragged the leading donkey along. For a time all went well.
The donkeys all followed. But when the leading donkey discovered that it was much easier and more convenient to be
dragged along than to go of his own accord, he allowed
himself almost to be carried, until Dobbs at last had such a
weight to pull that a whole railway train might have been

attached to the rope which was strained over his shoulder. He had to give it up and attempted once more to drive them along from behind, running the whole length of the caravan to collect any beasts who strayed.

Then there came a time when the caravan went along by itself without any trouble. The donkeys had settled down and kept well to the path. There was peace and quietness at last and Dobbs walked comfortably behind and lit a pipe. And as he had nothing else to do but stroll quietly along, he began once more to be busy with his thoughts.

I didn't make a proper search, he thought to himself. Perhaps he wasn't dead, only badly wounded. Now he's crawling through the bush and he'll end by reaching an Indian village. Then it's all up. Dobbs turned round with a start, for he thought he heard Indians close behind, pursuing him to give him up to the police.

But perhaps he won't get to a village. The villages are far apart and, even if he isn't dead, he's too hard hit to do more than drag himself along. I must find him and finish him off. In any case, it's attempted murder and brigandage, and that will mean twenty years in Santa Maria.

At last he saw nothing else for it but to go back and make a fresh search for Curtin, dead or alive. It occurred to him that there was one direction in which he had not looked at all. This was the opposite direction from the spot where he had left Curtin lying. He had never searched there at all, and it was quite clear that Curtin might have crawled off in that direction because it would lead him back to where they had seen that village at midday the day before. Dobbs had been fast asleep and neither seen nor heard anything. Perhaps, too, Curtin had avoided passing close by the camp in case he waked Dobbs and got finished off. He would have been de-fenceless. Yes, there was no doubt of it. Curtin had crawled off in that direction, and it was there he was to be searched for.

It was just before nightfall when Dobbs was once more back at the old camping-place. He did not wait to unload the donkeys, but began on his search at once. He searched in the new direction with the same feverish haste with which he had searched in the opposite direction during the morning.

But the night came quickly and Dobbs had to give up.

There was now only one thing left. He could not waste a single hour more on the search. He would have to get off at dawn and reach the railway at Durango with the utmost speed, sell the donkeys and tools at once and, taking the first train to one of the large towns, vanish from sight there. For the time he could not think of Laredo, Eagle Pass, Brownsville or any other station on the frontier, for, if Curtin had really reached a village or if Howard was on the road, then he would be looked for first of all along the frontier.

At noon, on the day before, Dobbs had seen from a bare mountain height the smoke of an engine in the far distance. It could not be so very far now.

Chapter Twenty-one

Dobbs was on the way before daylight. The caravan went along fairly well once it had settled down. The beasts were more willing than on the day before, because they had not been kept standing so long and they were already familiar with first part of the way. Nevertheless, one donkey broke away and Dobbs was unable to round it up. He had to let it go, as he had no more time to lose. Its load bumped against trees while Dobbs was chasing after it and the girths broke. The donkey cantered off without its packs. Dobbs took the trouble to distribute the load among the other donkeys, for the runaway would no doubt follow and join up again of its own accord at night.

Dobbs had now an almost unbroken view of the railway line in the distance, and the track led downhill the whole way towards the valley. That very afternoon he could easily have reached a station at Chinacates or Guatimape, but he would have caused too much of a stir with his caravan in these tiny villages, all the more now when he was quite alone. It would look suspicious. Besides, in little places like that no one would buy his donkeys, tools and the other stuff which he had to sell in order to buy a ticket and pay the freight charges.

So he had no choice. He had to go on to Durango, where he could transact his business without exciting much attention. This meant another two days' hard going, perhaps even three. If only he knew whether Curtin was dead or not, but after all one must always leave something to luck.

When Dobbs pitched camp for the night he felt calmer than he had for two days past. It was not really conscience that had vexed him. It was rather the uncomfortable feeling one has after leaving a job half done. And he had left his job less than half done and it took its revenge by making him feel uneasy. He ought to have smashed Curtin's skull, plunged his knife into his heart and put him under the ground there and then. That would have made a proper job of it and set his mind at rest. 'Do your job well and do it at once', he had been taught as a child, and yet when it had come to the pinch he had neither done it properly nor at once.

Anyway, there came the donkey which had broken away, trotting up to join its companions. Two of the grazing donkeys raised their heads and brayed. They were, no doubt his intimate friends, but the runaway went up to one of the other donkeys and after snuffling and nibbling its neck began to graze beside it as unconcernedly as if it had only wandered away for five minutes instead of having trotted along miles behind the caravan for a whole day.

'That's a bit of luck,' Dobbs said with a laugh when he saw the donkey trotting up. 'That's fifteen pesos to the good. Another two days and I can write the old boy a letter to send the other swine a doctor. I can snap my fingers at them then.'

He was in such good spirits that he began to whistle and at last to sing, and he passed that night much more quietly than the night before, during which he had started up several times, frightened by every sound.

Towards noon of the next day when the path went over a hill, he could see Durango in the distance. Durango, the lovely jewel of the Sierra Madre, which, bathed in golden light and softly fanned by gentle breezes caressing it with the tenderness of a feminine hand, nestles between protecting hills. 'The Town of Sunshine' it is called by those who, once having seen it, are homesick for its endearing loveliness. Mother Earth, who is not stingy when once she has a mind to make a present, has placed on one side of it one of her miracles of nature, the 'Cerro del Mercado', a mountain of pure iron, six hundred million tons of pure iron ore.

That evening he camped for the last time. Next evening he would be in Durango and on the following morning in the train for Canitas. The sale of the donkeys and the rest of his gear would take little time, as he would ask no more than he stood in need of for his journey.

He was jubilant. He was in sight of port. When the wind was in the right direction he could hear the whistle of the goods trains in the silence of the night. And this shrieking whistle of the engines, which often sounds so mysterious and ghostly, made him feel that he was already in an hotel close to the station. It was the cry of civilization and this cry was his assurance of safety. He had a longing for law and order, for the solid masonry of the town, for everything which would serve to guard his treasure. Once within the sphere where property is protected by law and where strong forces make law respected, he was safe. There everything and every accusation had to be proved, and, if nothing could be proved, then the possessor was the lawful owner, whose property would be protected by the bullet and the prison. But he would certainly avoid putting himself in need of proving his title. He would carefully keep out of the way of every stone or pebble over which it is so easy to stumble when you have to keep a look-out on every side. What could Howard do? Nothing. If he attempted to invoke the police or the law he would be up against it himself, for he had dug for gold and removed it without the permission of the government. He had robbed the state and the nation, and so he would take good care before making any move against him. And Curtin? Even supposing he were alive, what could he do? Just a little. He too had robbed the state and could make no accusation without confessing it. Dobbs had not robbed the state. No one could prove it against him. Attempted murder? Curtin could not prove that either. There had been no witness. As for Curtin's wounds, who could say in what scrap or robbery he might have got them? Dobbs by that time would be a well-dressed and prosperous gentleman who could afford the services of an expensive lawyer. Everyone would believe him when, with a casual wave of his hand, he pointed to the other two as bandits. To look at them would be enough, and, besides that, they were by their own confession robbers of the state. He would hold that over them. They would never get at him, not when he once had the protection of the law. Law is a good thing after all.

It was only in the interval before he reached the station and before he could take shelter within the protecting arms of the law that the two could do anything against him. But they were far away and tomorrow he would be safe. Perhaps a long time hence they might by pure chance come across him somewhere, in the States or in Cuba or in Mexico or even in Europe. They could, of course, call him murderer, bandit and shameless swindler to his face. They could do that, but, though he could not stop them, he would not turn a hair. Or, if they went it too strong, he would bring a charge of slander against them. No court in any civilized country would ever believe that such things were done anywhere on the earth. Not nowadays. A hundred years ago, or even fifty, but not today, anywhere. Such lawless places are no longer to be found. Every judge knows that, and he would laugh at such slanders. And then the slanderer would have a heavy fine to pay, or else go to prison, for Dobbs is an honourable and prosperous man, who has made his money by perfectly lawful speculations.

The old man or Curtin might of course murder him. They could do that in spite of all the laws in the world, but they would hang for it or take their seats in the electric chair. They knew that all right, and therefore they would think twice about it.

The whistle of another engine sounded in the darkness. For Dobbs it was music, the music of security.

Strange that Curtin never made a sound when he shot him down, not a groan, not a whimper, not a rattle, not a sigh. Nothing at all. He collapsed like a felled tree, and lay there full length as though dead. Only the blood flowed and soaked thickly through his shirt. Nothing else moved. And when Dobbs took the burning branch to see him by, expecting something horrible, all he saw was that white staring face. He couldn't in any case have felt any horror, for Curtin lay so oddly cramped that Dobbs almost laughed at the grotesque appearance of his body.

And now Dobbs laughed aloud to himself. He thought it so funny, the sight of Curtin struck down and lying there dumb, so funny to think that a whole life can be quenched for ever with just a touch on the trigger of a gun.

Wherever could the body be? Carried away, found and brought into safety? Or dragged off by a lion or a tiger? But that he must have seen. Could it be that he wasn't dead?'

Dobbs grew restless and began to shiver. He raked the fire together. Then he turned round and looked across the bare expanses and beyond them to the bush. At last he could lie still no longer and got up to walk about. He told himself that he did it to get warm, but in reality it was because he could see on all sides more easily when he was on his feet. Sometimes he thought he saw someone stalking him. Then he felt sure he heard someone coming up to the fire. Suddenly he had the sensation of someone standing close behind him. He even felt his breath on his ear and the point of a long knife at his ribs. With a quick jump he sprang forward and whipped round with his revolver in his hand. But there was nothing to be seen. Nothing but the dark shadows of the donkeys, who were unconcernedly grazing or lying down. Dobbs excused himself on the ground that you have always to be on your guard. He had done nothing ridiculous, not anything that had any connection with fright or conscience. No one could travel alone through the wilds with such a valuable cargo and not be nervous. It was quite natural, and if anyone pretended otherwise he was only deceiving himself. He did not sleep quite so well that night as the nights before. But the reason was obvious. It was only because he was overtired. He was delayed in his start next morning, as some of the donkeys had strayed to a distance and had to be fetched. Dobbs had been careless when he hobbled them. He lost fully two hours.

The road improved and by midday Dobbs could reckon that three hours more would take him to Durango. It was not his intention to make straight for the middle of the town. He meant to halt at the first Fonda he came to on the outskirts and unload there. He would arrange with the owner of the Fonda to introduce him to buyers for the donkeys, unless the man would take them himself at a low price for the sake of a bargain. Then he would load all the rest, that is to say, the sacks containing the real goods, on a wagon and have it delivered at the express goods station. In this way he would avoid arousing suspicion. The stuff could be consigned as hides. He would pay the highest rate for merchandise and then no questions would be asked.

The track was deep with sand and dust. On one side there was open country, but on the other there was a steep bank of dry, friable clay and crumbling, weathered stone. Thorny bushes and maguey plants were dotted here and there, withered and parched and thickly covered with dust.

Whenever the wind rose or a sudden squall came over, a column of suffocating dust swirled up, and you could scarcely breathe. The fine sand was driven into the eyes, making them smart and blinding them for minutes together. When the squall had passed over, the still air weighed on the land with a metallic glare; then in the blazing atmosphere the dust seemed to singe and roast the skin. The earth, after waiting months for rain, could no longer bear the oppression of the sun and threw back its light with a tormenting brilliance. The dancing shimmer of the merciless sunlight struck through eyes and brain of man and beast, until they staggered on dazed, with closed eyes and not a thought for anything but the end of their torment.

The donkeys struggled on with half-shut eyes. Not one strayed or left the path. They walked like automatons, scarcely moving their heads. Dobbs too had his eyes shut. If he opened them by so much as a chink, the cruel glare flooded into them and he felt that his eyeballs would be burnt up.

Then through his eyelashes he caught a glimpse of some trees by the wayside. He decided to make a brief halt there, just five or ten minutes for the sake of leaning a moment against the trunk of a tree and opening his eyes in the welcome shade to rest them. The donkeys would gladly stand for the sake of a moment's rest in the shade.

When he came to the trees he ran to the front to turn the leading donkeys, and the caravan came to a halt. Of their own accord the animals thronged into the shade and stood quietly. Dobbs went to his water bottle and after washing the dust out of his mouth had a drink.

'Say, got a cigarette?' he heard someone ask him.

He gave a start. It was the first human voice he had heard for days.

For a moment he thought the voice must be Curtin's; then Howard's. But in the same second he realized that the words were Spanish and that therefore it was not either of his two companions. He turned his head and saw three men lying under the next tree. They were Mestizos, down and out and in rags, fellows who perhaps had worked for some mining company long ago and now had been for months without work of any kind. They drifted to and fro on the outskirts of the town, sleeping, idling, begging, and if they saw the chance of some petty theft they took it as a gift from God, who allows no sparrow to starve even though it neither ploughs nor sows.

On the other hand, they might just as well be escaped convicts, or criminals not yet caught, who were lying in hiding until they had grown their beards and could hope to return to the town without being recognized. Whatever a town cannot do with, even on its rubbish heaps, it drives out on to the roads, which lead to it, out beyond the zone of rusting jam tins, broken bottles, leaky enamel ware, stoved-in buckets, yellowing newspaper and all the other refuse which a civilized town ejects day by day. It is just the same in the tropics as everywhere else. No beast produces such a mass of rubbish and filth as the civilized human being; and the disposal of this filth which he daily produces costs him as much trouble, labour and forethought as the production and use of all the things which he imagines he finds necessary.

Dobbs had been in the country long enough to know that he was now in as awkward a situation as any he could have looked for. He knew these outcasts from the towns, fellows who had less to lose than any destitutes in the world.

He saw now that he had made a bad mistake when he left

the road to have a quarter of an hour's rest in the shade. Not that he would have been any safer on the road, but at least he would not have walked straight into the trap.

'I've no cigarettes. I haven't had a cigarette for ten months.'

That sounded all right, and he added that he himself was a poor devil who couldn't afford to buy any.

'But I've a little tobacco left,' he went on.

One of the men asked for paper to roll a cigarette.

They were all still lying indolently on the ground with their heads turned towards him. Two were propped on their arms and the third lay stretched on his front with his head turned askew to look at Dobbs.

'I've got a bit of newspaper,' said Dobbs.

He took his bag of tobacco and a bit of paper out of his pocket and handed them down to the one who lay nearest him; for the man did not bother to get up to take the tobacco.

They all tore strips from the paper and shook tobacco on to them. Then they rolled themselves cigarettes and the one in front gave the bag of tobacco back.

'Cerillos? Matches?' asked the one who gave the tobacco back.

Dobbs felt in his pockets and brought out some matches. They even returned his matchbox.

'Going to Durango?' asked one of them.

'Yes, to sell the donkeys. I want money. I haven't a cent.'

That was a cute answer, thought Dobbs, for now they knew that he had nothing in his pockets.

They all laughed. 'Money, that's just what we want, too, eh, Miguel? That's what we're waiting for, money.'

Dobbs leant against a tree and kept an eye on all three of them. He filled his pipe and lit it. All sense of fatigue left him. He was looking for a way out. Perhaps, he thought, I could hire them as drivers. It will look better when I reach the town than arriving quite alone with the caravan. Then they'll be sure of a job and look for a peso each and drop any other ideas they may have. They'll be sure of food in their bellies and a few glasses of Tequila.

'I could do with two or three drivers,' he said.

'Oh, you could?' One of them laughed.

'Yes, the donkeys give me enough to do. They don't keep together.'

'What will you pay?' asked another.

'A peso.'

'Among the three or each?'

'Each. Not till we get to the town, of course, and I can put some money in my pocket. At present I haven't a centavo.'

Again Dobbs thought what a cute answer he had made.

'Are you by yourself, then?' asked one who was propped on his arm.

What shall I say, thought Dobbs. In order not to let them wait for an answer and arouse their suspicions, he replied: 'No, I'm not by myself. There are two others behind with the horses.'

'That's a funny thing, Miguel, don't you think?' said the one who was stretched out on his stomach.

'Yes,' Miguel answered, 'that's very funny. Here he is by himself with all these donkeys and lets his friends come behind on horseback.'

'Can you see anything of his friends on the horses?' asked the third.

'I'll have a look,' answered the one who lay flat. He got up slowly and, walking away from the trees, looked up the road, which could be seen for a long distance a little further back.

When he returned he said: 'Those two with the horses are a long way off yet, an hour at least. That's a funny thing, Miguel, don't you think?'

'A decir verdad,' said Miguel. 'I think it's very funny too. What's all this in the packs?' he then asked, and getting up went to one of the donkeys.

He punched one of the packs with his fist.

'Skins, I should say,' he said.

'Yes, there are skins there,' Dobbs admitted. He was feeling more and more uncomfortable, and wanted to get off.

'Tiger?'

'Yes,' said Dobbs indifferently, 'there's tiger among them.'

'They fetch money,' said Miguel with a knowing air, and stepped back again from the donkey.

To hide his uneasiness Dobbs went up to one of the donkeys and tightened its girths, although there was no need for it. Then he went to one of the others and gave a pull at the packs, as though to make sure they were fast. Next, he tightened his belt and pulled up his trousers to show that he was making ready to go.

'Well, I'll – yes, I must get on if I'm to be in the town by dark.' He knocked out his pipe against his heel as he spoke. 'Which of you will come as driver to Durango?' He looked at them and at the same time rounded up the donkeys.

Not one of them made any reply. They looked at each other and exchanged meaning glances. Dobbs intercepted one of these, and gave a push to one of the donkeys to get it going. The donkey trotted off and another lazily followed it, but the rest stood still and nibbled at the grass. Dobbs went up to one of them and shouted at it, and it too moved off.

The men were now on their feet. Without apparently meaning anything, they strolled up to the donkeys which had not yet moved and crowded them back or got in front of them if they made an attempt to follow the rest.

The animals, however, began to get restive when they saw the head of the caravan under way and already on the road, and so they pushed past the men. But the men had now come to life and seizing the reins they brought them to a halt without any disguise.

'Get off from those donkeys,' Dobbs shouted angrily.

'What's that?' said Miguel, impudently pushing out his jaw. 'We can sell them just as well as you can. They'll be none the worse because we sell them.'

The other two laughed and caught hold of another donkey.

'Leave go of those donkeys,' Dobbs shouted louder than before. He took a step back and pulled out his gun.

'You don't frighten us with your gun,' sneered one. 'You can only shoot one of us and he won't care.'

'Get back and let go,' shouted Dobbs.

Then he loosed off at the nearest man. It was Miguel. But there was only a hard, dry click. Again and again he pressed the trigger. Not a shot rang out. Dobbs stared and the men stared. From sheer astonishment they forgot to laugh or jeer.

But one of them bent down and picked up a large stone.

A pause of one single second followed. Yet his thoughts crowded upon Dobbs so quickly in this single second when his life was at stake that he could not help wondering how it was possible for anyone to think of so many things in one second. His first thought was how his revolver could have missed fire. But this brought a long story to his mind. On the night when he shot Curtin he had crept up to him while he was asleep, taken his loaded revolver from him and later shot him with it. Curtin had had both revolvers in his pockets, his own and Dobbs's. As both revolvers were marked and Howard could have identified them, Dobbs threw down Curtin's, with which he had fired the shots, beside the body after shooting him the second time. But he put his own revolver in his pocket. Thus it would appear, if Curtin's body were found, that he had been attacked and had defended himself. Dobbs's revolver was of a different calibre and the bullets could not have been fired from it. Dobbs forgot only one thing. He forgot, when he took back his own revolver, to load it. He forgot that Curtin unloaded it on the night when he took the revolver from him. Busy as his mind had been all these last few days, it had never once entered his head that the revolver was still unloaded.

Still in the same second Dobbs thought of another weapon. He was standing close beside one of the donkeys to whose pack a machete was tied. He made a grab to draw the machete and defend himself with it. This might have served him well, for with the machete in his hand he could perhaps have gained time to load his revolver with the few loose cartridges in his shirt pocket.

But the second had now run out and the stone came hurtling at his head. He saw it coming, but he did not turn his head aside quickly enough, because his mind was entirely taken up with the machete.

The stone stretched him out, more by the weight of its impact than the injury it did to him.

But before he had time to jump up again Miguel was on to the machete, to which his eyes were first directed by Dobbs's movement. With a practised hand he drew it in one sweep from its long leather sheath; the next moment he was above Dobbs, whose head with one short sharp blow he struck clean from his neck.

Less shocked than taken aback by the swiftness of it, they all three stared at the body. The head lay separated only by the thickness of the blade from the trunk, and the eyes quivered spasmodically and then, with a sudden jerk, remained three-quarters shut. The fingers of both hands stretched to their full extent and then were tightly cramped together. This they did several times, until, they gently opened and died, half closed.

'It's you who did it, Miguel,' said one of the other two in a low voice as he came nearer.

'Shut your mouth,' shouted Miguel in a passion and turned suddenly on the speaker as if to kill him. 'I know myself who it was who gave it him, you canary bird. If it comes out, you two will be shot as well as me. You know that, without me needing to tell the police. It's all one to me in any case and I am not your wet-nurse.'

He looked at the machete. There was scarcely any blood on it. He wiped it against a tree and pushed it back into its sheath.

Chapter Twenty-two

Donkeys do not as a rule concern themselves with human affairs in the way that dogs are so ready to do, and the caravan had gone quietly on; and as they have more intelligence than those who have had nothing to do with them believe, it had taken the road for Durango.

In their excitement, the men had quite forgotten the donkeys. They stripped the trousers and boots from the body and pulled them on there and then. Neither trousers nor boots were worth much, for they had seen more service during the last ten months than was ever expected of them. All the same, they were magnificent acquisitions compared with the rags these men wore.

But not one of them would have the shirt or put it on, although all three, in place of shirts, wore what can only be described as a network of tattered remains.

'Why don't you take the shirt and put it on, Ignacio?' asked Miguel, giving the body a push with his foot. There was nothing on it now but the threadbare khaki shirt.

'It's not worth much,' answered Ignacio.

'You have reason to say that, you dirty hound,' observed Miguel. 'Compared with yours, it's better than new.'

'I don't want it,' said Ignacio and turned away. 'It's too close to his neck. Why don't you take it yourself?'

'I?' asked Miguel, frowning angrily. 'I'm not going to put on a shirt which is still warm from that hound of a gringo's body.'

But the truth was that for Miguel too the shirt was too close to the neck of the corpse. There were no bloodstains on it, but all the same none of them would put it on. They had a foreboding that they would not feel comfortable in it. They could not explain the feeling and contented themselves with saying that the shirt was too near the neck and that this was why they didn't want it.

'The swine is sure to have some shirts among his gear,' said Ignacio.

Miguel turned on him at once. 'You wait till I've had a look, and if there's anything left over we can talk about it.'

'Do you think you are boss here?' now shouted the third, who for the last few minutes had been leaning against a tree, taking no part in the discussion. He had good reason, for he had got the trousers and Miguel the boots. Only Ignacio had come out of it empty-handed, since he would not have the shirt.

'Boss?' yelled Miguel in a rage. 'Boss or no boss, what have you done up to now?'

'Didn't I plug the stone at his skull?' shouted the third. 'You wouldn't have lifted a hand to him otherwise, you skunk.'

'A stone,' sneered Miguel, 'About as much good as a toothpick. Which of you two mangy cats would have got to work and finished him off? You bastards. And in case you don't know it, I can make use of the machete a second time and a third too, for the pair of you. I don't want your permission for that.'

He turned round, meaning to go to the donkeys.

'Where are the donkeys? To hell with it!' he shouted in astonishment.

They saw now that the donkeys had gone.

'If they get to the town we shall soon have a lot of police buzzing round,' Miguel shouted.

They set off running after the donkeys. They had need to run, for the animals, finding not so much as a dried stalk to detain them, had trotted briskly on. It took more than an hour before the men got back to the trees with them.

'We'd best put him under the ground,' said Miguel, 'or else someone with nothing better to do might want to know what the vultures had found here.'

'Yes, and perhaps you'll leave a label behind with your name on,' Ignacio sneered. What does it matter to us whether the carcase is found or not? He won't be able to say whose company he was in last.'

'You are very smart, my little cock,' said Miguel. 'If they find the swine and us with his donkeys, we'll have nothing to say. But if they find the donkeys with us and no sign of the body, then someone has got to prove that we helped the gringo to hell. We can say we bought the donkeys from the gringo. But if they find what's left of him no one will believe we bought his donkeys. So get on with it.'

The spade that Dobbs had meant for Curtin was now used for his own burial. It was quick work. They didn't trouble themselves much. They did what was barely necessary and then left the matter to the ants and the worms.

After this they set off and drove the string of donkeys back into the mountains again. They didn't venture into the town for personal reasons, and also because they thought they might meet someone there who knew Dobbs and was waiting for him. It was also quite possible that Dobbs had spoken the truth and that two others were really following him on horseback. For it seemed to them very unlikely that Dobbs should have driven the whole string by himself. So, in order to avoid the risk, they turned off from the track which, according to their reckoning, Dobbs had followed and took another mule-track up into the hills.

As soon as they were in the bush they could not restrain their curiosity any longer. They wanted to know what the booty was and what was to be found in the packs. It was dark by then and the mist made the place where they had halted for the night still darker; and to avoid betraying their camp while they were still in the neighbourhood they refrained from making a fire.

They got busily to work unloading the beasts and undoing the packs. They found another pair of trousers and two pairs of light shoes. There were also cooking implements, but only a handful of beans and even less rice.

'It doesn't seem he was a millionaire after all,' said Ignacio. 'No wonder he had to get to the town.'

'There was no money on him either,' grumbled Miguel,

while he looked into the pack he had undone. 'Only seventy centavos in his trouser pocket, the bastard. And the skins aren't up to much. They won't fetch above a few pesos.'

Then he came to the little packages.

'What's he got here? Sand, nothing but sand. I'd like to know what he lumps this sand around for all in little bags.'

'That's easy,' said Ignacio, who now came on the little bags in his pack too. 'It's clear enough. The fellow was an engineer from a mining company, who had been looking round the mountains and taking samples of soil back to the town, where it could be tested by the other engineers and the chemists in the office. Then the American companies know straight away where to stake out a claim.'

He shook the bag out. Miguel too emptied out the ones in his packs, and when he saw that the little bags were only made of worthless trips of canvas he cursed gods, devils and all gringos. It had got so dark that even if they had known more about it they would never have recognized the nature of this sand.

Angel also, the third man, found the same little bags in his packs. He gave another explanation. He said: 'The swine was a proper American swindler and liar, I can tell you that much. These little bags were all put nicely among the skins and then skins tied round them tight. 'D'you know why? He was going to sell the skins in Durango by weight, and to make them weigh more he put sand in with them, and so that the sand shouldn't run out he put it in little bags. He'd have sold the skins one night, and next morning, before the buyer found out, he'd have left by rail. We've upset his game for him, the swine.'

Miguel and Ignacio agreed that this was the best explanation and they made haste to get rid of the sand.

Chapter Twenty-three

While it was still night they packed up and went on. By midday they came to a village and asked an Indian whom they found in front of his house, whether he knew anybody who would buy donkeys, as they intended to sell some of theirs because they had no use for them. The Indian looked at the donkeys, walked round them and inspected the marks branded on them; then he also looked at the packs and gave a casual glance at Miguel's boots and Angel's trousers, as though willing to buy them as well. Finally he said: 'I cannot buy any donkeys, I have no money. But perhaps my uncle will buy them. He has enough money. I have none. I will take you to my uncle and you can see what he says.'

The three ruffians thought this promising, for in general you can go the round of half a dozen Indian villages before finding anyone to buy a single donkey. Usually the people have no money, and a peso is a large sum to them.

A few hundred yards further on they came to the uncle's house. It was, like most of the others, built of sun-dried bricks and roofed with grass, and stood on the large open space in the middle of the village where the market, the Independence Day celebrations, the festivities commemorating the Revolution and political gatherings were held. In the middle there was a modest pavilion where music was played during public festivities and from which speakers gave addresses. From this pavilion, too, the heads of the Public Health Commission addressed the inhabitants when they toured the country to instruct the Indian population in matters of health and the care of children. The Labour Government does more in this direction than all other governments put together since the arrival of the Spaniards.

The Indian went into his uncle's house to speak to him about buying the donkeys. It was not long before the uncle came out and went up to the three bandits, who were squatting in the shadows of a few trees near the house.

He was an elderly man, already grey-haired, but strong and wiry. His copper-brown face was alert and his black eyes glanced like a boy's. He wore his plaited hair fairly long and drawn back from the face on each side. Holding himself very erect, he walked slowly up to the men. After greeting them he went straight to the donkeys and had a good look at them. 'Very good donkeys, señor,' said Miguel, 'very good, verdad, you could not buy better at Durango market.'

'It's true they are good donkeys,' said the uncle, 'over worked and in poor condition. You must have come a long way.'

'Not so very far, scarcely two days,' Ignacio put in.

Miguel punched him in the ribs. 'My friend here is not quite right, we have only come two days' journey since they were last rested. But we've been some weeks on the road.'

'Then it's no wonder they're a bit down. But we'll soon feed them up again.' As he said this he looked more closely at their ragged clothing and their scoundrelly faces. But he did not let it be seen that he was observing them; it was rather as though he looked at them without thinking while his mind was occupied with the deal. 'What would you want for them?' he asked without taking his eyes off them.

Miguel smiled and, bending his head confidentially, suggested that twelve pesos would not be too much.

'For the lot?' the Indian asked innocently.

Miguel laughed as though he had heard a good joke: 'Not for the lot, naturally. I mean twelve pesos for each animal.'

'That is a very big price,' the uncle said briskly. 'I can buy them in Durango market for that.'

'You'd be lucky,' Miguel replied. 'They're a lot dearer there, fifteen or even twenty pesos. And then you have them to drive home.'

'That's true,' the Indian nodded, 'but they pay their way on the road. I can load them up with goods to bring back.'

Miguel laughed aloud. 'I see we have a smart man to deal with, and we don't want to stick out for our price. We'll say nine pesos and that's my last word. I know things aren't too good for you either and we've had a long dry season this year.'

'Nine pesos,' said the uncle quietly. 'I cannot pay that. Four pesos and not a centavo over.'

'Make it five and the donkeys are yours,' said Miguel, putting his hands in his trouser pockets as though he had got the money already.

'Four pesos is my bid,' said the uncle quietly.

'You pull the skin over my ears, señor; I am not out to make a fortune, but strike me blind if I am not making you a present of the donkeys at the price.' As he said it, Miguel looked from the uncle to the nephew and then at his two companions in crime, who nodded with an air of doleful resignation to show that they were giving away their last possessions.

The uncle nodded likewise, but with the air of having known the evening before that he would buy donkeys for four pesos apiece next day.

He went up to the donkeys again and said: 'Are you going to take the packs away on your back?'

'Yes, you're right, there's the packs,' said Miguel, taken off his guard, and he looked at his two companions; this time not so cocksure as before, but rather as though he expected their advice and assistance.

Ignacio understood the look and said: 'We want to sell the packs as well, we're going on by rail.'

'That's true,' Miguel went on fluently. 'We're selling them too, that was what we meant to do.'

As a matter of fact they had forgotten all about the packs.

'What have you got in them?' the uncle went on, and gave one of the packs a punch with his fist.

'Skins,' said Miguel. 'Good ones. Also our pots and pans and some tools as well. You won't want to take the rifle. That's too dear.'

'What sort of tools are they?' asked the uncle.

'All sorts,' Miguel replied. 'There are spades and pickaxes and crow-bars and a lot else.'

'How do you come to have tools of that sort?' the uncle asked casually, as though for the sake of conversation.

'Oh – the tools – well . . .' Miguel was suddenly in a fix. He felt uncomfortable and swallowed once or twice. The question of the tools took him by surprise.

Then Ignacio waded in: 'We've been working for an American mining company. That's where we've just come from.'

'Yes, that's it,' Miguel put in quickly and threw a grateful glance at Ignacio. He would never forget his timely help.

'Then you must have stolen these tools from the mining company,' said the uncle dryly.

Miguel laughed and winked at the uncle, as if he were one of them. 'Not exactly, stolen, señor,' he said. 'Stealing is no business of ours. It's just that we didn't hand the tools in when we finished our last shift. No one can call that stealing. We don't want much for them, perhaps two pesos the lot, just to save lugging them to the railway.'

'Of course, I can't buy all the donkeys myself,' the uncle now said slowly. 'I have no use for so many. But I'll get the rest of the villagers along. Each has a bit of money, and I can promise you, you'll soon be quit of the donkeys and the other gear as well. I will do my best. Sit down. Do you want water or a packet of cigarettes?'

Angel went in to the house with him and came back with a jug of water and a packet of Supremos.

The uncle said a word to his nephew, and the nephew went off to summon the men of the village.

The men came, old and young, singly and in twos. Many had their machetes at their sides, others carried them unsheathed in their hands, and others again carried nothing at all. All of them went first into the uncle's house and spoke to him. Then they came out again and after looking the donkeys over carefully they looked at the three strangers too. Perhaps they looked even more closely at the donkeys' owners than at the donkeys themselves, but very much more unobtrusively. The strangers did not notice that they were being so carefully examined. They took it for the ordinary curiosity of the Indian peasant.

After a while the men's wives came along too, creeping up slowly and a little shyly. They all brought their children. Some of the women carried their children slung on their backs, others had them in their arms. The children who could walk ran about round their mothers like chicks round a hen.

At last it seemed that all the men were assembled, for no more came up. Only an occasional woman slowly drew nearer to the house. The uncle now came out followed by the men who had last been in the house with him. They stood in a group. But the rest, who had come out earlier and had been examining the donkeys, remained where they were. Thus the bandits, without noticing it, were unobtrusively surrounded. Wherever they might turn, their escape was cut off. And yet there was nothing in it, since the men had only come to look over the donkeys.

'You are selling them very cheap,' the uncle said. 'The only thing that surprises us is how you can sell such good donkeys for so little.'

Miguel replied with a broad grin. 'You see, señor, we need the money, that's why, and so we have no choice but to sell.'

'Are the donkeys branded?' the uncle asked casually.

'Of course,' said Miguel, 'they're all branded.' He looked round at the donkeys to see what the brand was but the men got in front of the donkeys, so that not one of the bandits could see how they were branded.

'What mark are the donkeys branded with?' the uncle asked.

Miguel began to feel extremely uncomfortable, and his companions started turning this way and that to see the mark. But the Indians, apparently without design, edged them further away from the donkeys.

The uncle looked steadily at Miguel, and Miguel became more and more uncertain of himself. He felt the approach of something which would have a decisive effect on his continued existence, and when the uncle, without repeating his question, continued to look him straight in the eye, he knew that he had to answer. He hesitated a moment and swallowed hard and then said: 'The mark – yes, the mark, it's a ring with a stroke under it.'

The uncle called out to the men standing by the donkeys:

'Is that the mark?' he asked them.

'No,' they called back.

'I made a mistake,' Miguel said. 'It's a ring with a cross over it.'

'That is not the mark,' the men said.

'No, I'm wrong again,' Miguel said, almost beside himself. 'Of course, it's a cross with a ring round it.'

'Is that right?' asked the uncle.

'No,' the men said, 'it's wrong.'

'Yet you told me that they were your donkeys,' the uncle said quietly.

'So they are,' Ignacio broke in, unabashed.

'It's odd then that none of you knows how they are branded.'

'We never troubled to notice,' said Miguel, trying to look unconcerned.

The uncle turned to all the men present.

'Have any of you,' he asked them, 'ever seen a man who owned donkeys or any other cattle without knowing how each one was branded, even if the brands were different and the animals came from different breeders?'

The men all laughed and said nothing.

'I know very well,' the uncle said, 'where these donkeys come from.'

Miguel glanced at his two companions. They were all looking round for some way of escape, when they heard the uncle say:

'The donkeys come from Señora Rafaela Motilina of Avino, the widow of Señor Pedro Leon. I know his brand mark. It is an L with a P backwards on the stroke of the L. Is that right?' he called out.

And the men standing near the donkeys called back: 'That's right, that is the brand mark.'

The uncle looked about among them and called out: 'Porfirio, come here.'

One of the Indians came forward and stood beside him.

The uncle now went on to say: 'My name is Alberto Escalona. I am the Alcalde of this place, regularly elected, and installed by the governor. This man here, Porfirio, is the policeman in this place.'

There are differences between countries and climates, and differences in upbringing and in the influences to which people are subjected. In any case, if anyone in Europe announces his office and title, his object is to arouse a tremor and feelings of awe, so that the man he addresses, impressed by the sublimity of the occasion, shall respectfully incline himself and pay the holder of the title the honour due to his rank. Here, on this continent, a title counts for nothing, a name for little and personality for all. No one inclines himself, unless, on occasion, before a woman. And anyone who calls the President 'Your Excellency' would be as ridiculous as a president who expected it. The president is much less usually addressed as Mr. President or Señor President than as Mr. Coolidge or Señor Calles, as indeed the rule is almost without exception, and anyone who has business with the president shakes his hand when he arrives and when he goes, and talks to him as if he had eaten from the same spoon all his life. This is something that the freshly starched, top-hatted presidents of the brand-new European republics have still to learn. For European presidents take absolute rulers as their patterns, whereas presidents here take no one for their pattern, or, if they need a pattern, they take themselves as a pattern and so they are just such men as anyone else in the country. And if anyone here says: 'Our president is a great fathead', the president does not sentence him to a few months' imprisonment; rather, if he hears of it, he says to himself or his friends: 'That fellow knows more about me than I do myself, he seems to be a smart man.'

If anybody here mentions his office and says: 'I am a

magistrate of this place and this man here is the chief of police', it has quite another meaning than it has in Europe.

The three bandits knew at once what it meant and that there was an end of hand-shaking. They started up and tried to make their escape without taking their donkeys with them.

They would have sold the lot now for a peso or given them away for nothing, if only they could have left the village behind them; but there was no question of that now.

Miguel felt for his revolver. But he found his pocket empty. In his excitement he had not noticed that Porfirio had relieved him of it. The revolver would certainly have been of little use, for it was still unloaded. But the Indians could not know that and might perhaps have let him go if he had threatened them with it.

'What d'you want, then?' Miguel shouted.

'Nothing so far,' the Alcalde said. 'We're only wondering why you're in such a hurry to be gone without taking your donkeys with you.'

'We can take our donkeys or not, we can do what we like with our donkeys,' Miguel replied in a rage.

'Yes, but they are not your donkeys. I know the history of these donkeys. Señora Motilina sold these donkeys ten or eleven months ago to three Americans who were going hunting in the Sierra. I know the Americans.'

Miguel grinned and said: 'That's quite right. It's from these Americans we bought them.'

'At what price?'

'Twelve pesos apiece.'

'And now you want to sell them for four. It seems a bad bargain.'

The Indians laughed.

'You told me,' said the Alcalde, 'you had had the donkeys a long time. How long?'

Miguel thought for a moment and then said: 'Four months.' It occurred to him that he had said they had been working in a mine and had come a long journey.

'Four months?' the Alcalde remarked dryly. 'That is a funny thing. The Americans came down from the mountains a few days ago. They were seen in the villages. And they had all the donkeys which you bought from them four months ago.'

Miguel tried on his confiding smile once again.

'The truth is, señor, we bought the donkeys from these Americans two days ago.'

'That sounds better. So you bought them from the three Americans?'

'Yes.'

'But it cannot have been the three Americans, for I know that one of them is in a village on the other side of the Sierra. He is a doctor.'

'It was only one American we bought them from.' Miguel scratched his head.

'Where was it you bought the donkeys?' the Alcalde continued relentlessly.

'In Durango.'

'That is scarcely possible,' said the Alcalde. 'The American could not be in Durango by this time, and if he was you could not have got here.'

'We travelled all night.'

'Maybe, but why should the American sell his donkeys to you in particular when he was already in Durango where he could find plenty of other buyers?'

Ignacio now joined in: 'How do we know why he wanted to sell his donkeys to us and not to others? That was his affair.'

'Well, he must have given you a receipt,' said the Alcalde. 'A receipt with the price and the brand marks; otherwise Señora Motilina can claim the donkeys any time, because they are branded with her mark.'

'He didn't give us a receipt,' Miguel answered. 'He didn't want to pay the stamp.'

'You might have paid the few centavos yourselves in order to have a proof that you'd bought them,' said the Alcalde.

'Damnation,' Miguel shouted, clenching his fists. 'What is it you want from us? We go quietly about our business and you surround us. We'll make a complaint to the governor and have you removed. Do you understand?'

'That's a bit too much,' the Alcalde said, smiling. 'You come to our village and want to sell us donkeys. We want to buy the donkeys and we agree about the price. But after all we have the right to know where the donkeys come from. Otherwise, early tomorrow morning perhaps soldiers may turn up and say we are bandits and have taken the donkeys from their rightful owner after killing him, and then we should be shot.'

Miguel turned to his friends and gave them a look. Then he went on: 'We don't want to sell the donkeys now at any price, not even for ten pesos. We want to go on.'

'But you might sell us the tools and the skins, all the same?' asked the Alcalde.

Miguel thought this over, and as it occurred to him that the skins and the tools had no brand mark, he said: 'Right, if you want the skins and the tools – what d'you think?' turning to his friends.

'Very well,' said they. 'Let them go.'

'They belong to you, I suppose?' asked the Alcalde.

'Course they do,' Miguel replied.

'Why didn't the American sell his skins in Durango? Why are you carrying skins back here? You are only carrying water to the river.'

'Prices were not good in Durango and we thought we'd wait for a better time.' Miguel began to walk to and fro, though the Indians left him little room.

'Did the American go naked to the railway?' The Alcalde threw in this question unexpectedly.

'What do you mean?' Miguel went white.

'Well, you have his boots on and that other has his trousers on. Why has none of you got his shirt on? It was quite good. In any case, it was as good as new compared with the rags you're wearing.'

Miguel was silent.

'Why didn't any of you take it?' repeated the Alcalde. 'I can tell you,' he went on, 'why none of you wanted to put that shirt on.'

Neither Miguel nor either of the other two waited to hear what the Alcalde would say next. Each of them leapt upon the men nearest him. It was so sudden that the Indians were not quick enough to get hold of them, and they made their escape and ran down the village street, making for the open.

The Alcalde nodded to some of the men, and a few minutes later five of them were in pursuit of the runaways on horseback. They didn't even wait to saddle the horses. They only threw halters over their heads. The thieves had not got far. The Indians overtook them before they had reached the last house of the village. They were lassoed and brought back to the village square.

'Now we'll go and find the American and ask him what he sold you the donkeys for, and why he let himself be stripped naked and made you a present of his boots and trousers. We will bring his shirt, which none of you wanted, back with us.' The Alcalde said this as though it was for their information and required no reply.

The three were bound and then guarded by Indians, who squatted down opposite them with their machetes across their knees.

The other men saddled their horses, put tortillas in their bast pouches and set off. The Alcalde and Porfirio rode with them.

Chapter Twenty-four

It is very difficult for anyone to travel for long in these parts without being seen. Even though he tries to avoid all habitations and all encounters on the way, there are always eyes which see him, follow him on his way and observe all his doings. He himself as a rule does not know that he is observed. Long before he has seen them, the Indians have left the tracks and crept into the bush, where they wait for him to go by and do not come out again until he is out of sight. They have seen him, little as he thinks it, and so thoroughly inspected him from head to foot that a few hours later the whole village knows just what he looks like and all that he has with him. From water channels, from behind hillocks and rocks and bushes the eyes see every movement and every step the stranger makes.

The mounted men followed the track which Dobbs had gone and not the one which the bandits had taken. As they were on horseback and riding light, they reached the place where Dobbs had halted by midday. The spot was easy to find.

Two of the men followed the trail on towards the town. But they soon found that the donkeys had merely strayed and then been driven back again.

It was now a simple matter for the Alcalde, himself a full-blooded Indian, to reconstruct the whole affair. The donkeys had gone on by themselves, so no one had had time to bother about them. Hence something must have been going on at that spot which so absorbed the attention of all those who were present and whose footprints could be recognized, that they had not noticed when the donkeys began to stray. And whatever had happened must have been of some importance, for otherwise the donkeys would not have got so far.

The footprints of the American were not to be seen either from the trees to the spot where the donkeys were overtaken, or from this spot on towards the town. Even if he had gone barefoot it would have been easy to recognize his tracks. The form of his foot would not be so beautiful as that of an Indian's foot, because he wore boots which cramped the toes. Besides this, the feet of white men are much larger than those of Indians, whose feet are usually neat and small.

As the American's tracks did not lead on, it followed that he must be there. And as he had not been very deeply or carefully buried and as no rain had fallen, the men in a few minutes came on his grave.

No one can be accused of murder unless the body can be produced, as Miguel had said. In this he was right. This is the law, and one may call it a good law, for in such vast countries men can vanish so completely that a corpse is more easily found than a man who disappears of his own accord.

The body was found, and as the three bandits were in possession of the dead man's property without being able to produce any title to it, there was no need of further proof.

The Alcalde gave one glance at the body and then observed: 'Machete.'

Then the men took the shirt off the body and the Alcalde took possession of it. After this the Indians buried the body once more. They worked with bare hands and when they had filled in the grave, which they dug deeper than before, although they had only their machetes, they stood for some while round the mound without their hats. They did not pray, but with bowed heads all looked down upon the mound.

While they were standing there the Alcalde went to the nearest tree and cut off a small branch with his machete and then cut it in two pieces. He tied the two pieces together with string in the form of a cross and planted it in the ground at the head of the grave.

Next morning they were back in their village. The Alcalde showed the shirt to his captives, who looked at it and shrugged their shoulders.

212

Meanwhile two men were dispatched to the nearest station of mounted police and a detachment arrived during the morning. The inspector, when he had seen the men, said to the Alcalde: 'There's a reward for that one,' pointing to Miguel. 'I think it is three hundred pesos or two hundred and fifty. I don't know exactly. He's a bandit and has committed two murders already. The other two are no doubt birds of the same feather. I don't know them. The reward will come to you, señor, to Porfirio and the rest of the men here. Now what will you do with the donkeys and their packs?'

'Tomorrow we shall restore them to their owners,' said the Alcalde. 'I know where they are. One of them is a doctor and they won't let him go on the other side of the mountain. We want him here too for a week. He'll have his gear now and will not be in such a hurry to go on.'

The three bandits were now taken over by the police. They were no longer on the lasso. They went on foot surrounded by the mounted soldiers. There is the shirt, there are the trousers, there are the boots, there are the donkeys, there are the packs, there is the cross on the mound. It is not likely, then, that the further procedure will take more than two hours. There will be no costly scaffold erected and no white gloves put on. The state has not got the money for all that. Money must be saved for more important matters.

Chapter Twenty-five

Howard was a very busy man. He was not able to enjoy the leisure he had hoped for. He was famed far and wide as the great medicine man. The Indians of the uplands are all very healthy and live to an age which seems fabulous to the European. They are defenceless only against diseases brought in from outside. But though they all enjoy most enviable health they suffer, all the same, from ailments and infirmities into which they persuade themselves by dint of hard talking. They only need to hear of an illness and to have its symptoms described in order to be sure within three days that they have it themselves; that is why doctors, medical and clerical, do such good business in the country.

A woman came to Howard and wanted to know why she had lice, while her neighbour had none. What was Howard to prescribe? A ointment would have been the right thing. But as soon as it was used up, the lice would return, and the question would be repeated: 'Why have I got lice and my neighbour none?' Howard got out of the difficulty by a simple expedient, for he was a genuine medicine man. He said: 'It is because you have very good healthy blood and lice are fond of it, whereas your neighbour has very poor and sickly blood.' Whereupon the neighbour, a woman bursting with good health, came and asked him to prescribe for her poor and sickly blood. If she had gone to a qualified doctor in the town, he would have prescribed salvarsan, although she had not the least symptoms of any illness requiring it. But people imagine that salvarsan is good for the blood and so the doctor prescribes it.

Howard had no salvarsan by him. He had, indeed, no medicine whatever. His one and only prescription was hot water, two litres every day. For the sake of variety he might prescribe three litres or one and three-quarters or one and a half; then again hot water with lemon juice or with orange juice or with any herb or vegetable he was acquainted with and knew could do no harm.

Those who do not know the healing power of water may find it remarkable that the men, women and children who besieged the medicine man all got well. At least, so they said. And it is the case with all illnesses that, if you are convinced that you are ill no longer, you are immediately cured.

In the case of bodily pains when, as the people said, death lurked immediately under the skin and they could plainly feel it when they pressed on the place, Howard prescribed hot compresses, and again for the sake of variety, cold compresses, compresses on the head, on the neck, on the palms of the hands, on the pulse, on the pit of the stomach, on the soles of the feet or wherever the place might be. And in these cases too the people all got well. Death crept back again from under the skin, because it grew too hot or too cold for it, as the case might be.

As for fractures of arms or legs, strains or sprains, here the people needed no assistance. They had nothing to learn from any doctor. And there was no need, either, for Howard to act as midwife. They had no trouble with childbirth.

Howard's fame increased daily, and if he had more taste and liking for a life among a primitive people he might have been content to stay on here for ever in peace and happiness; but every day his thoughts were set on his departure. He thought again and again of his two companions, wondering whether they would duly hand over his share and whether they would get safely to the railway. His consolation was that there was nothing he could do, except rely upon their honesty and resource.

Then, one morning, an Indian came riding to the village and asked for the house where the great medicine man lived. He spoke first to Howard's host and then the two went up to Howard.

His host said: 'Señor, this man here is from a village over the mountains and he has a story to tell you.'

The Indian sat down, rolled and lit a cigarette and then began to tell his story.

'Lazaro was in the bush burning charcoal. He is a charcoal burner. It was early in the morning. He had just stacked up his wood. The he saw something creeping on the ground. And when he looked more closely he saw that it was a white man crawling along. He was covered with blood and could go no further. Lazaro gave him water to drink. Then he left his stacked wood and got the white man on to his donkey and took him to his house in the village.

'When the man had been laid on a mat in the house he was dead. But then another man came and looked at the white man and said: "He is not quite dead. He is only very sick and very weak. Filomeno must ride over the mountain to the white medicine man because Filomeno has a horse and a donkey does not go so fast."

'I am Filomeno, señor, and I have a good and fast horse and here I am. You can certainly help the sick white man if you come at once.'

'What does the white man look like?' asked Howard.

Filomeno was able to describe him as clearly as though he stood beside him and Howard knew that it was Curtin.

He got ready to go at once. His host and three other Indians accompanied him.

It was a long and hard ride. But when they arrived Curtin had recovered a little and seemed to be out of danger. Curtin had told the people of the village no more than that he had been shot on the road, by whom he did not know. He wanted to avoid Dobbs being followed, because in that case all would be up.

'The dirty swine shot me down in cold blood,' Curtin told Howard, 'because I wouldn't go halves on your lot with him. He tried to pretend it was in self-defence. I saw at once what he was after. I might have agreed to the share-out and then, when we got to the town, put the matter to rights again. But you might perhaps have joined us before I expected and then you'd have believed I'd agreed to do you down. You'd never have believed I'd only made a pretence of it. He gave me one in the left side and left me lying in the bush to rot.

But now I find I was shot twice, though I can only remember the once. I almost think the skunk came back when I was unconscious and put another into me, just to be sure of making a good job of it. I came round late in the night and dragged myself away from the place as fast as I could. I thought to myself: he'll be sure to come in the morning before he gets off and if he finds there's a breath left in my body, he'll finish me off. Then I came on an Indian burning charcoal in the bush. He was afraid and ran away at first. But I spoke to him and told him that I was at my last gasp, so he helped me at once and brought me here. Without his help, I was finished. I could go no further and no one would ever have found me.'

'Then he's made off with the lot?' Howard asked.

'Sure.'

The old man reflected for a moment. Then he said: 'Actually he wasn't a crook. At bottom he was a decent fellow. The mistake was his going on alone with you. It's a damnable temptation to travel day in and day out with a heap of gold, along tracks and paths through this Godforsaken bush, and only one man at your side. The bush keeps whispering and whispering and shouting its temptation in your ear: "I tell no tales. Here's your chance which will never come again and I am as secret as the grave." If I was as young as you two, I don't know that I could have resisted such a hellish temptation day after day. It is only a matter of a second, one single second, and you can count for yourself how many seconds there are in a day of four and twenty hours. For the flash of a second the mind loses its grip and before it grips the cogs again you have loosed off. Then there's no turning back and you have to finish the business.'

'The swine had no conscience,' said Curtin.

'He had just as much or just as little as the rest of us who know we have to use our elbows to get on top. When there is no chance of being run in, conscience is as silent as an empty brandy bottle in a dusty corner. Conscience only shouts when it has a good backing. That's the reason for prisons,

hangmen and the pains of hell. Had the armament manu-
facturers, who made their money by helping the peoples of
Europe to massacre each other, any conscience? Had Mr.
Wilson any conscience when he left fifty thousand of our
young fellows be murdered because Wall Street was afraid
of losing its money and the munition makers wanted to do
even better business? If he had, it's the first I've heard of it.
It's only the small fry who have to have a conscience; the
others don't need one. Our friend Dobbs will find his conscience very lively as soon as he knows that he only killed
you by halves. You can leave conscience out of it. I don't
believe in it. All we have to think of now is how to recover
the goods.'

Howard's idea was to ride straight off to Durango in order
to overtake Dobbs, or, at least, find him in Tampico before
he fled the country. Curtin was to remain in the village getting well and come on afterwards.

When Howard explained to his host that he now must see
to his property because Curtin lay there sick, they gave their
consent to his departure even though it grieved them that he
should go soon.

Next morning Howard was ready to set off for Durango.
But his Indian friends refused to let him go alone. They
wanted to accompany him and see him safe to the town, in
case he might meet with the same fate as his friend Curtin.
So they all rode along with him.

They had just reached the next village when they met the
Indians, with the Alcalde at their head, who were on their
way to take the donkeys and the packs to Howard.

'But where is Señor Dobbs, the American who was
taking this string of donkeys to Durango?' Howard asked
after looking round and seeing nothing of Dobbs.

'He has been killed,' the Alcalde said quietly.

'Killed? Who by?' Howard asked mechanically.

'By three bandits, who were taken up by the soldiers yesterday.'

Howard looked at the packs. They seemed to him to have
shrunk strangely. Running up, he opened one of his own

packs. The skins were all there but the bags were gone.

'We must overtake these bandits,' he shouted. 'I've got to ask them something.'

His escort was quite ready. They left the donkeys to go on to the village where Curtin was. All the rest of them made a bee-line after the soldiers.

The soldiers had not been hurrying. On such occasions they always visit every place lying off their route to hear what's going on and to show the peaceful inhabitants that the government does not forget to give them its protection. The prisoners whom they take along with them only deepen the impression made on the Indian peasantry that they can quietly pursue their labours and that the government looks after the righteous and lays all bandits and footpads by the heels. Bandits, and any others who might have a thought of taking up the business, are warned by the sight of the prisoners, whose end is clear to all, that there are drawbacks to the career of robbery on the roads. Such warnings are more effective than reports in the newspapers – which are never seen in such places and which in any case no one could read.

They overtook the soldiers next day. Howard was introduced to the officer by the Alcalde as the owner of the donkeys and their loads and was given permission at once to question the bandits.

He didn't want to hear any more about their murder of Dobbs, as the Alcalde had already given him a full account of it. All he wanted to know was where the bags had got to.

'The bags?' Miguel repeated. 'Oh, those little bags – we emptied them all out. There was nothing but sand in them to make the skins weigh heavier.'

'Where did you empty them out?' Howard asked.

Miguel laughed. 'How am I to know? Somewhere in the bush. One bag here, another further on. It was dark. Then we went on during the night, so as to get away – we didn't put any crosses up where we emptied them out. You can get sand anywhere for the picking up. And if it's that particular sand you want, perhaps as a sample, I don't suppose you'd find a grain of it now. We had a terrible downpour the night before last, and even if we knew the place it'll all be washed away. Otherwise I'd tell you gladly enough for a bag of tobacco. But I don't know and so can't earn my tobacco.'

Howard did not know what to say. All he could do was to let out such a shout of laughter that the other men and the soldiers too could not help laughing as well, although they did not know what the joke was. But he laughed so heartily that no one could resist joining in.

Howard threw the bandit a bag of tobacco, thanked the officer and then rode back with his friends.

'Well, my boy,' he said, sitting on the edge of Curtin's bed,' the gold is back where it came from. Those fine gentlemen took it for sand and thought we were going to cheat the dealers by having it weighed in with the skins, and the precious innocents chucked it all away. They don't know where, because it was dark. And anyway, the rain-storm the night before last has just put the lid on it. Otherwise, all we slaved ten months for was to be had for a bag of tobacco.'

He began to laugh so hard that he had to double up in case he hurt himself.

'I'm damned if I see what there is to laugh at,' Curtin said half angrily.

'I don't understand you,' said Howard, still laughing. 'If you can't laugh now till you burst, then you don't know what a good joke is, and that would be a pity. It's a joke worth ten months' hard labour.'

And he laughed till the tears ran down his cheeks.

'They have made me into a medicine man,' the old man chuckled, 'and I have more cures to my credit for less medicine than the best doctor in Chicago. And you were twice shot dead and are still alive, and Dobbs has so entirely lost his head that he will never be able to look for it again. And all this for gold which is ours and yet nobody knows where it is, and it's going begging for a bag of tobacco worth thirty-five centavos.'

Now at last Curtin began to laugh as hard as the old man had the whole time. But Howard put a hand over his mouth.

'Not so loud, my boy, otherwise you'll burst your lungs. And you must keep them, because otherwise we won't get to Tampico. We shan't manage it by railway. We shall have to ride the donkeys, and those we don't need for riding we must sell, so that we can have tortillas and frijoles to eat, the millionaires that we are.'

'What are we to do when we get there?' Curtin asked.

'Well, I had been wondering whether I wouldn't settle down here as a medicine man. We could run the show together. There's more than I can do alone. I need an assistant, and I'll make over all my prescriptions to you. They're good ones, I can promise you.'

When Howard began to look through all the packs one by one, he found one pack in which the bags had not been emptied out. Either it had been overlooked or else the bandit who had possessed himself of it was too lazy to empty it there and then and thought he would leave it over until later, when they were not in such a hurry to get on.

'This will just pay for – pay for what?' asked Howard.

'Not a cinema,' Curtin said.

'It wouldn't run to that. But I thought perhaps a little delicatessen shop?'

'Where? In Tampico?' Curtin said, raising himself on one elbow.

'Of course, where do you think?' Howard replied.

'But during the last month we were in Tampico, four big delicatessen shops went bust in six months.' Curtin thought it important to remind the old man of this.

'That's true,' said Howard. 'But that was twelve months ago. Things may have altered. We must risk something.'

Curtin thought a moment and then said: 'Perhaps your first idea was best – we'll try the medicine business for a time first, then at least we're sure of board and lodging. Whether this would be so with the delicatessen shop, I shouldn't like to say.'

'But you sit right in the middle of it, you only need your tin-opener and you can open a tin of what you like.'

'That's all very fine. But I'd like to know what you'll have

221

to eat when they come and seal up your delicatessen shop. Then you won't get at your tins any more.'

'I hadn't thought of that,' Howard said sadly. 'It's true we couldn't get at the tins then, and the best tin-opener would be no use at all. I agree that it will perhaps be better to leave the delicatessen alone for the time and stick to medicine. Besides, it is a highly honourable profession. After all, any fool can be a grocer, but not a medicine man by any means. It's got to be born in you. And I have good right to say so. Come along to my village and you'll soon learn something. You'll take your hat off when you see what honour I'm held in. A few days ago they wanted to make me into a legislative body. But what they mean by that I haven't been able to find out.'

At that moment his host came in.

'Señor,' he said. 'We must now ride on. There is a man just arrived on horseback. He says there are so many people in the village wanting to see the doctor that the village is getting anxious. So we must get off at once.'

'Do you hear that?' Howard said, turning to Curtin and shaking his head.

Curtin laughed and said: 'In three days I'm coming to see the medicine man myself.'

Howard had no time to reply. The Indians had picked him up, carried him out and put him on his horse.

Then they rode off with him.

TRUE WAR – AVAILABLE IN MAYFLOWER BOOKS

Alan Burgess Seven Men at Daybreak	35p	☐
Kendal Burt & James Leason The One That Got Away	95p	☐
Leonard Cheshire VC Bomber Pilot	95p	☐
C S Forester Hunting the Bismarck	35p	☐
Francis S Jones Escape to Nowhere	75p	☐
Ka-Tzetnik House of Dolls	95p	☐
Olga Lengyel Five Chimneys	95p	☐
Fred Majdalany The Battle of Cassino	75p	☐
Ian Mackersey Into the Silk	95p	☐
Dr Miklos Nyiszli Auschwitz	75p	☐

All these books are available at your local bookshop or newsagent, or can be ordered direct from the publisher. Just tick the titles you want and fill in the form below.

Name ....

Address ....

....

Write to Panther Cash Sales, PO Box 11, Falmouth, Cornwall TR10 9EN.

Please enclose remittance to the value of the cover price plus:

UK: 25p for the first book plus 10p per copy for each additional book ordered to a maximum charge of £1.05.

BFPO and EIRE: 25p for the first book plus 10p per copy for the next 8 books, thereafter 5p per book.

OVERSEAS: 40p for the first book and 12p for each additional book. *Granada Publishing reserve the right to show new retail prices on covers, which may differ from those previously advertised in the text or elsewhere.*